PERSONALS

PERSONALS

STORIES FROM THE SEX WARS

R. M. BURKE

THE BORGO PRESS
MMX

PERSONALS

Contents

KEVIN'S MOM

So I had this friend Kevin. He was a bit of a dweeb—one of these guys who always smiled sheepishly, as if he was constantly embarrassed about something or apologizing about something, mostly himself. Maybe that's why he liked me. He was damn smart, but he couldn't have gotten into the cool crowd without me. I was a jock—football, baseball, and track—but I was no dope: I was already set to go to Michigan State after we graduated this summer, and you better believe I'd do something better than major in business administration or something twerpy like that. Sure, I was going on an athletic scholarship—but maybe, once I got into the NFL or was playing center field for the Cubs, I'd surprise the jock reporters by saying I majored in comp lit or something like that. They probably wouldn't know what comp lit is.

I liked Kevin, and not only because he served as a good punching bag whenever I felt like roughing him up a little, just for fun. Nothing hard, just a few jabs to the shoulder or the biceps (he had no muscles to speak of—flabby as a girl). I figured it was a good lesson for him—he needed to learn what raw power and strength could do. Of course, he'd be the one to say "I'm sorry" when I hit him. But I really did like him: we actually talked philosophy and stuff, something that none of the other "student athletes" in school could do even if someone was about to cut their balls off. Kevin taught me a few things, and maybe I taught him a few others. He knew I'd come from a rough background (I may get into that later)—a background he just couldn't understand. Well, maybe he could in a way: his dad bolted the scene when he was, like, maybe thirteen. Kevin didn't know why, and he could never talk about his dad without face all crumpling up like a wad of waste paper. But I had some idea.

A real good idea.

It had to do with Kevin's mom. I'll give her one thing—she was hot. But I think she was one of these broads who didn't know how hot they were, or were embarrassed that they were hot. You couldn't have asked for a more housewifey sort of woman than Maureen Jacobs—even that name has June Cleaver written all over it. Short—Kevin was already way taller than her—and curvy, with nice firm tits for a gal who must have been at least forty, and an ass to die for. Well, maybe that's a bit of a stretch—but it was nice: round and *tight*, no flab anywhere. Damn nice legs too—kinda short, but worth drooling over whether in stockings or bare.

But, Gawd help me, she was just the fussiest, most persnickety woman I'd ever met—worse than my grandma, who thought every single thing you did in life had to be governed by some rule or other, a rule only she knew and made sure to tell you about. Get a load of this: Maureen had different coats for Kevin depending on how warm or cold it was outside: every ten degrees, another coat, only marginally heavier or lighter than the one next to it in the line. Don't they call that anal retentive? Or is that obsessive-compulsive? Guess I like that first term better.

I don't blame Kevin for getting out of that house as much as he'd dare. I don't blame him for hanging around me, in spite of all the abuse I gave him—that was the closest he could get to defying his mom and being a bad boy who wouldn't play by her rules or anyone else's. Of course, he had internalized a lot of those rules by this time, and so he really couldn't be anything like the rebel he thought he was; but I guess you need some kind of safety-valve.

And I have no doubt—no doubt at all—that all this is why Kevin's dad got the hell out of there. Fourteen or fifteen years of this constant babying from his own wife must have been too much for him.

So I figured I'd help Kevin's mom just the way I was helping Kevin.

As I say, Kevin was a brain. Languages, math, science—you name it. I don't think even he knew what he was best in; he was good in everything. Except in sports: he was damn relieved when p.e. became optional during the last two years of high school. One of the things that obsessed him was chess—it has all these *rules*, man, but at least they're not rules made up by his mother, and they're ones that you can learn and that didn't change erratically depending on the time of the month or whatever. So he liked chess; and when our school formed a chess club, he was one of the first to join. Me, I thought chess just the dopiest game imaginable. Oh, I'm sure you gotta be smart to play it—but where did it get you in the end? But Kevin liked it because you could get wrapped up in a single game for hours, maybe days.

And that's why the chess club starting meeting Thursday evenings, around 7 p.m. They'd started meeting after school, but people got to complaining that they couldn't really get into the games if they went on for more than two hours—got too hungry, had to go home for dinner, parents would get worried—so they shifted to evenings. I guess the parents didn't worry if their brainiacs didn't come home till 10 or 11.

So there I was, in front of Kevin's house at 7:15 p.m. on Thursday. I rang the doorbell. Kevin's mom answered.

I love the way people's faces go blank when they encounter something they don't expect. Even an Einstein looks like a dope then. The next thing that happens—if you're an upstanding member of the bourgeoisie—is that hesitant half-smile, as if that will ward off some social scenario that might turn awkward. Sure enough, Kevin's mom gave me that smile, and I now knew exactly where Kevin got it. Not only did I predict exactly what she was going to say, but I almost predicted the exact words she was going to use.

"Hi, Tony." She really didn't like me, but she had to pretend she did, just because she knew how much I meant to her precious boy. "Kevin isn't here right now. He's at . . . ."

I cut her off. "I know he isn't here. It's you I want to see."

You gotta realize that I said this in a kind of flat monotone—no smile, eyes looking right into hers, maybe taking a pointed glance at her boobs.

Her mouth fell half open, and a wisp of worry flitted across her face. *Here's a situation I don't know how to deal with—a situation I'm pretty sure I don't want to be in.* She didn't have to say the words—they were written all over her.

She backed up a little from the doorway, not so much as an invitation for me to come in—I'm sure she wished I were a hundred miles away right then—as to keep us at a distance where I didn't invade her personal space. But I was too quick—or maybe decisive—for her. I walked right in, pushed her firmly—not violently, mind you, just firmly—to a blank space on the wall of the entryway, and planted a kiss on her mouth.

Now remember: I'm not stupid. I kept my mouth glued to her lips, but I didn't go much farther than that—yet. Sure, I had my hands fixed to her shoulders, just to keep her from wriggling—she wriggled anyway, or tried to, but she had no chance to escape me—but that was it. No fondling—yet. No tongue in the mouth. Yet.

I could hear her muffled moans or squeals—they kinda made her lips vibrate, and that felt good. I knew something about kissing, so I didn't press super-hard—no pain yet. I had a plan—or you might call it an experiment. After about half a minute I took my lips off her mouth, but I still held her firmly to the wall. She gasped for breath, and her eyes looked frightened, shocked, mad—mostly shocked, I think. Once again, I could tell what she was going to say before she said it.

"What do you think you're doing . . . ?" She was such a wuss she couldn't even say *What the fuck do you think you're doing, you fucking shit?* And I don't have to tell you she didn't try to knee me in the balls or scratch my eyes out or anything else to free herself from my grip. You see, these middle-class broads—and guys, too, for that matter—are so unused to being physically challenged that they simply don't know how to respond. Their world is so safe and sanitized that they just can't imagine having to use their fists or a knife or a gun. That's not how things are done in their world, and so they're totally helpless when their world comes tumbling down.

Anyway, all I said back to her was: "You're a hot little piece, Mrs. Jacobs, and I think I can make you very happy."

Man, you ought to have seen her turn crimson. Imagine a forty-year-old mother blushing! She turned bright as a strawberry. But after a few seconds of that, she turned pale—because she knew, or sensed, what was coming. It would take her a while to wrap her conventional little brain around the idea, but she was starting to get the message.

But I wanted to go to slow. As I say, this was a kind of experiment.

I first placed my left hand on her jaw and planted another kiss on her mouth. A surprisingly gentle kiss—she was expecting another violent one that might bruise those wet lips of hers, and actually tried to back further into the wall as if she could somehow disappear into it; but it was of course no use, and the kiss I gave her was soft as a bashful lover's. That was only the start. After that I kissed her cheek, her throat, her eyes (I could taste the mascara she was wearing—it was her one concession to dolling up), even her ear, which made her groan softly in surprise.

It was only then that I placed my right hand on her left breast.

She was wearing this cotton dress that came down to her knees—no stockings, of course, as it was already a warm day in spring. Even through her clothes I could tell that those tits were as firm as they looked—even though I figured Kevin had had his share of pulling on them when he was a baby.

At this point she really started to writhe and groan. Whenever my mouth wasn't fastened to hers she moaned, "No, please," and made weak attempts to get my hand off her boob. Well, I let that tit go soon enough—but only to pull her away from the wall a bit. This dress had a long zipper in the back, and there was no way I could reach it otherwise.

With the zipper down, I reached both my hands to her shoulders and pulled that dress right off her. Believe it or not, I was trying not to rip it—but maybe it ripped a little. But she was a good seamstress, and she could fix it sometime. So there she was, shivering—not from cold, either—in her bra and panties. Too hot to wear a slip on a day like today. Her face, neck, and even her shoulders were all red from rage and shock and fear. I'd never seen her more tempting.

There was this weird little period where time seemed to stand still. But it wasn't long before I moved into action. Again I shoved her against the wall, and this time I mashed my lips into hers a bit harder. And I used my tongue this time. Feeling her boobs over the bra wasn't much fun, so I just ripped it off of her. Those tits felt mighty fine in my two hands—they were as good as advertised. With my mouth on hers, she couldn't speak, and her moans had gone from anger to terror to pleading.

After a while I reached my two hands to her hips and pulled her panties down to her knees. Pulling her back from the wall again, I gave her butt a nice rub with one hand while I held her waist with the other. She was now hitting me in the shoulders with her little fists, but with my leather jacket on I hardly felt them.

My right hand—I'm always best with my right hand—went between her legs. Here was the first part of my experiment. I was right.

She was wet.

Here was this woman whose husband had left her four years before. There was no chance she would try to find someone else right away, and I'd never heard Kevin say that she was on a date or even that she was looking. She just turned her attention to being even more of a mom than before, doing her best to make sure that Kevin didn't grow up and become a man who would treat some other woman the way her husband had treated her. (She forgot the way she had treated him.) To say she was sex-starved would be an understatement. Did she even play with herself? Probably—but I bet she did it with shame and embarrassment, and maybe cried afterward at what her bodily needs were forcing her to do.

And so she was wet after my tender ministrations. Of course she tried to lock her legs so my hand wouldn't reach her spot, but it was no use—I got there sooner than she expected, and locking her legs only held my hand in place. After a while she unlocked them and tried to use her hand to pull mine away. No chance—she was a weakling. But remember, I'm no dope: I wasn't being rough or harsh, and in fact I kind of eased up after a while. I didn't want to rush this. So, as I was kissing her lips and neck, I was feeling her up all over—sticking a finger or two into her pussy, rolling her clit with my thumb, and on the whole just giving her the full treatment. And all the while, I was asking myself the question of questions:

Is it rape if she comes?

Of course, I guess there's no answer to that—it's what you'd call a moral quandary. But I wasn't thinking much of philosophy just then. I just wanted to make sure she came.

There wasn't much to worry about on that score. Since she probably hadn't been felt up in at least four years (and probably longer than that), she came almost as fast as some of the sophomore and junior girls I regularly serviced. And when she did, her whole body gave this big shudder, and she groaned so roughly that I thought she'd need to suck on a cough drop. And those arms that had been weakly fighting me suddenly went limp, and then they went around me—not (or not entirely) because she had suddenly come to believe I was her Prince Charming, but because she was so weak in the knees that she'd have fallen down if she didn't have something to hold on to. And that something was me.

She buried her face in my shoulder too, and I could hear her moan turn into weeping. I just held her in my arms—rather tenderly, if I do say so—while she bawled her eyes out. She cried like a baby.

Well, that went on for a while, but I got bored with it and pulled her away. I let her rest on the wall, her face streaked with tears, and got down to business. Off went my leather jacket; the T-shirt underneath could stay. A flick of the wrist, and my jeans were undone and down to my ankles, after which I kicked them off. My briefs had come off along with the tight jeans. At that point Kevin's mom caught sight of my big hard-on.

You ever seen a person's eyes get so big you can see the whites all around the pupils? Well, she was like that. I was going to say: *C'mon, lady, haven't you seen a cock before?* But maybe her husband's cock hadn't been exactly like this. Had he ever fucked her more than the one time that led to Kevin coming out of her cunt? Well, that was probably unfair, but I couldn't believe how startled—bug-eyed, jaw-dropping startled—she was at the mere sight of a male organ.

Maybe it was more than just the sight of it. After staring at it for several seconds, she slowly moved her glance up to my face, and I could read the question written all over her: *You're not really going to . . . ?* My eyes, I'm sure, told her all she needed to know: *Yes, Kevin's mom, I'm really going to . . .*

The problem was where. Remember, I didn't want to hurt her; and anyway, I had more in my mind than just this one-time bang. But that matter was settled quickly. It took me no time at all to realize that the floor was fully and deeply carpeted. So I took her by the waist and drew her firmly but gently to the floor on her back. She was surprisingly docile—I think by now she had grasped the notion that resistance was futile. Once she was flat on her back, I took both those lovely breasts in my hand and kissed and sucked them all over, even their oh-so-tender undersides. My lips ringed her nipples so they were almost dripping with my spit. After that I mounted her. Nothing rough, mind you—but when I was fully in she groaned deep in her throat. Her eyes were tight shut, but her lips responded to mine when I planted another kiss on her. And her hips began rocking in rhythm to my own thrusts. Oh, yeah, she was liking this.

Well, I have to confess that I came a little faster than I wanted or expected. I guess I was pretty hyped up about the whole thing, more than I'd realized. When I came I just stayed in her for a bit, putting my weight fully on her. Some women like that, and she did, because her arms went tightly around my neck and shoulders, and she even planted a virginal little kiss on my cheek. That made me give a final little spurt, and at that she gave a kind of high-pitched squeal.

Well, we rested on the floor a bit, and then we did it all over again. Of course, I was on top—don't like women on top, the rhythm's all wrong—and I took a lot longer. I'm sure she came at least once more, maybe twice. There was this dreamy look of pleasure on her face most of the time.

So after the second time I was just lying there on my back, having rolled off her. I've always thought that that was the very best moment a woman could gain her revenge on a guy for bopping her, for a guy is as weak as a kitten then. I am, anyway. But she didn't do anything. But after a while the abnormality of the whole situation seemed to get to her, and she suddenly got up and picked up the dress, just holding it in front of her as if I hadn't already seen everything she had to show. I was still on the ground, my cock lolling off on my thigh and dripping a little—whether from her juices or mine or both I couldn't tell—and I was just giving her a kind of amused and quizzical look. *Yeah, what now, Kevin's mom?* She tried her best to look stern and adult and motherly, and she said:

"Tony, I think you'd better go." A deep and ragged breath. "You really shouldn't have done that."

You really shouldn't have done that! Man, how lame! I swear to you, I laughed out loud, and bounded up in one motion and grabbed my jeans, putting them on without bothering with the briefs. After I'd gathered up the rest of my clothes, I gave her this look—I think they call it conspiratorial, like: *You and me have a secret, babe, and we're stuck with each other from now till whenever*—and grabbed her face to give her one more kiss. She tried to pull away, but no luck: I planted a wet one right on her mouth.

Then I left.

* * * * * * *

Of course, that was only the beginning. Every Thursday I'd mosey on over and give her the treatment. I'm pretty sure she knew that was the way it was going to be, because the very first Thursday after our memorable encounter, she opened the door, saw it was me, looked down at her feet, blushed to the roots of her hair, and let me in without a word. This time we went to her bedroom—the very room, could it be, that Kevin had been conceived?—and closed the door, as if somehow that made it better or more private or whatever. Still without a word, she began reaching behind her back to unbutton her blouse—she was wearing a blouse and skirt this time—but I put a stop to that, looking at her with the clear expression That's my job, lady. We kissed a couple times, and I undid each button one at a time. The skirt had a zipper on the side, and when I pulled it down the skirt just fell off. She made no motion to get to the bed, and in fact reached for my hand and put it between her legs—I guess she liked having it done to her standing up. Sure enough, she came as before, shuddering all over and holding me tight in her arms.

Over the course of the next few weeks, I showed her a few things. Of course, there was all kinds of oral stuff. She seemed reluctant to do it at first—typical middle-class prejudice against "dirty" sex—and I think she was even more ashamed of having it done to her than doing it to me. She sucked cock as if it were some kind of unfortunate duty she couldn't escape, and of course she hated doing it the way I liked best—I standing up with legs spread wide, and she kneeling in front of me. No, she didn't like that at all. But she really didn't like—but, actually, she did like—being licked. She didn't even want me to do it the first time I made the effort. I had started by doing a number on her boobs with my mouth, then gradually headed downtown. But when she realized where I was headed, she almost squealed and tried to pull me up by the shoulders; and again there was that ridiculous cry, "No, please. . . ." But I wasn't going to let that kind of foolishness stop me:

I moved right down to my destination and licked her for all she was worth. She actually put an arm across her eyes, as if she could somehow shield both her eyes and her mind from what was happening. But her moans—including that final rough one that I now recognized so well—told a different story.

Then there was anal stuff. I'll be honest and say that she *really, really* didn't like that at all—and I guess I don't blame her. When I first suggested it she gasped like a schoolgirl and cried, "Not on your life!" But I kept after her, even once turning her over roughly on her stomach and rubbing my cock between the cheeks of her butt. And when I told her the best lube was cold cream (and it is), she gave me this look that all but shrieked: *You must be the worst pervert in creation!* But that's only what you'd expect a broad like this to say or think. Well, we tried it, and I could tell that her groans were more of pain than of pleasure—she even started puffing air harshly through her mouth, as if that would help her bear the pain of my tunneling into her butt. But we only did that a couple times, and more to say we'd done it than because either of us liked it much.

And where was Kevin in all this? He was as clueless as ever. I got to know that he would stay at that chess club till as late as he could manage, and there was no chance of his getting home much before 10:30 or so. I'd often stay for three hours, but after 10 I knew I was pushing the envelope. I really didn't want to hurt the kid—and I don't suppose anyone likes to catch his best friend banging his mother. I very much doubt if he noticed how overheated and overexcited she was when he came home.

I figured everyone would be surprised when I decided not to go to Michigan State but attend the local college. After all, you don't turn down an athletic scholarship for no reason—and of course I couldn't give the real reason. I don't say that I was, like, falling in love with Kevin's mom—that would be too lame and stupid; but I do say that she was really good in bed—better than the ditsy girls at school I'd had to bop for years—and getting better all the time. After she had gotten over the horror and mortification of having an affair with a seventeen-year-old boy—even a boy who was built like no man she'd ever had, and who made her ex-husband look like Caspar Milquetoast—she, shall we say, got into it. With the passing of months she really loosened up. And I have to admit that

I really got kind of addicted to those tight little breasts of hers. I couldn't stop sucking them. I couldn't believe how firm they were—it was almost as if they were fake. But smaller breasts do tend to be firm, even ones that have suckled a child or two. It's the big bazooms that are horribly shapeless and flabby. No thanks!

Well, I moved into a dorm room on campus—had to get away from dad and his awful burned dinners and drinking and fighting—and stopped by Kevin's mom's house pretty regularly. For of course, Kevin himself had gone off to Wellesley or some other former all-girls school on the East Coast, and so he was out of the picture. We actually stayed in touch by e-mail, but there was plenty I didn't tell him. I guess I was servicing Mrs. Jacobs about three times a week, often staying overnight when I didn't have an early class. She made a mean breakfast, and I liked to eat it naked in her kitchen nook while she would mosey around in a kimono or something, sometimes tight around her and sometimes flapping loose. She'd sometimes sit on my lap and feed me mouthful by mouthful, kissing me after each bite. Once she gave me a bubble bath.

The girls at college weren't quite so silly as the ones in high school, although of course a fair number of the girls—and guys—from our class ended up going to the college in town, either because they were too scared to brave the big wide world or because they couldn't get in anywhere else. College does mature you a bit, but not enough for me: the girls—and I could have had my pick, for it didn't take me long to became a star on our mediocre sports teams—just didn't do it for me. When I had someone as experienced as Kevin's mom, why the hell would I bed down with a girl who was little more than a recently devirginized teenager? When I could have someone halfway intelligent to talk to, why would I want to yak with a girl whose vocabulary was bounded by giggles and "Omigod"?

And talk we did. I learned a lot about her, and what had happened with her ex. He was a real jerk, although I have to say—and Maureen admitted this herself—that she was not entirely without blame. What happened was this:

After having Kevin, Maureen kind of freaked out about the whole motherhood thing. Aside from having to tend to her baby and get her figure back, she didn't feel like having sex for a really, really long time—maybe a year or more. Her husband—Don, I think his name was—took it in stride for a while, but eventually began freaking out himself. Acted real snippy and short with Maureen, which she repaid in kind. I think that's when she became the super-fussbudget she turned into: it was as if turning into a little domestic tyrant was her way of getting revenge on her loathsome husband.

They did have sex, but at real infrequent intervals—maybe once every two months. Once she caught him playing with himself—but she was such a middle-class prude that she didn't use that as a springboard for some kinky sex, but just backed away and never spoke of it again. (I once tried to get her to play with herself in front of me, but she squawked so much she almost broke down in tears—and anyway she couldn't get herself off. I didn't have that problem: I came on her face any number of times—it kinda made me feel I was a porn star.)

Anyway, it went from bad to worse. A year, two years would pass between sex. And so the inevitable happened: the guy ran off with his secretary. So before I came along, Kevin's mom hadn't had sex for, maybe, six years. I asked her if she'd ever tried to date, but she seemed horrified at the idea. So I figured I was doing her a favor by bopping her regularly: good for the soul, you know?

Once she asked about me. What about my parents? She didn't know them—we weren't exactly in the same social circle, if you know what I mean.

So I just said: "Well, my dad is a construction worker, makes terrible meals, beats me upside the head when he drinks too much, and in general is a guy I wouldn't mind seeing dead."

She tried to hide her shock at that, and all she could say to change the subject was:

"How about your mom?"

I said blandly, "My mom left us when I was five," and fell asleep with my mouth glued to her nipple.

PEEPING TOM

Believe it or not, I'm not a peeping Tom.

Not by nature, at any rate.

But what are you going to do when a shapely and attractive woman parades herself in front of her large picture window for all the world to see?

Here's the set-up. I live in a big apartment building that's really two buildings in one, divided by a "courtyard"—if you can call it that—that looks like something out of *Metropolis* or *Brazil*. It's not meant to be used or even occupied by any of the tenants, and in fact there's no convenient access to it; which is no doubt why the lady in question feels no compunction displaying herself in the buff in front of her window. She's in the south building, her window facing north, and I'm in the north building, my window facing south. So I have what might be called a front-row seat.

Now you gotta understand that I'm really not interested in naked ladies. Well, of course I am, but I'm not exactly going to do something illegal to get an eyeful of them. But this woman seems to have no shame—or, perhaps, no interest—in what she is doing.

The first time I saw her was when I got up way earlier than usual—for me—to relieve myself. I work freelance, so I don't have to hit the pavement with all the other wage-slaves of the world; but the call of nature is imperious, and my bathroom is located in such a way that I have to cross the living room—and *my* large picture window—to get to it. And as I was going there, or maybe coming back, there she was.

She clearly *was* a wage-slave, although perhaps a somewhat more classy one than usual. So far as I could tell, she had a full-length mirror set up in her living room, and when she came out of *her* bathroom she went right up to it. She had nothing on. Her apartment is one floor above mine, so I couldn't quite see her full figure: the best I could see was her up to her knees. But that was good enough. She was slim, curvy, blonde, with incredibly erect tits and a bush that could have been a kind of Amazon jungle for any tics and lice that I'm sure were not there. In these days of shaved pussies it's been a long time since I saw a lush delta like that. I took her to be in her later thirties.

Why she didn't dress, or put her makeup on, in the privacy of her bathroom or bedroom was anyone's guess. She was entirely unself-conscious about walking around without any clothes on and with the curtains wide open. She simply didn't care. I don't think she was an exhibitionist: she was (peculiar as this may sound) too *self-centered* to be. I never saw her standing directly in front of her window and saying, in effect, "C'mon, guys, look at my hot bod!" She knew she had a hot bod, and couldn't be troubled to interest or tease anyone who might be trying to take it all in.

So it happened that for the most part I saw her only in profile. That's how I could tell she had fabulous boobs that didn't need a bra to hold them up, and a lovely curved butt without an ounce of fat, and that dense forest of dark fur at her groin. When she leaned over to the mirror to put the finishing touches on her face, I thought I would just about explode.

Then she crisply put on a power business suit, slipped on her shoes, and got the hell out of there. It was twenty to nine. However high-powered an executive she may have been, she didn't want to be late.

So what do you think I did after that? Yep, you got it in one: from that day forward, I set my own alarm for about eight a.m. and took in the view. Day after day it was pretty much the same: she would come out of her shower at around 8:15, go naked to her kitchen to make some coffee, and while that was brewing she would make up her face. She taught me how some women put on a bra, clasping it in front and then spinning it around to put the straps on. Very clever—I would never have thought of that. I guess that's why I don't wear a bra. And I swear to you that one time she actually combed her bush. I'm sure I'd never seen *that* before.

It's pretty interesting to try to figure out a person's life, mood, and character just based on seeing them—whether naked or not—without hearing a word they say. After a while I got to know this broad pretty well. Usually she'd come home around 5:30, make dinner, watch TV, or read a book or magazine—nothing unusual. Sometimes she'd have people over, although usually no more than four, since all our apartments are pretty small. On weekends she might dress in a light cotton dress and wear a bonnet. Once or twice she dressed up in tennis gear.

Then, of course, there was her husband.

Sorry I forgot to mention him; naturally, he didn't figure very much in my thoughts. But he was there—or at least someone I took to be a husband of some kind. I hate to say this, but in some ways he was more interesting than she was. I will confess that he wasn't exactly appealing physically—balding, paunchy, with one of those loosely hung faces that look too big for the body it's attached to. He seemed older than her—maybe mid-forties or even more. I could never figure out exactly what he did, if he did anything. Sometimes he left the apartment in the morning, but most times not. He didn't seem to have a regular job. Many times he wouldn't even be up before she left the house. And on those times that he was, he would just lounge on the sofa and read the paper—that's right, *read the paper*—while she paraded around naked in front of him and everybody else.

What gives here? Is this what marriage does to you? I wanted to go right over there and throttle the poor bastard, saying: *What do you think you're doing, guy? You can get a large helping of the most luscious eye-candy that ever fell into a man's lap, and you're seeing whether your stocks went up a fraction of a point yesterday.* (Actually, they were probably her stocks.) I vowed that if I ever got married, and got lucky enough to nab a hottie like her, I'd make sure she knew how special she was. Of course, if *my* wife decided to parade around naked in the place, I'd make sure the blinds were closed.

The wife—I decided to call her Francine, for that name suited her somehow—seemed to regard her husband with a mixture of contempt and condescending affection, as if he were some old pet that she'd had for years and couldn't be troubled to have put down. Just as he hardly gave her a second look even though he could have slapped her butt half-a-dozen times as she walked back and forth in front of him getting dressed, she scarcely looked at him sitting like a lump on the sofa, and could be bothered only to give him the most token wave of the arm when she left the place. He really didn't seem to know what to do with himself, and oftentimes I never even saw him—he must have gone back to the bedroom to sleep away consciousness until dinnertime.

To give him credit, he would do a lot of the cooking, although like all urban couples they went out for dinner a lot or brought in take-out. There was one time he bought a live lobster, and when she came home he playfully shoved it in her face. It was the one time I saw them engaging in anything like horseplay. I guess Francine wasn't really the sort of woman who would take kindly to horseplay.

I think there must have been times when she got tired of his shiftlessness, for I could have sworn that one day, while he was sitting as usual on the couch, she berated him (clothed), waving a section if the newspaper (maybe the want ads?) in his face. He just shrugged and tried to look away, at which point she just threw the paper down and stalked off. I guess he figured that she was making good enough money for both of them.

So, you wonder—I certainly did—what kept them together. Was he some kind of Adonis in bed? Could I in fact figure out anything about their sex life? I think there was *one* time—only one—when she came out of the bedroom, naked of course, and maybe just a little sweaty, although it was hard for me to tell from so far away. Her hair was mussed up, which it otherwise never was except when she came right out of the shower. All she did then was to mosey on up to that full-length mirror and look herself over, raking her hair with her fingers and actually giving her breasts a bit of a feel—maybe to make sure they were still firm after hubby had tugged on them to his heart's content. I never saw *him*—*he* never paraded naked in front of the picture window, thank Gawd for small mercies—but I'm pretty sure he was there. *Someone* was there, anyway.

So you ask, where's all this leading to? Well, I'll be honest that I really got to like getting an eyeful of naked Francine every morning—and it was *every* (weekday) morning that she announced to the world that her body was available to anyone who wanted to look. She was like clockwork. She didn't stay naked long enough for me to get myself off, but most of the time I got hot enough that

I managed to finish the job myself a bit later. I was, to put it tactfully, between girlfriends, and so I really didn't have much going on in that direction just then. And since the last breakup wasn't the most entertaining thing I'd ever gone through, this kind of silent visual relationship was just about what I could handle.

But you know how things go. After a while you get to thinking ... *what if there was a time when hubby wasn't there?* As I say, our apartment complex was a big one, and there were front and back entrances to it, so it wasn't easy to actually make acquaintances with anyone not within your immediate vicinity. Did I mention that one time Francine actually saw me peeping at her? (OK, OK, I'm a peeping Tom—are you happy now?) Picture this: Here she is, going back and forth naked, coffee cup in one hand and some makeup implement in the other; she stops cold and looks directly out her window (giving me a fabulous full-frontal view of her magnificent tits and that heavenly bush, not to mention curving hips that Aphrodite would have died for) and looks right at me; here *I* am, giving my member the business while looking straight out *my* window (were there peeping Tomettes looking at me?). Well, I guess I'm really kinda shy, because the sight of those flinty eyes boring in at me made me go limp—in every sense of the term—and I just fell to the floor, ducking under the window and out of view of that luscious but terrifying beauty. I must have stayed there for half an hour, because when I finally pulled myself up and poked my head fractionally above the windowsill to see what was going on across the courtyard, Francine's place was empty.

So that's how it stood . . . until the time when I saw her coming out the back entrance of the building while I was going in. I was so stunned that I just held the door open like a comatose doorman while she sauntered out, looking right into my eyes and saying "Thank you" in a low, clipped voice that said all kinds of things without saying them: *I know who you are; I know what you're doing; I think you're a poor loser, but if you want to look at my fabulous body, go ahead . . . I can't even begin to tell you how little I care.*

Well, that was kinda the last straw. I really wasn't a loser—you can take a survey of my dozen or so ex-girlfriends if you want—and I decided I'd prove it to her, somehow.

The chance came sooner than I thought. Of course, there was no way anything could be done on weekdays, for she was in such a hurry getting herself dolled up like a female Donald Trump that it would be hopeless to make a move then; and anyway, hubby was surely lurking in the bedroom or somewhere. And as for weekends, well, again hubby was the problem. Why couldn't he just go on a long vacation by himself, or something? I don't recall a single time when *both* of them went on vacation for more than a day or two.

But one Saturday morning proved to be my opening. I don't know if he'd decided to go shopping for one of his specialty meals, but I saw him get up before her and trundle out of the house before *she* got up. Maybe she slept in on weekends after her hard week's work at Morgan Stanley or wherever. So he was, at least temporarily, out of the picture. What would she do?

It was pretty much the same as before. I could actually see steam coming out of where I knew the bathroom was: like me, she liked really hot showers. Well, I might make it a little hotter for her.

Eventually she came out, in all her naked glory. This time she was drying herself in front of the picture window with this big towel, and as she energetically dried her back she may have cast a glance at my window, wondering idly if she had her usual audience. She did, but it wasn't for long.

I had already bolted out of my apartment and headed to the basement, where there was an underground walkway to the south building. I knew which floor she was on, but I wasn't absolutely certain which door was hers. But I'd reached the stage where caution was definitely thrown to the winds.

So there I was, standing in front of the door that I *thought* was hers. No use being shy now. I knocked sharply, creating almost an echo effect down the whole corridor.

There was a moment of dead silence. Then, in a surprisingly tentative voice: "Who is it?"

It was her voice. I knew it—I could never forget that smarmy "Thank you" she had flung at me that time. By now, my whole body tingling with adrenaline, I figured I had to go through with it; so I just said: "You know who it is."

Another dead silence. Either she would ignore me altogether or else she would laugh uproariously and say something like, "What chance do you have with me, bud?"

But she did neither of those things. Instead, she opened the door. She was still entirely naked. She just stood there, looking up at me.

I was a few inches taller than her, and I'm pretty well built, so I just stalked right in, forcing her to back off. I wouldn't say she was anything like a shrinking violet; but I knew that with women like her, strength works better than politeness. Anyway, it's a bit hard to be polite to a woman standing naked in front of you.

After a few moments of silence, she said sharply: "Well, what do you want?"

I was prepared. Muttering, "I think you have a pretty good idea," I displayed myself.

I forgot to mention that I had come over there wearing only my bathrobe, with nothing on underneath. Now I dropped the robe to my feet.

My boner was jutting proudly forward. She looked at my face, then looked down at my groin, then back at my face. There was just the faintest curl of a smile at her lips—and just the faintest shadow of dread in her eyes.

I took things quite literally in my own hands, marching right up to her and wrapping my arms around her waist. The first contact of flesh on flesh was electrifying, especially when my cock seemed engulfed in that forest of fur at her crotch. I pasted a kiss on her mouth: she resisted just for a second, then gave in, enfolding her arms around my neck and mashing those lovely tits into my chest. For my part, I moved my arms down and clutched the cheeks of her buttocks, satisfied in my guess that there was no fat to be found there. Soon I reached one hand around to her front, slipped it between her legs, and found a surprising amount of wetness dripping out of her pussy lips.

She wasn't slow on the uptake either. While our lips were glued together, she took one hand away from my neck and grasped it firmly around my hugely swelled cock. I don't know when I've ever felt so big. She gave it a bit of a rubbing, then, somewhat to my surprise, simply parted her legs and let it slip into her pussy.

There we were, fucking each other standing up for anyone—if there was anyone—to see. The curtains were wide open.

I held on to her buttocks with both hands while pumping her. She raked her nails all over my back, causing a little blood to flow. Maddened, I turned my head and bit her earlobe, at which point she gasped and almost screamed. Her noise helped to cover up my own, because I shouted at the top of my lungs when I came.

For a while we must stood there clinging to each other, more to prevent ourselves from falling down than because we had any kind of tender affection for each other. Breathing heavily, we must both have pondered what we had just done. I had just fucked another man's wife in his own apartment—a woman I had met (the little encounter at the back entrance hardly counted) about two minutes before I plugged her. For her part, Francine (or whatever the hell her name was—I still didn't know and never found out) must have been thinking: *My husband walked out the door. A strange man who has been playing peeping Tom for weeks or months has just come in, all but naked. He has seen me naked dozens, perhaps hundreds of times. After the most cursory protest, I let him fuck me standing up.*

Well, we didn't have much time for reflections of that kind. The doorbell rang.

Splitting apart with a kind of wet sucking sound, we stood there in alarm like two burglars when an alarm goes off. My come was dripping off of me and making its oozing way down her legs, but I was shrinking rapidly. She quickly said, "Oh, God! It's my husband!" and shooed me into the bedroom, telling me to stay in the closet until the coast was clear. A few seconds afterward she threw my bathrobe in after me.

So here I am in her closet. This is too ridiculous for words. What kind of bad soap opera had I stumbled into?

Then I got to thinking: *Why the hell would her husband ring the doorbell? Why wouldn't he use his key and come right in?*

Well, maybe what Francine said was just the first thing that came into her guilty conscience. Clearly, *someone* was at the door; even if it was just a delivery boy, it was better for me to keep under wraps until it was safe to slink back to my own apartment.

I could hear the door opening. For a moment there was silence. Then a man's voice said, "You look even better up close than at a distance."

Very soon thereafter there were various sounds of kissing, sucking, licking, and so forth. I thought to myself: *Well, this is one scenario where three isn't a crowd.*

I came out—naked—and joined in the fun. But before that, I made sure the curtains were drawn.

PERSONALS

Carla shivered as she entered the café. At sunset the temperature had begun to drop rapidly, and there was the threat of snow later in the evening. Carla didn't mind the cold or the snow, but she hated getting out of work when it was dark. You arrive in the bright sunlight of the morning, and by the time you leave it's already pitch dark. It's as if the whole day is wasted, Carla thought, even though she liked her job.

The café was large but informal; it was only six, but already it was filling up. She looked around nervously, but didn't see any man sitting alone. Am I early? she wondered. She didn't think so . . . well, maybe a little. She saw a sign saying "Please Wait To Be Seated," but there was no one there to seat her. She stood indecisively, wondering whether she should simply go to a table, when finally someone who looked like a maitre d' (if he could be called that in a place as casual as this) came up.

"Table for one, miss?"

(She hated it when people called her "miss," but thought it was inevitable, since "Ms." seemed so awkward to pronounce.)

"No, for two . . . ."

The maitre d' made what she thought was an elaborate effort to see if she had a companion and, when it was obvious that she did not, raised an eyebrow.

"I mean, I'm expecting someone . . . ."

With amazing alacrity the maitre d' nodded "Ah!" and began guiding her to a table toward the back. She followed without thinking, and found herself being led to a table where an elderly woman was seated alone. The woman looked up, and Carla's eyes met hers for an instant.

"Here you are, miss," said the maitre d'.

"No," Carla said, "I think there's some mistake . . . ."

The waiter's eyebrow went up.

As if on cue, both Carla and the woman spoke the same words together:

"I'm waiting for . . . ."

Both stopped abruptly, and turned to look at each other. Then both spoke again together.

". . . a man."

It might have been rehearsed! Carla said to herself, and giggled aloud. The other woman merely smiled. But in any event, enlightenment dawned upon the maitre d' and he said, "Yes, of course," as if remembering something he had forgotten. He led Carla to the table—for two—next to the elderly woman's and held the chair for her. Only at that moment did Carla notice, disconcertingly, that her coat and the woman's were nearly identical. She suddenly remembered seeing some eighteenth-century painting of two couples who had met in a sunny, open square in Venice, with the two women glaring at each other almost with hatred because they were wearing nearly the same long, red, bell-like dress. *What vain creatures we are!* Carla thought.

The two women looked at each other tentatively and with some embarrassment, not knowing how to begin a conversation or whether there should even be a conversation. Finally Carla said:

"Are you waiting for your husband?" (She knew this wasn't the case—the woman wasn't wearing a ring—but she couldn't think of anything else to say.)

"No, no," the older woman said, but failed to volunteer more.

Carla was about to ask if she was waiting for a boyfriend, but almost giggled out loud wondering, *Can women that old be said to have boyfriends?* It was a cruel thought—the woman couldn't have been much more than sixty.

"Actually," the other woman finally said, a little abruptly, "I'm on a blind date."

Carla was startled. "Really?" was all she could manage.

"Yes, I know you must think it silly, at my age, but I answer personal ads from time to time . . . just to see what might happen. You never know."

"And you've not met this man before?"

"No," said the woman. "I don't even know what he looks like. Of course, I've spoken to him on the phone, and he described himself to me, so I think I can recognize him. He sounds very nice."

Carla said nothing for a while. Then she blurted out:

"You know, this is really remarkable, because *I'm* on a blind date also . . . I've never met *my* man either. I hope he doesn't confuse us!"

Carla laughed at her own jest, but the other woman only smiled politely. For an irrational instant Carla wondered whether this woman was in fact here to meet *her* date. But no, that couldn't be! Surely the man she had spoken to on the phone didn't sound like the type to play that sort of joke. He was also "nice," of course—Carla would never have anything to do with a man who wasn't—but there was so much more. . . . She had felt a real rapport with him even during their twenty-minute phone conversation.

She recalled seeing the ad in the magazine. She had initially subscribed to the magazine two years ago because she had generally agreed with its editorial policy and felt that many of the articles were very thought-provoking; but gradually she had begun turning immediately to the back of the issue and seeing whether there might be some presentable males taking out personals. She still read the magazine itself, although she had somehow gotten three or four issues behind, but she always read the personals. Occasionally she would answer some (she could never bring herself to take out a personal of her own); sometimes she would hear back from the men, and then meet them. Nothing serious had happened yet, but you never know.

This ad had appealed to her immediately. *Lonely man, hopelessly romantic, seeking well-bred, intelligent, attractive woman, 30–35, for serious relationship.* "Lonely"—well, that was certainly honest! She had hoped it was not some eccentric recluse, but felt that if he wanted someone "well-bred" and "intelligent," he must be those things himself. She had taken heart that he had listed "attractive" after the other qualities he sought; not that she really had anything to worry about on that score, but it must mean that he didn't set quite so much on personal appearance as most men do.

So she had written a letter to him, to be forwarded by the magazine. She had only given her first name, and she had given only her telephone number, not her address (she would never give out her address to a man unless she knew him well, and would never, never give her address *and* phone number together). She suspected that he was a little older, maybe thirty-five to forty. Funny how men want women who are younger, and women want men who are older, she thought. And isn't it funny how men mostly want women who are shorter than they are, while women generally favor men who are taller . . . . She sighed, thinking that some sexual stereotypes might never be overcome.

The two women hadn't spoken for some time, and Carla had hardly noticed the other. But now the woman removed some papers from her handbag and began leafing through them. *Well, that's a little rude*, Carla said to herself, but then chided herself, thinking that she and the woman, in spite of the similarity of their situation, really had nothing to talk about. But the other woman looked up and said abruptly:

"This is a story my man sent me. Would you like to read it? I have another copy."

Without waiting for a reply she handed Carla a set of typewritten sheets. Carla took them without thinking. Then the peculiarity of the situation struck her: Why would this woman have two copies of the story with her? Did her man send her two copies? Did she make a copy just so she could give one to someone else? Carla looked at the first page: "A Night at the Movies, by Samuel Winsor." A nice name, sort of old-fashioned—how fitting for this old maid! Carla bit her tongue, again chiding herself for her unkindness.

She was hardly one to talk, anyway. Here she was, thirty-two years old, and still unmarried. The personals had really been a bit of a disappointment. She had remembered what a thrill it had been to write off to these mysterious men at the beginning—maybe they were lonely millionaires, or struggling novelists, or even some educated workman who wanted some feminine refinement in his life. But then she found that many of the men didn't even call her, and those who did often sounded so ordinary. . . . Still, she had met some of them, and had had a pleasant enough time, but she knew that they weren't for her. It was always a little ticklish at the end of a date: if you really didn't like the person, or at least didn't think you wanted to see him again, you had to convey it politely and not hurt his feelings . . . . "Thanks for a lovely time," "It was great fun meeting you," even "Keep in touch," even though you really didn't mean it and hoped to heaven he wouldn't call back . . .

Of course, you had to be careful with some of these people. She knew that the magazine wouldn't allow ads for people who just wanted sex, but she had the feeling that some of the personals were covertly seeking just that. She didn't answer any that stated that the man was "passionate," and certainly not the ones who wanted "fun and frolic" . . . that was really too obvious. Fortunately, she had had no disastrous experiences as yet.

But the possibilities for trouble were always there. She wondered about the situations where one person liked the other but wasn't liked in return. This could become very awkward. It really hadn't happened to her, although she did remember the time when she had met the schoolteacher and thought they had really hit it off, and hoped he would call—that was when she had gotten an answering machine—and he never had. But what if a man really wanted you and you just didn't want him? Would he call incessantly, forcing you to disconnect your phone or turn off your answering machine? Would he run amok and try to hunt you down? Maybe he would follow you home from work (she usually told her men where she worked—that seemed safe enough) and fall to his knees on your doorstep, pleading with you to go out with him, maybe even crying in that rough, uncouth, half-ashamed way men cry. That would be just too awful.

She looked down at the story, which she saw the other woman reading with a neutral expression. Probably she's read it before, Carla thought, and is refreshing her memory so that she can talk about it with her man. It seemed to involve a couple named Henry and April (what a stupid, artsy name!) who evidently knew each other reasonably well but who, the author implied, hadn't yet become "intimate" . . . . He actually used that word, and again Carla thought it a little old-fashioned but charming in its way. They had gone to some film which they had both enjoyed, but now it was late and very dark, and they were simply walking about.

Carla turned around in her seat and looked toward the entrance. She wished she hadn't been placed with her back to the door of the café, since she couldn't see who came in. There was nobody waiting at the "Please Wait To Be Seated" sign, certainly not a man of thirty-five to forty. . . . Surely he would know enough to come in and look for her? Would he be waiting *outside*? No, it was too cold, and now Carla thought she saw the first few flakes of snow starting to fall. He was now definitely late, and she hoped he had some good excuse.

The strange thing was that she couldn't even remember much of the phone conversation she had had with him, even though she did remember his deep baritone voice and his slow, precise way of talking. He was definitely well-bred and intelligent, and she hoped she had presented herself that way also. They seemed to have a lot of common interests—music, museums, films, long walks in the park—and she thought there was a real possibility of something significant developing.

In the story Henry had offered to walk April back home. Carla, already caught up in the story in spite of its rather dry and plain style, began feeling a little nervous. *Why don't you just take a taxi, you silly?* she expostulated to April. And yet, Henry seemed the perfect gentleman, only holding April's hand chastely, not trying to put his arm around her waist and certainly not fondling her out in the open, even though they were now in a residential section where all the people were safely in their homes.

The other woman was reading also, but not as intently. And she also seemed a little farther behind than Carla, which Carla thought strange if she had read the story before. Maybe the woman was just a slow reader; perhaps she wasn't even very well educated, although her clothes certainly indicated she was well-bred enough. Every now and then the woman (*funny that I never asked her name, Carla thought, or gave her mine*) would look up from her reading and smile, a little tiredly. Where was *her* man? He must be even later than Carla's. But the woman didn't seem to mind so much.

Now Henry and April had arrived at April's apartment building and were saying their goodnights. They must have known each other reasonably well, for the writer had them embrace and kiss for some time at the doorstep. Carla's hands seemed to be shaking for some reason, and she had trouble reading the words clearly. Then she groaned inwardly as April hesitantly invited Henry in for a drink. *No, no, you little fool!* But it was done, and they were heading up the stairs toward April's third-floor apartment.

Carla knew what was coming.

No sooner had April turned the key and opened the door than Henry shoved himself in and slammed the door, leaving the key outside in the lock. He grasped April by the shoulders and pushed her against the door, kissing her roughly. April incongruously felt his moustache tickling her nose. As Henry began kissing her neck and throat April got her breath back and gasped, "Stop it, you—"

"Beast!" Carla said.

But Henry wouldn't stop. Now he was fumbling at the buttons of her blouse, leaning against April so that she was pinned between him and the door. April inwardly cursed herself for wearing a brassiere that unsnapped from the front, for this made it that much easier for Henry to remove it. April was growing dizzy and faint as Henry fondled her breasts, one knee jammed between her legs.

Carla was now clutching the pages spasmodically, unable to stop reading but unwilling to finish. Suddenly she looked up at the other woman and was amazed to find that her placid expression had not changed. Perhaps she was not so far along in the story. Then Carla remembered that the woman must surely have read the story before, so that she knew what was coming. She couldn't believe that an almost complete stranger had sent this woman a story like that. The idea! And what did this woman mean by giving her such a story to read?

On the last page of the typescript the text ended about half way down, and below this there was a crisply rendered pen-and-ink drawing. It was really rather horrible. The artist (the author? a friend of his?) had shown a window of an apartment building with gauze curtains over it, and two shadow-figures within. It was a little hard to make out, as the picture was pretty small, but it seemed to show a woman bent over a kitchen table with a man standing behind her and holding her down. The skirt had been rucked up to the woman's waist, and Carla thought she could see the woman's breasts mashed against the hard surface of the table. And was the man holding the woman by her hair . . . ?

Abruptly Carla stood up. She realized it was close to seven, and she was certain her man wasn't coming. The other woman looked up with those placid, resigned eyes of hers, but said nothing. Carla grabbed her coat and almost ran to the front of the café, now almost full with couples and groups of people in the midst of their dinner. The maitre d' was there, lounging idly in front of the

"Please Wait To Be Seated" sign. He looked at her without interest, not even raising an eyebrow.

"Has anyone come by . . . ?" she said breathlessly.

He just shook his head.

Then she remembered that she still had the story written by the other woman's man. She felt she ought to return it, even though it was a pretty awful thing, and she thought she might even give the woman a piece of her mind for giving her a story like that. She turned around to go back into the café.

The other woman wasn't there.

For a moment Carla was dazed and confused. How absurd! Had the woman decided at that moment to leave also? She had clearly been stood up herself. But if so, where had she gone? There was no other exit to the café. Carla drifted back to where she had been sitting. There was a nearly full glass of water at the other woman's table. Had she ever drunk from it? Carla couldn't remember. She lifted the glass, hoping to find some lipstick on the rim, or *any* sign that the woman had been there. But there was none. Without thinking, Carla took a sip of water from the glass. It was flat and tepid.

Carla stuffed the story in her handbag and wandered back up to the front of the café. Nothing to do now but go home. She couldn't even call up her man, for he had not given her his phone number. Maybe there would be a message on her answering machine, but she knew there would be none.

At that moment the door of the café opened and a cold blast of wind, along with a few snowflakes, blew in. A man entered alone. His eyes met Carla's for an instant, then turned indifferently away.

"Table for one, please," he told the maitre d'.

Was it him? It sounded a *little* like his voice, although the telephone did funny things to voices. But he had said he was tall and broad-shouldered, and this man was only slightly taller than Carla and not really very well-built. Surely he couldn't be the other woman's man, for he was not nearly old enough. And anyway, he had asked only for a table for one.

The maitre d' guided him almost obsequiously to the table at which Carla had been sitting.

Flustered, almost crying now, Carla fled from the café, running down the street, which she knew would be deserted, and back to her apartment, which she knew would be empty.

ONE TOO MANY

"Amor me docuit castas odisse puellas."
—Propertius

I grabbed her wrist before she had a chance to turn on the light, or even get the key out of the lock—I saw it fitting snugly there for an instant before I dragged her into the room, slammed the door, and thrust her, face forward, against the wall. At the first contact of my hand she uttered a gasp—one of those silly, high-pitched, pathetic little gasps that women let out all the time. Now, as I pushed her against the wall of her own room—fool! why do you wonder how I got in, when you leave your windows unlocked all day long?—I wondered if it hurt her to have her breasts flattened by the wall: I could see those foul lumps of flesh, ugly and distorted, through her dress. She wasn't wearing any makeup, but she had some sickening perfume on—how typical. I hoped she could smell my sweat, my lust, my rage.

I drew out my switchblade and let her feel it against her back. "Make one sound, you bitch," I whispered, "and you'll end up in a thousand pieces all over this room." She closed her eyes tightly, and a tear crept down from one corner. No, you don't, you slut—it won't work to gain my pity. I wanted to laugh, for I suddenly thought of an aria from a Vivaldi opera: *"Son tutto crudeltà"*—"I am all cruelty." It's amusing to be an educated criminal.

I whirled her around, tore off the front of her skimpy dress with one hand while unzipping my fly with the other. Her panties came off with one stroke of my switchblade, and she stood there in her stockings like any common whore. I pounded her until she cried out at each thrust: she was probably enjoying it, the slut—all the girls in X-rated movies cry out like that. When I came I let out a sort of growl and let her sink to the floor. I became suddenly calm—I always do after sex—and arranged my clothes and walked right out the door. Before closing it I took the keys out of the lock and threw them in her lap.

* * * * * * *

I didn't like the way that girl in the front row was looking at me. What was her name? Diana, I think. Diana—what a virginal name. *Dea virgo, custos nemorum* . . . Surely she couldn't be finding my lecture interesting—I certainly wasn't. How many times had I given it?—"Samuel Johnson and *Rasselas*." What did Juvenal say about such things? *Crambe repetita*—"rehashed cabbage."

I made a mistake, though—in my arrogance I casually referred to my own article on the subject in *ELH*. As I was walking quickly to the door, she came up to me. She must be new, I thought—everyone knows I speak to students only by appointment.

I stopped grudgingly and looked at her.

"Do you have a copy of your article?" she asked in that piping and childish sort of voice which most girls never lose, however old they are. "I'd like to borrow it."

People tell me I have a cold glare to my eyes which ranges from hostility to contempt. I was giving Diana my most withering look, but she didn't seem to notice.

"I think I have an offprint in my office," I finally said.

We walked along the corridor, talking about *Rasselas*. I was surprised—she had actually made an effort to read the thing before class. I tried to avoid the masses of other students walking in the opposite direction, but couldn't help rubbing shoulders with some of them. One girl—she had taken my Dryden and Pope course two years ago—smiled at me as she passed, and I swear she intentionally rubbed her bosom (of course she wasn't wearing a bra) against my arm as she passed. Whore.

We reached my office, and I found the offprint as quickly as I could. I handed it to her.

"Here you are," I said.

"Thanks—I'll return it real soon," she chirped.

"Don't bother. You can keep it—I have many more."

Another mistake. I could have bitten my tongue.

Her eyes widened and a foul, naive little smile creased her face. "Thanks, Professor Jameson—thanks a lot."

She turned around and left.

* * * * * * *

This one was a brunette—I rather prefer brunettes—and she had a sort of mousy face with small features which I suppose I could have gotten to like if I tried. She was wearing makeup, but at least it wasn't whorish. She was biting her lower lip over and over again, as if her lipstick were bothering her—or perhaps she was remembering someone's kiss that evening. Small breasts—narrow hips—slim thighs. God, if I didn't know better I'd think she was a virgin. She was no college student, though—probably a secretary.

She seemed to be whispering to herself (why is it that even a girl's whisper is distinctive?) as she walked casually to the front door of her house. This was a "good" neighborhood—nothing ever happened here. It was also far enough from the university that no suspicion would ever come my way.

When I jumped out of the bushes she gasped—God, I hate that!—and stood still.

"Open the door, bitch—fast!"

"Please don't—" she started.

"Do it—now!"

She fumbled in her handbag and got the keys. She gave some hurried glances around—but her neighbors were either asleep or safe in their houses. Watching television, probably.

Her hand was shaking when she put the key into the lock. As she turned it I opened the door and pushed her in—she almost fell, but stumbled against the corridor wall. Even in the darkness I could see the whites of her round eyes.

I closed the door, got out the switchblade, and warned her about screaming as I had done with that other bitch the week before. *Hey*, I thought—*I'm getting rather good at this.* I recalled that Aristotle had something to say about habit being useful for moral training.

She was cowering against the wall, but I grabbed her arm—no muscles there, of course—and dragged her to her bedroom. I threw her on the bed and unzipped my fly.

She saw it and said: "No! God, no . . . ."

"Shut up," I said.

Her arms were crossed over her breasts. I must have surprised her, though, when I roughly rolled her over so that she lay on her stomach. She started to say:

"What are you—?"

"Shut up," I said again, sending a blow to her neck with my hand.

I didn't tear her clothing this time—I merely placed one hand on the small of her back, lifted up her skirt (it was a short one—you could have guessed) and cut away her panties with my blade as before. She finally began to realize what I was going to do, and started to complain again before I clubbed her head enough to make her groan and start sobbing.

She was in such a pathetic position—there I was, controlling her with one hand. Plato had said women were the equals of men in everything, except that they were weaker. They were weaker.

When I jammed my rod into her asshole she screamed, but I squeezed her face into the pillow. Her hair fell rather seductively over her cheeks and her long lashes were closed tight. Her eyelids squeezed every time I thrust.

I took my time about it—I'd already jerked off beforehand—and I must have been in her for about ten minutes. After a while she stopped struggling, so that I could grab the cheeks of her ass and thrust the harder. By the time I came I was almost entirely on top of her, my breath making her hair sway over her face. That sickening perfume smell almost made me vomit.

When I left the room I saw that she hadn't moved.

* * * * * * *

The knock on my door surprised and alarmed me. It was far too early in the semester for anyone to be worrying about final exams or term papers, and the timorousness of the knock ruled out any of the faculty.

I suppose, though, I should have guessed. It was Diana.

She was all excited, she said, about my article (fat chance! how does one get excited about dry literary scholarship?), and wanted to talk to me about it. I looked at her closely to see what ulterior motive she could have, but she simply gave me that naive, wide-eyed smile which I find so irritating in girls. It's so—so schoolgirl-ish.

I let her in and we talked. I must say she was rather bright—she'd read Johnson's poems with some care—and I actually found myself half enjoying the talk.

Or would have if a nasty thought didn't occur to me.

She looks like Cindy. Damnably so.

And she did—round face with full cheeks and finely chiseled features, figure that was not plump but well filled out, absence of makeup but faint perfume, chaste attire bordering on the prudish. She was a blonde, though, not a brunette.

I asked her if she was new. She was—had transferred that semester from Lehigh. It was her senior year, and she even hinted that she would like to write her senior thesis under me. I steered the conversation in another direction.

She had seen some of my other books and articles, and was amazed how much work I'd done at so early an age.

"I'm not so young," I said. "I'm thirty-four."

That wide-eyed look again. "Are you serious? You look as if you're in your late twenties."

I silently approved the fact that she used *as if* instead of the now universal solecism *like*; but I couldn't help glaring at her coldly.

"Thank you."

"You know, Professor," she started hesitantly, "there's one other problem I'm having. . . ."

I didn't speak for a moment. Then: "What's that?"

"Well, I've been trying to find Johnson's complete *Rambler*, but it doesn't seem to be in the library. Someone's checked out the Yale edition. Do you know where I could get a copy?"

"You do have Jackson Bate's paperback selection which I ordered for the class?"

"Yes, of course—but I'd like the whole series."

Damn you, what do you want from me?

"There's one thing you could do . . ." I said.

"What's that?"

"I have some spare copies at home. Why don't you come by sometime and pick one up?"

The schoolgirlish smile. "Oh, could I?"

"Certainly."

"Tonight?"

"If you like."

"Well, I think I'll do that. What's your address?"

I gave it and she left.

She really did look damnably like Cindy.

"I never knew you felt this way . . ." Damn your unctuousness!

"Michael, I mean, we've had a lot of fun together, and you've given me so many nice things, but I don't think I could . . ." You bitch. You bitch.

"I thought you knew I was seeing Paul. . . ." But who could have thought you were serious about him?

"Yes, I suppose I will marry him. . . ."

I hope you have, bitch. And I hope he fucks you up the ass every night. I hope he makes you swallow his come every night. I hope he pounds you until you can't walk. Bitch.

"Hi."

"Hi. Come on in."

I had been listening to Haydn—so clean, pure, and wholesome. Music was my only real joy—the one time when I didn't have to think. I used to watch television a good deal, but finally got fed up with it. God! what cheap, prurient sex there was everywhere! Titillation for the mindless middle class. You couldn't escape it—even the commercials were sex-oriented. Sex, sex, sex. How disgusting.

"Is this Haydn?" she asked.

"Yes," I replied, surprised. "How did you know?"

"I've played it—it's the *Farewell Symphony*, isn't it?"

"Yes. What do you play?"

"Flute, and a little keyboard."

Suddenly she caught sight of the harpsichord in the parlor. That foul, feminine gasp followed.

"Oh! a harpsichord! My parents have one! Can I play it, please?" She gave me this pathetic, pleading look. I could have smashed her face in.

"Yes, go ahead." I went to turn the stereo off.

Mistake after mistake. As she sat down at the instrument, I sat on the sofa nearby.

She had to do it. She had to play Bach's "Prelude in C" from the *Well-Tempered Clavier*. My favorite Bach.

I closed my eyes tightly. A tear crept down from one corner.

When she finished, she came over to me.

"That's such a beautiful—" she began chirpily, then saw my expression.

"Are you all right?"

I opened my eyes. "Yes—I'm fine."

"Are you sure?"

"Yes." I hadn't meant to raise my voice.

I got up abruptly. "Let's go to my library."

* * * * * * *

When we got upstairs, she gave more wide-eyed stares. I didn't have an especially distinguished library, but it was voluminous—and I had my share of eighteenth-century printings, which look expensive but in fact aren't.

I wanted to make this as quick as possible. I pulled down a four-volume set of *The Rambler*—Philadelphia, 1812. It was not rare or textually valuable, but looked nice.

"Here."

"Thanks a lot—I'll return these very soon. And I'll be sure to treat them nicely."

I paused for a moment.

"Why don't you keep them?"

God! Why do I do such things?

Her mouth slowly dropped. She looked confused, and a little worried.

"Oh, but I couldn't . . . ."

"Sure you can. I have at least three other sets. I picked this up for £4 in Bath."

"Are you sure it's all right?"

"Yes, of course."

She suddenly put the books down on a table and flung her arms around my neck. She gave me a little kiss on the cheek, and I could feel her breasts against my chest. And I swear she intentionally grazed her belly against my rod.

"Thank you, thank you—you're so sweet."

I got away from her clutches. "Let's go downstairs."

* * * * * * *

I must be some sort of masochist.

"Would you like a drink?"

She looked up, then smiled. "Okay."

"What would you like?"

"Gin and tonic, if you have it."

"Fine." I started to go to the bar.

"Can I put on some music?"

"Sure."

When I came back I saw that she had put on some Handel—the *Concerti Grossi*, Opus 6.

You know the way girls sit on their hips, with their legs flowing out demurely at their sides? Diana was sitting like that on the carpet before the stereo. She was reading the program notes to the album.

She didn't seem to hear me come in. Soon I was standing over her, the two glasses in my hand. If she had been wearing a sexier blouse, I suppose I could have looked down at her cleavage.

She kept on reading. I could see the smooth roundness of her cheek and the corner of her closed lips. There was the faintest of smiles on them.

I began clenching the glasses hard with my hands. My teeth gnashed, and I could feel the muscles of my neck throbbing.

You bitch. You bitch.

She looked up suddenly—and smiled.

"Hi."

"Hi. Here's your drink."

"Thanks."

* * * * * * *

I was crouching behind the wall—it wasn't very high, but it was high enough—waiting. She finally showed up—but what was this? She had a boy with her. He couldn't have been more than fourteen—hardly older than she herself. This was rather an annoyance—but it was getting late, and I was getting impatient.

Probably they were going to sit in the schoolyard before going home, where he would probably fuck the daylights out of her. She looked young and innocent, but I'm sure she knew the ropes. All high school girls are sluts anyway.

As I suspected, they entered the schoolyard. They seemed to be heading for the swing. I saw them holding hands—how sweet.

As soon as they crossed the gate, I leaped out from my position and opened the switchblade.

"Keep your mouths shut or I'll slit you open," I said.

They stood stock still. I saw their mouths drop open.

I frankly didn't know what to do with the boy. Why did she have to bring him? I shrugged, grabbed him by the hair, bent his head back, and slashed at his neck with the knife. For a moment I thought I had missed, for I didn't seem to feel any resistance—but I knew otherwise when he started to choke and fell to the ground, writhing. It was dark, and I couldn't see the blood.

The girl put her hands to her mouth—she seemed about to scream. She was probably so frightened that the intimidation of my knife wouldn't have much effect; so I clubbed her over the head, and continued to bludgeon her till she was unconscious. Now I could take my time.

I was very careful about unbuttoning her blouse. Her bra was one of those that unclasp in the front—rather convenient. Small, delicate little breasts. Virginal. Virginal, my ass.

The skirt's zipper was on the side, and I had to undo a button before I could reach it. After I took it off, I used the switchblade to tear through her panties—might as well be consistent, even though it might cause suspicions. (But I don't intend to keep this up much longer.)

Well, what do you know—she *was* a virgin. First time for everything, I suppose. After I rammed her for a while I pulled open her mouth, stuck my rod in, and finished the job there.

Afterwards I sat there for a while. Then, almost without thinking, I plunged the knife into her chest.

* * * * * * *

That was it. I wasn't going to take this any longer. Diana has asked me to go to a Halloween party with her. She says she still doesn't know many other people on campus, and thought we would have fun. Like a fool I accepted. But that's not for another two weeks. Somehow I don't think she'll live that long.

Ours is a nice campus. Oh, we hear about robberies and attempted rapes—but the latter turn out for the most part to be drunken boyfriends trying to have their way with sweethearts after frat parties. How pedestrian. The university is a sheltered conclave in an otherwise big city. Maybe that's why girls aren't afraid to take the short cut behind the Engineering Building after dark. It's the shortest way from the library to the dorms. That's where I was tonight. I knew Diana would be coming there.

I didn't know whether to kill her first and then rape her, or vice versa. I confess I'd gotten rather a kick from the pseudo-necrophilia of last week—but I certainly wanted to let her know whose affections she was trifling with.

There they came—a whole stream of them, men and women both. God, it looked like a party. Maybe they'd had their fun in the library restrooms.

It was early, though—only 10:30. The library would be open another hour. Studious Diana would surely be one of the last to go.

"I didn't know you felt this way. . . ."

Shut up!

"Thank you, thank you—you're so sweet!"

Shut up, damn you!

Journey's end in lovers' meeting. . . . Then come kiss me, sweet and twenty: youth's a stuff will not endure.

There she is. Books folded across her breasts, like a good college girl. Singing to herself—sounds like Mozart. Yes—*The Marriage of Figaro*.

I grab her and pull her into the bushes. She gives a little scream, her books fall to the ground. She stumbles, her knee is soiled by the dirt. She starts to speak, but I club her in the face with my fist.

Her hair is all tousled—over her forehead and cheeks. Probably intended that to happen. I tear at her blouse—the buttons pop off. Her breasts, now only half encased by her bra, bounce and writhe. She moans and tries to fight me off. She hasn't looked me in the face yet. I grab her chin with one hand and pull it in my direction.

Wide-eyed stare. Not very becoming this time.

A moment of silence. Then:

"Professor . . ."

I don't say a word, but keep ripping at her clothing. Her skirt is made of tougher material than I bargained for. May have to get the knife out.

"No, please . . . stop! Professor . . . please . . ."

"Shut up, you whore! Do you see this?" I thrust the knife in her face.

"Why . . . ?"

"You know," I say slowly, "that I'll have to kill you."

"Professor . . . please, Michael"—how did she know my name?—"please, listen. . . ."

She stops struggling, but grabs my face with both hands. She gives me a long, soft kiss.

"I love you," she says.

I stare at her.

She kisses me again. One hand goes around my neck. The other gently eases the knife from my clutch. It falls to the ground.

Picture us: she with her clothes in shreds, I in my usual costume of leather jacket, jeans, and beret. She kisses me on the lips, the cheek, the eyes, the neck. "I love you. Maybe we can make something happen. . . ."

"Maybe," I whisper.

I start to put my arms around her—gently this time. But what— Oh, God! what's she done! The knife! God, this fire in my chest! Where are you going? Who's that screaming, you or me? What have you done? I'm Nero—*qualis artifex pereo*—"what an artist dies in me. . . ." I knew I should have stopped before this—just one too many.

You bitch. You bitch.

AFFAIR

The guy kept looking at me.

God only knows what possessed me to go to lunch at that fast-food joint—which I will not name because I refuse to acknowledge that I've ever set foot in it—but I suppose a hard morning's shopping addled my wits. The riffraff that usually haunts these joints would ordinarily make me cringe—immensely fat retirees, male and female, the latter distinguishable only by the flabby, shapeless balloons at their chests; high school kids who talk more than they eat, and make more noise eating than talking; and, worst of all, those poor losers eating alone and finding tables as far away from any other sentient creature as humanly possible. Don't get me wrong; there's nothing wrong with dining alone—why, I'm doing so myself—but it's obvious that these loners are lucky to have had a solitary date sometime in the last millennium.

But this guy was, at least, different. Sure, he was eating alone—and on top of that, he was reading a book. Not a magazine, not a newspaper, but a book. Not a new one, but an old one (I'd say from the thirties of the last century), sans dust jacket, propped precariously against one corner of his plastic tray. But aside from this token of nerdiness—perhaps to be expected in this college town—he looked rather good. Dark hair, well—and expensively—cut, soft but not effeminate features, and a kind of twinkle in his eye as if he too were saying, *Yeah, I'm slumming here, but it's kinda fun, you know?* And I guess one of the things he wanted to do to make the time go by was to look at me.

And, by God, why not? OK, I'm forty-something, but I'm a dish. Got that? Pure blonde (not out of a bottle either), chiseled features (all right, some people might say they're a bit sharp or harsh, but my face could have been sculpted by—well, somebody famous like Michelangelo), tits that retained their shape even after all the guys that had tugged on them in the days of my wild youth, legs that go on forever . . . you get the message. I know what I've got. Too bad a certain someone doesn't know it—or know it enough. I'll get to that in a bit.

This guy had come before me, and so naturally he finished before I did. But, as if reluctant to get up and stop staring at my lovely self, he kind of fidgeted there in his chair, with all the messy wrappers and the pitiful inedible fragments of his mass-produced meal in front of him. He at least did one sensible thing and took all the debris to the huge wooden wastebaskets spaced strategically around the place (near every door, for maximum convenience), dumped the contents of his tray into one (almost losing the tray in the bin in the process), then . . . went back to his seat! Whereas all the other temporary denizens of this rat-hole—except the noisy teenagers, who figured this was as good a place to hang out as any—made a beeline for the exits as soon as they'd finished shoveling the unhealthy contents of their meal into their bellies, this guy went back to the same seat he occupied—did it have his name on it, or what?—and continued reading . . . and looking at me.

Well, that didn't last long. I guess his book wasn't as interesting as he'd made it out to be. So after about a minute he got up and headed toward the door—in the process of which he would have to pass right by my table. As he went by, I figured I'd take the plunge.

Now there are a couple of ways you can do this. The genteel, Victorian way would be to say something like: "I couldn't help noticing, sir, that you were casting several glances in my direction." And the thirties, *noir* tough-guy way would be: "Say, what's the idea of giving me the eyeball?" I compromised between the two, saying quietly: "So you like staring."

I hadn't even looked up at him when I said that. *I* didn't have anything to read, not even a magazine or those incredibly wasteful sheets of coupons that inevitably end up right in everyone's recycling bin, so I was just looking down at my suddenly unappetizing food and doing my best to down it. Maybe my mouth was full, maybe it wasn't. But he heard me well enough.

It was like someone had prodded him with a taser or something. He gave a little jump and stopped cold. But he was smooth, this guy: for someone who seemed like nothing but a brain on legs, he was pretty quick with the savoir faire. All he said was:

"Yes . . . when it's someone like you."

He was smiling, as if saying: *This really isn't happening. I don't speak to strangers, and neither do you. This is a movie, right? We've just come from central casting. So what's the next scene going to be?* In other words, he wasn't taking any of this seriously, and he knew I wasn't taking any of it seriously. Just a little harmless banter between two people who, after they went out that door, would never see each other again and scarcely remember that they'd ever spoken.

Well, let's see how far this would go. I couldn't exactly kick a chair in his direction to get him to sit in it, since these goddamn rotating seats were affixed to the table; but I could at least nod my head and say: "Well, get a better look."

He shrugged almost imperceptibly and sat down—a bit gingerly, as if the hard plastic seat had a whoopee-cushion on it.

"Do you have a name?" I went on.

Yes, he did: it was Michael. Nice name, and it suited him—there was no chance anyone would call him Mike, if you get what I mean. I said, "My name's Roxanne. Call me Roxy."

His eyes widened just a tad then, as if he were digesting the thought that he might have occasion to call me by my name many times in the future.

So we got to talking. He wasn't exactly a great conversationalist at the start, but he warmed up eventually. Seems he was some kind of science researcher at the U, looking up all sorts of arcane stuff in the science library (not far from this hellhole) for some bigshot professor who collected—and went through—grant money as if it were M&Ms. Hard to imagine someone making money at that kind of thing (I'm referring to Michael, not the prof), but it seems he did well enough.

I of course noticed the thin gold band on his finger. And I'm sure he caught a glimpse of the huge rock stuck to the band on my own finger.

I told him that spending my husband's money was a full-time job, and I did it pretty well. He laughed at that, a bit nervously—whether at the very mention of my husband, or his money, or my little joke, I don't know. He at least had the tact not to ask what

I was doing in this joint, for which I couldn't have given him a plausible answer to save my life.

Well, it went on like that. It was lots of fun talking with him—talking to any presentable man (and he was presentable—with a goofy, crooked smile that actually did things to my insides that hadn't been done in a long, long time) would be fun, even though I had at least a decade on him. I asked him if he had to vamoose that instant. His eyes widened just a bit at that, and he murmured, almost reluctantly (he was one of these people, I realized, who just couldn't lie), "Well, no, not really. . . ."

"Good," I said shortly. I got up, leaving the tray for him to put away, which he did.

I walked out the door, he following like the good little puppy that he was. Got to my car—Cadillac, of course—and stood by the driver's side door. He came up to me, hands at his sides, not having the faintest idea what to do.

I sighed inwardly, gave him a smile, and planted my lips on his—and wouldn't let go.

At first contact he made a queer little moan of surprise, but it didn't take him long to get up to speed. I had thrown my arms around his neck, and he abruptly dropped the little book bag he was carrying and wrapped his arms around my waist—but gently, as if I were a vase he might break in his clumsiness.

His lips tasted nice, as I knew they would. When my slim little tongue went into his mouth, I could feel his member immediately spring to attention. Funny how that gets them every time.

Now you gotta believe me on this. I've been married for better than fifteen years, but I haven't yet strayed. God knows I could have, or should have, but I haven't. Why? Well, let me be blunt: I like my creature comforts more than I like sex. My husband lets me live in a lifestyle to which I've gotten myself accustomed, and if he's a little slow as far as his marital duties are concerned, well, that's OK. I have my toys, after all.

So I'm a virgin as far as the extra-marital stuff is concerned. Maybe I haven't looked in the right places: I can't possibly carry on with anyone in my own social circle, for the chances of detection are far too great. And, believe it or not, I rather like my husband—he's kind of a teddy bear, and you can't say that about too many investment bankers.

So here I am, kissing this guy I only met twenty minutes ago, right out in public (although, mercifully, not in a part of the universe where anyone is likely to recognize me), and wondering how far I—or he—will go. I won't deny I was a bit shivery—or maybe tingly is the better word. It was like someone was tickling me with a feather all over.

Well, I stopped kissing Michael, mostly to get some air. He needed it too, for he made a huge gasp and looked at me as if I were an alien from another planet. I just smiled and said, "Get in."

For someone who supposedly lives by his brain, Michael was a little slow on the uptake. "Wha . . . what do you mean?" he blurted out.

I opened the back seat for him. Still smiling, I said, "Get in. There. Right now."

He was good at following orders, so he ducked his head—rather as if he were laying himself down for the guillotine—and got in.

The car had tinted windows, of course. And the back seat was pretty spacious. That's what these GM luxury cars are built for—fat Americans who need a lot of room. Neither Michael nor I was fat, but we needed some room.

He sat down on the couch and just waited for developments. I could tell he was rock hard. So I squatted in front of him, unbuttoned his shirt, pulled it back so I could see his (nice) hairy chest, then got to work on his belt buckle. He looked at me, and it, as if he couldn't believe what was happening: I'm sure he was thinking, *I really am in a movie—but not the movie I thought I was in.* Pulling his pants down to his ankles was easy, especially since he finally got with the program and raised himself up a bit off the seat. The briefs came off with the pants. His boner sprang in front of me like a rubber stick that has been bent back and then suddenly let go.

In it went into my mouth. He somehow managed to draw a huge intake of breath and groan at the same time. His cock had a really nice texture, and his balls weren't loose and flabby like some old steer's. After a while of that, I figured it was my turn. I got up and squatted over his legs, pulling off my thin sweater in the process. My breasts were right at his eye-level, and he was fixated on them as if they were some kind of hypnotist's watch. I leaned into him, and he got the message: he reached his hands behind my back and unfastened my bra, with only a minimum of fumbling. The bra came off, and I all but asphyxiated him with my melons. He, for his part, licked and sucked at them like a man dying of thirst at an oasis. Good boy!

Now I suppose I should have worn a skirt to make the next part easier; but I didn't wake up that morning with the idea, "OK, I'm going to have sex with a stranger, so I need to make sure my cunt is within easy striking range." So there I was, with my slacks rubbing up against his hard-on while his hands clutched at my breasts. Somehow I managed to get away from him long enough to shed the pants and then get right back on him. He slipped into me with the greatest of ease.

He still wanted to suckle my breasts, overgrown baby that he was. (All men are overgrown babies.) All I can say is that he felt really good inside me—I like this position for all kinds of good reasons. Every now and then he rubbed my back and grabbed my butt, but his hands kept coming back to my hooters as if they were some kind of magnets.

Just as I was getting in the spirit of things, he came. He almost shouted, although whatever sound he made was all but muffled by my knockers. He kept pumping for a little bit, then stopped. He was clinging to me, his head still buried in my chest. I pried his face away and held it gently with my hand; I could swear his eyes were glistening a bit. I just smiled at him, gave him a little kiss, and got off, plumping down on the seat next to him.

I will be honest and say that, even with hubby, the few moments after sex are just about the most embarrassing and awkward that I can think of. What the hell do you do? Say thank you to your partner? I could tell that Michael was a bit ashamed for being so quick on the draw; it seemed he almost wished to cover up his nakedness and get the hell out of Dodge. He didn't even look at me, even though under ordinary circumstances I'm sure he would have been glad to feast his eyes on an entirely naked woman sitting next to him in the back seat of a car.

He did start to mumble, "I'm sorry I was . . . ."

I finished the thought for him: "A little fast on the trigger? Well, there's always the next time."

And with that, I got down on my knees in front of him and began servicing him again. I knew that men's organs are very sensitive after sex, so I held his very gently and just licked it a bit, enjoying the mingled juices that dripped from it. It wasn't long before it was ready for action again—sooner, I think, than he expected. So I rode him again, and this time we took it nice and slow. And this time I got off also.

* * * * * * *

And so that was how it started. Of course, we didn't keep on doing it in the car. I told him to meet me at a certain parking lot of a certain grocery store near my house, and then we drove back together. I couldn't have him just come to my house, on the off chance that the master of the house was home sick or the landscape gardeners were around or something of that sort. When we got back to my house, I could see his eyes bugging out at the size of the place: well, really, it wasn't all that big, but I guess it was more than a cottage. We walked right in, went right up to my bedroom (separate from my husband's, of course—it's the only civilized way), and got down to business.

This time I let him undress me first. We were nearly the same height—maybe he was an inch or two taller—and that made certain things convenient. Like doing it standing up. I don't think he'd ever done that before, because he was clueless how to manage it, and I had to stick him into me as if handling a tampon. Like the typical man he in many ways was, he didn't ask about birth control—but sensed that I had that angle covered.

There was something a bit appealing in the faint flabbiness of his midsection—too much time spent in a sitting position, no doubt—kinda like baby fat. But he was no baby in other ways. Once he got over the shock and novelty of having sex with a strange married woman, he did his job like a trouper. He would come two or three times a session—although I could tell that the last one was a bit of a strain, and perhaps not even a whole lot of fun. But he knew well how to please a woman, how to use his hands, lips, and tongue, and every now and then he surprised me by taking charge in no uncertain terms and showing me that his brute strength was no match for my own wiry toughness. I don't usually let a guy manhandle me, but I let him do it: it was almost as if I were a disembodied spectator watching myself.

It wasn't long before we got to talking. I really had to figure out why he strayed without so much as a second thought. Do all men discard their marriage vows so easily the moment an opportunity presents itself? OK, I guess I came on pretty strong in that parking lot of the fast-food joint, but still, he could have said, "No thank you, ma'am," if he really wanted to.

So there I was, resting my face on his chest and getting my nose tickled with the fine down around his nipple, and I said:

"So, do you love your wife?"

He looked at me aghast, as if I had asked him if he were an anti-Semite. "Of course I do! How could you ever think . . ."

He stopped then, finally realizing how comical he sounded.

But I took pity on him—I didn't want him to feel more rotten than he must have felt. "Is it just that I'm so seductive, or do you have some 'issues'?" (I hate that word, but I guess it fit the context here.)

He frowned, almost scowled, as if I'd put to him a particularly difficult problem in differential equations.

"Well, the thing of it is . . . I really love Mona in every way—except sexually." He gave me this pleading look: *Don't you understand? How can I explain this to you without talking from here till Kingdom Come?* "We've been married about eight years, and it's just fabulous. . . . We never argue, we get along great, we have lots of fun doing things together, I love going on vacations with her, getting together with our friends. . . ." He paused, then went on, as if the words were being forced out of him: "But I . . . I really don't find her sexually appealing anymore. . . ."

I propped my elbow on his chest and looked him in the face. "And why is that?"

He couldn't stand to look me in the face. "Oh, lots of things. . . . She's gotten a bit heavy, and I guess I don't care for that. She's still very shapely and beautiful, but there's just . . . a little more of her than I wish there were." He breathed heavily. "But that's not really it. What it is . . . is that she's just so sexually unadventurous. Wants to have sex the same way every time. Doesn't like oral sex—sucks my cock as if it were an unpleasant duty, and doesn't like being licked at all. Doesn't like unusual positions. Closes her eyes during the whole process. . . . And when she comes, it's almost as if she's done something to be ashamed of."

I looked at him a bit quizzically. "Is she Catholic?"

His face showed a bit of surprise. "Yes, how did you know?"

"Oh, just a guess. . . . But you have no children?"

"No," he said. "You don't either?"

"No." My tone of voice basically said: *I really don't believe in the propagation of the human race.*

He tried to turn the tables on me.

"So how about you? I guess I'm only the latest of many lovers you've had."

I really startled him by telling him he was the first. When he asked why I'd waited so long, since I was plainly dissatisfied with my husband, I just said, "You were just the first who fell into my lap." But both he and I knew that was a cop-out. I guess I was as tongue-tied as he was in explaining how and why my marriage had gone awry.

"Look, Michael, my husband is a real nice man . . . hard-working, kind, considerate . . . not exactly an Errol Flynn in the romance department, but it takes a special man to be like that. And I really don't stick around just for his money—that would be too contemptible. Life is too short for that. I may not love him anymore, but I like him—a lot. I would never do anything to hurt him—which means there's no way he'll ever find out about us. But I don't need to tell you what happens, sexually, when you get married. . . ."

He took up the thread right away. "I know exactly what you mean. You're involved with so much mundane stuff with your spouse—balancing the budget, mowing the lawn, going to the grocery or the drug store, entertaining your friends . . . you basically become roommates, don't you think? You work so hard to keep the place looking nice, you kinda feel like a servant in your own house."

That was a novel way of looking at it. Of course, I couldn't quite agree with him on that score, since I had a little army of maids and gardeners to do that kind of thing for me. But I got the gist, and fundamentally he was right. The bottom line is: *Sex ceases to be romantic or forbidden or naughty or exhilarating when you get married.* There's just no getting around it.

In my case, the metamorphosis was real gradual. Fred and I used to fuck like rabbits when we were dating. I remember a time when we were getting pretty serious, and we went to visit his mother (his father had died years before) in a remote old ex-farmhouse upstate. We were so horny that we fucked in our guest room on the main floor in the morning, then fucked again in Fred's old bedroom upstairs later that afternoon. Fortunately, his mother was deaf as a post, so she heard nothing. When we first got married we made it a point of pride to have sex every day—and that lasted for months. But inevitably things came in the way—a late-night session at the bank, a longer-than-usual outing with friends, the occasional illness ... you get the point. I once remember freaking out because we hadn't had sex in four days. At that time that was something of a record.

So it went from sex every day to sex every few days to sex once a week to sex maybe once a month, if we were lucky. It stabilized at that point. Fred didn't seem quite as inhibited as Mona, but I will say it got just a tad repetitious after a while. You really do get to be like roommates. And that isn't all that bad, really: there's a kind of quiet comfort in just sitting together watching TV or reading in separate chairs, knowing that you're linked forever and ever (well, at least until the divorce lawyers show up on the scene) in the eyes of the world. But it doesn't make for good sex.

So what can be done? I once suggested to Michael that he slowly try to get Mona to loosen up a bit. OK, there wasn't much chance that she'd take it up the ass—after all, Michael himself had been a bit taken aback when I told him to fuck me in the butt, and he was mighty clumsy about it even with the K-Y liberally applied—but how about letting her ride him? I knew from first-hand experience that he liked that position, and I couldn't imagine why any woman wouldn't. Just bring an armless chair into the bedroom and sit in it with your cock riding high—she'd get the message.

Well, he came back a week or so later and said he'd tried it—but it was a disaster.

"She really didn't like the idea, but went ahead with it to please me. But she just sat there on me, not moving—expected me to do the work. Didn't realize that she had to do her part. So after a while we just had to go back to the bed and the usual missionary thing .. ." He looked about as frustrated as if he'd flunked an exam.

So I said: "Why don't you try someplace other than the bedroom? The whole house is one big sex arena. The kitchen, the bathroom (ever try giving her a bath?), the living room floor, for God's sake? You do have carpeting, don't you?"

"Yes," he mumbled.

"Well, then, try it!"

I sent him away with that, and he came back even more depressed than before.

The upshot of it—so far as I could get any coherent story out of him—was that he had practically raped Mona on the living-room floor. They were sitting on the couch, watching television or something, and he reached over and began snuggling with her (she needed a lot of snuggling before she was ready to perform). After a while, his arm, which was around her waist, moved up to her breast, and they began kissing and fondling. She was a bit surprised—they usually didn't have sex until much later in the evening—but she seemed to be getting into it. But Michael was determined to lend some novelty to the whole thing, so he basically dragged her to the floor, lifted up her dress, and pulled her panties down to her knees. At this point Mona became alarmed and began struggling, trying to get up and away from Michael, but he held on fast. First he plunged his face into her muff, at which point she almost screamed, and then, having pulled down his own pants clumsily to his ankles, plunged into that spousal pussy before she was quite ready. This time she really did scream, and her little fists began pounding at his shoulders. But Michael—who, if anything, was a thorough lad—carried on resolutely and finished the job, at least as far as he was concerned.

After it was over, he just rolled over, breathing hard. Mona was breathing hard too, and when she opened her eyes (they had, of course, been shut fast the whole time) she looked up as if some major part of her world had come unglued. She quietly pulled her panties up, pushed her dress over her knees, and got up without a word. She never spoke to him about what had happened.

They didn't have sex again for three weeks.

I told him I was really sorry and that I wouldn't offer any more advice; but he let me off the hook and said that it was all his own fault. He had tried to do too much at once.

"But by God!" he cried out, slapping the mattress in frustration. "Why is society so fucked up? Mona and I get along perfectly in every way—except sexually. So why can't I get my rocks off with someone else and be done with it?" He quickly spotted my amused glance and added: "Yes, I know, that's what I'm doing—but it's all secret and skulking and behind closed doors. . . ."

"So," I said, "you basically want to remain married but not required to maintain sexual exclusivity?"

"That's it!" He looked at me as if I'd just explained the unified field theory. "Sexual exclusivity! That's what's wrong with marriage . . . or at least with some marriages. Can I help it if my urges and needs aren't the same as my wife's?"

"I guess not," I said.

He made a point of showing me what those needs and urges were, and I didn't say no. He really was a nice guy to have in bed—both for sex and for talking. Maybe a little naive, a little boyish—but I realized that in many ways I was in the same boat.

* * * * * * *

Well, after several months of this, the inevitable happened.

After a particularly energetic bout that involved just about all the orifices that either of us had, Michael lay spent on the bed and held me clutched tightly to his chest. After his breathing had gotten to something like normal, he whispered into my ear:

"I want to leave Mona."

I pulled away from him and looked him right in the face. "No, you don't."

He gave me that frown/scowl that said: *Are you questioning something I've said?* Only an academic can give you that look. "Yes, I do," he shot back, with the faintest tinge of a whine. "And I think you should leave Fred too."

I just smiled at him and patted his cheek gently. "Now, you just forget any such ideas and just give me some more of that cock. . . ." I reached for it, but he actually slapped my hand away.

"Roxy, listen," he said earnestly—I hated that look, for I knew that things would take a turn for the worse unless we were real careful. "What's keeping you married? Money? OK, I don't have much money, but you could get a big settlement from Fred. You'd be just as comfortable as you are now. Don't we have a wonderful time in bed?" He gave me that pleading look again. "You know, I think I love you."

I wanted to cover his mouth with my hand, as if that could have somehow made the words go back down his throat.

"No, you don't, Michael, you love Mona, and you'll stay with her. And you know why?"

He didn't reply, but gave me a defiant look that said: *OK, you've staked out a really crazy position and you'll have a damn hard time defending it.*

But I wasn't daunted. "You love Mona in every way but sexually. I like Fred and don't want to hurt him. And here we are, having this nice affair that hurts no one, and things are just fine." I paused for breath. "And do you know what would happen if we got together? What are you talking about, marriage? Going to the store, mowing the lawn (OK, maybe my gardener can do that), and so on and so forth? You know the great thing about dating, and having affairs? It's that *we both go home afterwards*. We see each other once or twice a week, have a wonderful time, and leave. In marriage, your spouse is around you *all the time*. No one leaves. It's the great romance-killer. Economically and socially it may make sense, but there's no romance in it, and there's not meant to be any romance in it. Raising kids—which is what, I guess, marriage is for, as far as society's concerned—is not supposed to be romantic. Even living together and running a household without children is not supposed to be romantic—and it isn't. It's boring and tedious and repetitious. Some people can shoehorn romance into it somehow—but I guess we two can't. And so we're having this affair."

My look said: *Q.E.D.* He looked at me as if he didn't want to believe it, but he knew I was right.

"So then what?" he cried, almost whined.

"So," I said, getting up and heading to the bathroom to wash away the various sex molecules that covered me, "you go home. And we meet again on . . . what . . . Thursday?"

DOLL

You know she's going to have to die, don't you, Frank?
"Yes, I know."
I just didn't know whether she'd die before or after I fucked her.

* * * * * * *

Wanda was waiting for me when I got home at 5:30. She always was—she had nowhere to go. That didn't bother me a bit—a kinda liked the idea of a nice, warm, cuddly thing with nothing to do but look forward to her man returning home after a hard day's work.

As she lay there on the bed, I undressed slowly. I was tired, but not too tired—I never am. She was wearing that nice red camisole I'd gotten her a while back—can't remember which catalog I got it from, but it made her look scrumptious. I got hard just look-ing at her as I slowly took my shirt off, then my pants, then my underwear.

She knew what I liked, so she let me fondle her breasts with my hands, then with my mouth. After that I mounted her. She was deliciously tight, and the red lips of her mouth were always invit-ing. After a while I flipped her over and finished the job in her butt. She knew that was the way I liked it best, so she never complained.

After that I got up to fix dinner.

* * * * * * *

I think Wanda is the best of my latest round of live-in girl-friends. I will say I've gone through a fair number of them of late. I don't know what it is, but somehow they don't always work out.

There was this Asian girl, Komiko, who was cute as a button, but a bit small—I won't deny that I'm a hefty guy, so I need a little more bulk than what Komiko offered. Anyway—and I hate to say this—after a while I did get kinda tired of looking at those almond eyes and high cheekbones. They're OK for a change of pace, but not as a steady diet—not for me, anyway. Don't get me wrong—I love girls of all races, and even of all shapes and sizes, but it's just a matter of a certain comfort level.

There was a really long-legged girl named Tanya who was fun for a while, but somehow she too overstayed her welcome. I couldn't quite put my finger on what went wrong, but after a while it became obvious we just weren't suited to each other. Possibly her tits were too small. Not that I'm one of those guys who like huge bazongas, which I know can be really flabby and shapeless. But Tanya's were just a bit *too* small and *too* firm, if that's possible. So pointy they made indentations on my chest when I was on top of her.

And as for that blonde bombshell named Toni, well, she was more my size—a lot to hang on to, but things went wrong there also. Her skin was so pink you'd think she had rosacia all over. Striking at first glance, but over time it came to seem almost repulsive. Her face was also not exactly to my taste—eyes a little too wide apart, always seeming a little startled or surprised, her mouth too much of a big O.

She needed a bit more repair than I cared to give. I guess my bulk was a bit too much for her.

* * * * * * *

What is it about women? I just can't believe how evil and nasty they can be. And they learn so young.

High school was hell. You'd think the girls would understand that not everyone can be a jock. Wake up, girls! What do you think these jocks are going to amount to when they grow up? You think everyone's going to become a star quarterback in the NFL or a point guard in the NBA? Better think again. You girls all want guys who can be "good providers"—well, what's a better provider than a good brain?

I wanted a girl so bad, but it was no dice. Man, you'd think I had some kind of infectious disease, just because I had a little extra flesh on my bones. Even the fat girls didn't go for me. You think I liked jerking off every night and keeping my groans to myself so my parents wouldn't hear? All I wanted was a little flesh-to-flesh contact. Even to come within smelling distance of a girl was something that made my day. But the way the girls laughed at me, or turned up their noses, or had this blank look on their faces at the mere idea of doing something together. . . .

After that, all I wanted to do was . . . well, you know. I knew that someday I'd get even. But how? The idea of calling in prostitutes was too disgusting—not that I didn't have the money for it: you have plenty of money when you're a C.P.A. and don't go out much or even take vacations. But the idea of buying affection was just too vile. Every moment I'd know that all these girls would be thinking of was, "When is this porker going to blow his wad so I can get clear of this joint and move on to my next gig?" These whores can't act worth a damn—they don't even pretend they like being with you.

But that changed with my dolls. They were just the ticket. Did exactly what I wanted, didn't waste time yammering, and got quietly out of the way when I was done with them. Just what a girl should do. No complaints about my size or my smell, no squawks about what I wanted to do or when I wanted it, no demands that I get them stuff or take them out or crap like that. Sometimes I'd put them away in a closet; sometimes I'd leave them on the bed, so they'd seem like a nice little wifey curling up to go to sleep after being well fucked. But a wifey who didn't make any unreasonable demands on hubby.

Why couldn't all women be like that? Or even just one?

But I have to say Wanda was different. I couldn't quite put my finger on it . . . she seemed to look at me funny sometimes. I think I was a bit *scared* of her. I knew she wouldn't like being put away in a closet, so I kept her on the bed day and night. I knew she liked to try out all the skimpy lingerie I had bought for her, so I made sure to change it often. I treated her better than I treated any of my other dolls—and she knew all about the other ones.

I know. She told me.

There was a time when I saw this weird sneer on her face. I stared and stared at her, and finally said out loud:

"What are you looking at?"

Silence. But still the sneer.

"What's up with you, Wanda? What do you want? What's your beef?"

No beef. Just looking at you, kid.

Yeah, that's what she said. It seemed to go right into my brain.

"What do you mean by that?"

I'm the best, aren't I?

"The best?" I pretended not to understand, but I knew what she meant—and she knew I knew.

The best of all your squeezes, lover-boy.

I smiled sheepishly at her. "Sure you are, Wanda. You know that."

Do I? Then why don't you say it?

"O.K. . . . you're the best, Wanda." I tried to put some enthusiasm in it, but it didn't come out so well. This was freaking me out.

You don't sound so sure. How am I the best?

"You just are, Wanda. . . . I don't have to describe it, do I?" I hated the way I sounded so scared.

Tell me, big boy. Just tell me.

"Oh, Wanda . . ."

You like my mouth? My boobs? My pussy? My ass?

"Sure, Wanda, sure, they're wonderful. . . ."

Tell me. Make love to me with your words instead of with your cock.

I must have blushed—felt hot all over. "Wanda, please . . . you're just the best. I love your hot little mouth, the way it clings to my cock. . . ."

You like to shoot your wad into my mouth, you dirty little boy?

"Yeah, Wanda, it's fun. . . ."

You wanted to do that with Janice back in high school, didn't you?

I stared at her. "How did you know about Janice?"

I know all about you, Frankie my lad. What about Katie the cheerleader? You almost came in your pants when you saw a little flash of her underwear.

"That was a long time ago, Wanda. . . ."

Yeah, and now you have me. I'm better than all of them, aren't I?

"Sure you are."

And I'll always *be better than all of them, won't I?*

"Yes, of course."

I'm not going anywhere, am I?

"Where would you go?"

Nowhere, guy. I'm here to stay.

* * * * * * *

The trouble began when Marcy showed up in the office. She was a C.P.A. who had been transferred from our main office the next town over, and she was a real breath of fresh air. Aside from our secretarial staff, we had precious few women in the office. When Marcy came, we figured we'd have to cut down on the guy-talk—football, beer, the tight ass on the office receptionist—but Marcy surprised us by being one of the boys, although we did let up a bit about the receptionist's butt. Marcy had big auburn hair and a big body—but with curves in all the right places. She was what, in the '30s, would have been called (flatteringly) a broad.

I saw no reason to think that Marcy would be particularly interested in me, but after a few lunch dates with the whole crowd of us, she once asked me to have lunch just with her. I didn't think the gleam in her eye when she asked me was meant just for me—she just looked at everyone that way. And I didn't think that having lunch with a nice, attractive, fun-loving woman meant anything more than a nice way to pass an hour between the tedium of office work. But it was a nice hour.

When I came home that evening I didn't quite enjoy Wanda so much—oh, I'm not saying I didn't get off (I always do), but there was something missing somehow. And I could have sworn that Wanda *looked* a little different afterward—disappointed, maybe, or crestfallen. Don't think I'm crazy—you don't know Wanda the way I do. After you live with someone for months and months, you get to have a pretty good idea of their moods and feelings.

So things went on with me and Marcy. She was divorced, and one of the reasons she had asked for the office transfer was to get away from her bastard of a husband. Fortunately there were no kids involved, but this guy was a real jerk—nasty, vindictive, do-ing everything he could to mess up Marcy's life just to gain a bit of revenge. So she was now looking for someone calm, placid, low-maintenance. I'm not saying she had targeted me from the get-go, and of course she, like everyone, knew that office romances were potentially troublesome, but for some reason she took to me. Said I was the nicest, least stuck-up person in that office. And since she was a little on the hefty size, my girth didn't bother her.

So how was Wanda taking this budding romance? I know what you're going to say—"She's just a doll, how can she say or feel anything?" But I tell you that Wanda was more than just a doll— she *had* to be, to last as long as she did with me. I mean, why had I cast off all these other gals and stuck with Wanda for months and months?

And I have to say this right now: Wanda wasn't pleased.

OK, you can say she had no reason to be jealous—yet. I mean, there she was, lying seductively on my bed all day long just waiting for me to come home and get my rocks off with her—or on her, or in her. What girl could possibly want more? She had me wrapped around her little finger. There wasn't a day when I didn't service Wanda—sometimes more than once. On weekends I'd wake up with her next to me, and sometimes I'd just roll over and give her the business right then. She was the center of my whole existence. So what possible reason could she have for being upset?

Still, I could feel that she was. And I didn't know what to do about it.

When Marcy and I began to go to dinner and movies together, things got really tense between Wanda and me. I felt like a cheat-er—I was a cheater, even though I'd come home and make tender love to her the moment I came in. Sometimes I'd do it twice just to prove how much she meant to me. But it didn't seem enough. A certain coldness, a certain distance began to develop. I could tell Wanda was just going through the motions. She didn't want Marcy in my life.

You can predict what happened. One time Marcy invited me over to her place after a movie, and we started cuddling. I have to tell you, it had been years since I'd done it with a real girl, and I was nervous and clumsy as a schoolboy. But Marcy was all under-standing, and we just kissed and fondled a little bit before I said I'd better go. She patted me on the cheek and said OK, but I could tell from her eyes that next time she wanted more.

* * * * * * *

You're going to have to stop seeing Marcy, you know.
"But how?" I pleaded. "She's right there in my office . . . ."
Working with her and bopping her are two different things.
"I haven't bopped her. I haven't done anything with her. . . ."
Then why do I smell her all over you?
"Look, it was just a little snuggle session. . . ."
Well, what do you think I am, chopped meat? Who's been your main squeeze all these months?
"Why, you have, Wanda, but—"
And who lets you fuck her every which way whenever you want?
"You do, Wanda—"
And what if I stopped? What if I told you my body's off limits to you from now on?
I must have blanched with horror. "No, Wanda, no—not that...."
Well, buster, then you'd better get your act in gear. I don't want her cheap perfume hovering over you like a cloud anymore.
"OK, Wanda, I'll stop. . . ."

* * * * * * *

But of course I couldn't. The next time I was over at Marcy's place, I knew what was coming—it was almost as if I was another person, watching myself going through the motions. We stood in the middle of her big living room, just holding each other tight. She did smell really, really good, even after a long day's work. Just holding her was something so wonderful I didn't want to do anything else. But when she felt me getting hard, she just slipped a hand down to my waist, unbuckled my belt, unzipped my pants, and let them fall to the floor. Without speaking, she just kneeled down and put me in her mouth. I probably would have come if I weren't so petrified—of Marcy, of Wanda, of where all this was heading. . . .

After we had taken our clothes off, she led me into her bedroom—which was so small there was barely enough room for a full-size bed. But it was big enough. Her breasts were pretty big, but their texture was heavenly—I can't remember when I've felt anything so soft and tender. And when I went gently into her, we both moaned as if we were two young kids doing it for the first time. It was like nothing I'd ever felt before.

And I hated myself for thinking it, but it was way better than what Wanda could offer.

* * * * * * *

Well, I ought to have guessed it.

You two-timing bastard! How dare you sleep with that porker of a slut?

"Wanda, she's a nice girl. . . . I haven't had a real girl in so long. . . .

What am I? Some kind of fake? You think I'm just going to wait all day for you and take you into my arms and my bed after you've already poked someone else?

"Well, Wanda, maybe it's time . . ." I couldn't say it—couldn't even think it.

Time for what, you stinking oaf? Time for what?

"I don't know. . . ."

You thinking of dumping me?

"No, no—never!"

Yes, you are, you fucker! You're gonna dump me!

"No, Wanda, I'd never do that!"

Then there's only one thing left to do.

"What, Wanda?" But I knew what she was going to say.

You know she's going to have to die, don't you, Frank?

"Yes, I know."

* * * * * * *

Marcy could tell something was up. She saw instantly that I was nervous, even a bit scared. But I think she felt it was just a result of our sudden intimacy. I mean, it's not every day that you fuck someone and then walk into the office and see them in the desk next to yours.

I would have liked to have a day off to think things over, but Marcy wasn't going to go for that. That gleam in her eyes could mean only one thing—she'd found a man and she wanted to keep him. So there was no chance of my being able to get away from going out with her—and doing other things—that evening.

Dinner was a fiasco—at least, it seemed so to me. I could scarcely take a bite. Marcy didn't seem to notice—she was talking a mile a minute, and reaching over every now and then and stroking my hand, or playing footsie with me under the table. Every time that happened, I could hear that horrible voice in my head—*You know what you have to do*—and then I could barely look at Marcy in the face.

I mean, how can you look someone in the face when you know they're going to die in the next couple of hours?

So when Marcy suggested that we go to *my* place, I almost wet my pants. She wanted to see what kind of bachelor pad I had. I think she took my look of fear as a joke—as if I was ashamed of having a dirty apartment, or something like that. Of course, I couldn't explain anything to her. . . . *You see, I have this doll on my bed and she's telling me to kill you.*

I wasn't sure exactly how this was going to work. When we came back—arm in arm—to my place, I figured I would have to do some fancy footwork. It turned out easier than I expected . . . because Marcy just made herself at home in my living room and didn't bat an eye when I dashed into the bedroom without explaining why.

There was Wanda on the bed.

You ought to have seen the look of evil and hatred she gave me. I could hardly bear to touch her. But I had to do it. I opened the closet and—

What the fuck are you doing, you son of a—

I managed to close the door before I heard any more.

The next thing was . . . how and when to do Marcy.

When I came back to the living room, Marcy was already ready . . . she had quietly removed her skirt and blouse and stood there right in the middle of the room, arms akimbo on her hips, giving me this look that said, *I know I'm gorgeous and I know how much you want me.* For a minute I couldn't tell if it was Marcy or Wanda whose words were boring into my brain.

There was nothing I could do except go right to Marcy and engulf her in my big, brawny arms. My cock was so hard through my pants that it was almost painful. Marcy looked right down at the huge bulge in my crotch and smiled this wonderful smile . . . proud of herself for making me so hot, and proud of me for responding to her so fast. We kissed, each of us simultaneously sticking our tongues deep into each other's mouth. I grabbed her butt with both hands over her panties, but as I was starting to pull those panties down she backed away, as if saying, *Not yet, buster.* She looked me up and down and then began undressing me . . . slowly. First the shirt, button by button. After that came off, she pulled my T-shirt over my head—she loved the feel of my hairy chest, and in fact she bent her head down and rubbed her face all over my pecs, licking and sucking my nipples so they became as rock-hard as my cock. Then she unbuckled my belt, pulled down the zipper of my pants, and just let them fall to the floor as she had done in her place a few days before. My briefs were so bulging with my hard-on that it looked as if I'd stuck a rolling-pin down there. They came off too, and she both looked at my big cock and grasped it gently with her hand, giving my balls a little stroke also.

I returned the favor, although I didn't have much to do. Turning her around to unclasp her bra and sliding her panties to the floor took seconds. There we were, standing up in front of each other, naked as the day we were born. I grasped her breasts in my two hands and kneaded them, licked them, sucked them, smelled their heavenly aroma.

Then she took my cock and put it right in her. We were pretty much the same height—it wouldn't have worked otherwise—and she was dripping wet. I slid right in, and I must have blanked out for a second from the ecstasy of it.

We didn't fuck like rabbits . . . no, this time it was slow and loving. Little moans came from each of us as we stroked each other's face, shoulders, back, and bottom with our hands. At one point we just looked into each other's eyes and then kissed gently and tenderly. It was like nothing I'd ever experienced before . . . and I began to think she hadn't either.

I wish I could have held it in and made it last forever, but I came way sooner than I wanted. But that didn't matter; I stayed in her, and knew she wanted me to stay in her, and we just held each other close for minutes. I licked her ear and whispered, "I love you, Marcy," and she whispered back, "I love you too, Frank." God, how corny it sounds! I guess you had to be there. . . .

Finally we separated. But of course we weren't done yet. We walked hand in hand to the bedroom and, climbing into the bed, resumed. It seemed we went on for hours. I can't even remember all the things we did. But it wasn't anything like sexual gymnastics or a porn show. It was just two people making love.

So finally we stopped, and Marcy fell into an exhausted sleep.

And all of a sudden I heard that harsh, raspy voice that I knew would come to me sooner or later:

Frank, you son of a bitch, you fucking adulterer . . . you know what you have to do, don't you?

Yes, Wanda, I know.

Well, then, do it, you stinking pig.

OK, Wanda.

I rose from the bed. Marcy was out like a light. I went into the kitchen; it was dark, but I knew my way around. Keeping as quiet as I could, I pulled open a drawer. No, a steak knife probably wouldn't work. I didn't have anything like a hatchet or meat cleaver, so what could I use? Well, maybe this long, serrated knife with a sharp point would do. Yeah, I think it will do very nicely.

I closed the drawer and headed back to the bedroom.

Marcy was lying face down on the bed, her hair tousled all around her head and shoulders, her arms bent away from her body. She looked dead already.

I stood over the bed.

Then I turned to the closet, opened the door, and slit Wanda's throat clean with one blow. She deflated at once and fell with a kind of puzzled exhaustion to the floor.

I threw the knife on top of her, closed the door, and came back to bed. I fell asleep with an arm around Marcy's waist.

TOMMY, ANNE, AND VERONICA

Ninth grade!—what a blast! First year of high school! Yeah, O.K., the juniors and seniors looked down their noses at us (whenever they could be bothered even to notice our existence), but that gave us something to look forward to in two or three years. Junior high seems so . . . in-between. You're not a kid anymore, but you're not quite a "young adult" (gag). But by ninth grade you're finally at the (lowest) level of the top rung—and that's something. I went to a small K–12 school, and so all the little tykes knew immediately that you were in "high school" . . . they said it with a kind of reverence in their voice.

Anyway, my new-found status allowed me to focus on my two favorite occupations—sports and girls.

There was this kid (I guess I shouldn't call him that, he was only six months younger than me—but that made him a whole year behind me in school) who lived right behind us—our back yards were divided by a high shrub, but our constant going back and forth had made a pretty clear pathway just big enough for us if we stooped a little. His name was Tommy. A good kid. He didn't go the same school as I did (weird zoning laws in this town). When my family moved into this house three years ago, I felt all alone—we'd come from a different state, I didn't know anybody, didn't know what sixth grade would be like. So there I was one day, bouncing a tennis ball against the side of our garage. I was, like, totally bored. A gorgeous summer day, but I didn't feel like doing anything. Well, the noise of the ball seemed to attract Tommy, so he came through the bushes and said hi. (The pathway wasn't quite as big then.)

It was pretty uncanny. He was just a little bigger and stronger than me, but I was just a little faster and—lemme just say it—smarter than him. So we got to playing all sorts of sports and games. My school was too small to have a football team, so we just played with the kids in the neighborhood. Man, you can't imagine the kind of energy we put into finding the perfect football field! None of our families' yards was quite right. You needed a long field—forty or fifty yards woulda been good—not too wide, no annoying trees in the way, thick grass (didn't wanna get injured), and pretty level. We kept rotating between two or three fields, none of which was *quite* right but would do in a pinch.

Tommy had this way of coming into my yard and yelling up at my upstairs window, "Hey, Josh, you there?" The moment I heard it, I dropped everything—even the homework that was so easy I could do it in my sleep—and rushed over to meet him. Sometimes we'd take long bike rides all around—and beyond—the neighborhood, going out onto the country roads where even cars didn't come very often, so we could ride in the middle of the street and no one would care. If we got bored with the usual round of baseball, football, basketball, or soccer, we'd *invent* new games on our own. There was one time we came up with a weird variant of kick-the-can that lasted for days—and I remember the look of delight and gratitude he gave me when I freed him from "prison." Once I got poison ivy and Tommy gave me this cream that cleared the thing right up. He was immune, lucky stiff.

So that's how it went for a couple of years. By the time I got to ninth grade, both Tommy and I were pretty big and strong, and so we dominated our "gang," which ranged from several boys our age to various little brothers as young as five. Usually he and I were on opposite sides, but every so often we managed to persuade the gang to let us be on the same side. When that happened, we always creamed them—you know, 35–7, 49–14, stuff like that. (No field goals, of course—none of the fields had goal posts—and extra points had to be made by running or passing.) I wasn't so good at baseball, but Tommy was pretty good at everything. His fastball was unhittable. But maybe I fielded just a bit better than him—or am I kidding myself?

So every day after school I'd race back home and look for Tommy—or he'd look for me. I couldn't tell if it made much difference to him that I was in high school and he wasn't—maybe he didn't tackle quite so hard. . . .

Now about girls . . . . I'll have to say this was a kind of recent hobby. I don't know what it was about going from eighth to ninth grade that suddenly made the girls seem . . . special. Before that, they were just slow, soft little runts (except those weird girls who were actually *taller* than you—man, you stayed away from *them*!) who couldn't throw a football to save their lives. But now . . . aside from the fact that they all smelled nice, they just seemed *wantable*. In fact, let's be honest—they were terrifying. And they were *all* beautiful in their different ways. Suddenly you wanted to talk to them—but you *couldn't*. If, by the greatest of luck, they decided to talk to you, all you could do was gape at them or say something so stupid that half an hour later you wanted to go back to them and say, "Can we have this conversation over again? I know what to say now."

There was this girl, Anne Franklin. She had come from another junior high school, so I'd not seen her before. Can I describe her? It's pretty tough, for reasons I hope you'll understand soon. It wasn't that she wasn't pretty—as I say, almost *all* the girls were—but most people might think her a bit . . . plain. Just a blonde, with hair that hung straight down to her shoulders. Pretty nice figure, although the clothes she wore didn't show it off much. But it was her face. There was something about her face that could just express all kinds of emotions in a flash. Usually she had this strange sort of sad/solemn look, as if she was mourning something or someone. But then all of a sudden she could burst into a smile, and when I saw that my heart kind of turned over.

Maybe I'm getting ahead of myself.

I really didn't notice her right away. I was too busy being a freshman. There was one math class—Introductory Algebra—where another boy, Bill Gaines, and I were (I have to say it) obviously better than everyone else. The teacher, Mrs. Rasner, quickly saw it and put us to work. Remember, we were a kind of loosy-goosy school, where pretty much anything went, and so the teacher let Bill and me work way ahead of everyone, since she saw that we were pretty bored with the pace she was going at. But there was more than that. During study hour, she would encourage Bill and me to be kind of her tutors, explaining the day's lessons for the other kids. I remember big long lines stretching back from each of our desks—some of the questions these bozos would ask were so dopey that I couldn't believe they'd actually graduated from junior high. We tried to be as patient as we could, but every now and then I guess I got a little, um, sarcastic.

So once, in my line, was Anne Franklin. It was really the first time I'd paid any attention to her. She was no dope, but she was doing a lot of stuff with foreign languages, and math didn't come easy to her. So she plopped her book on my desk and asked me to explain something—I don't even remember what. To me it seemed easy as pie, but she was stuck. I tried to explain it as simply as I could, but, even though her face had this deep frown from concentration, she just wasn't getting it. I felt a little uncomfortable, since I still had kind of a long line of other students to help. She picked up on that, so she asked if I could sit down with her after school. I said sure—mostly just to get rid of her. Don't get me wrong—I liked her, liked the way she looked, even liked the way she smelled—but I had other clowns to tutor, and I needed to move things along.

In fact, I'd pretty much forgotten about our "study date" by the end of that school day. But she caught me just as I was heading out the door and said, "Hey, Josh, wait. Can you help me?"

At that I felt pretty bad—actually, really bad. A weird sort of hot and cold feeling went all over me. I grinned at her and said, a little shakily, "Yeah, sure, of course."

So we sat down in the library—it was pretty much empty—and I went over that cussed problem real slow. She kept nodding at each point, looking so intently at that math book that it might have been the Holy Grail. Then, all of a sudden, a kind of light seemed to go off in her head. She looked up at me, mouth just a little open, and then smiled. She didn't have to say it: she got it now.

I felt weirdly proud. Remember, she wasn't stupid—it's just that math wasn't her thing. But for a few seconds I felt that math *was* her thing—or could be. Anyway, it was a nice feeling.

I suppose I should have expected what she did then. But I didn't. She put one arm around my neck and gave me a little smack on the cheek.

Man, I don't know when I've been so flustered. I must have turned beet red. I couldn't say anything, couldn't look at her, could only look down at that blasted math book and hope that those numbers and figures would somehow stop my heart from beating so hard and so fast. God only knows why I felt this way—it was just a girl, whom I scarcely knew, giving me a little bit of thanks for helping her with something.

She started to laugh. I'll say right now that Anne didn't laugh much—I don't know why. It wasn't that she was an unhappy person. She smiled a lot—although mostly it was that kind of half-smile where your lips just curl up a bit and you don't show any teeth—but laughter didn't seem to be in her genes. But she laughed now.

"Don't be embarrassed!" she said. "It's just that you've been so sweet."

That really wasn't the thing to say to a guy. I almost scowled at her and said, "Oh, it was nothing. Glad to help."

With that, I felt I had to get out of there—but she grabbed my arm (gently) and basically asked me silently to sit still a moment.

"Are you doing anything now?" she asked.

I looked at her almost scared. "Wh-what do you mean?"

She half smiled again. "Oh, nothing. I just thought we could hang out."

I really didn't want to say, *Well, you see, I have this friend named Tommy and we kind of have this deal where we play sports after school.* That would be so . . . junior high. So I finally said, "Sure. I don't have much going on."

And that was the start of it. First we hung out with other friends, then we began going out on our own. Nothing special—pizza, burgers, movies, walks in the park (yeah, I know, that sounds pretty corny, but it was nice), long bike rides into the country, stuff like that. Unlike most girls, Anne didn't really say much—but she liked to listen. Like me, she was an only child—maybe that helped.

I'm not sure I can tell you how it was like when we first kissed—I mean, really kissed. More than pecks on the cheek. We'd gone out to get a pizza with some other friends, and afterward the others wanted to see a movie, but Anne and I didn't. We'd almost become a "couple" then, but not quite. But when we said we wanted to go off and do something else, the others—three boys and a girl—all looked at us with this look that I would really, really have liked to wipe off their faces. I sort of glared at them, took Anne's hand,

and walked away without looking back. I could hear them making some remarks.

We weren't too far from my house, so I figured we'd go back there. I was still a bit steamed, and Anne could tell. So instead of just holding my hand, she kind of wrapped herself around my arm, resting her head on my shoulder. (I'll say this made walking a bit difficult.) I really liked that, but all I could think of was: *Thank God we're out of sight of those others! This would really set them talking!*

Anne didn't say anything for a while, but finally she said: "Are you angry, Josh?"

I stopped walking and looked down at her. Her face just looked so beautiful in the twilight, with a cool autumn breeze blowing her hair a little. The anger sort of fell off me, and I looked down at her and smiled. "No, of course not. Why should I be?"

She was smart enough not to press that point. Instead, she just reached up a hand to my cheek and said, "You know, I really like you."

What else could I say but "I really like you too"? And of course I did.

So she smiled and stood on tiptoe and . . . kissed me on the mouth. It was very fast—so fast that I didn't have the chance to pucker or anything. The feel of those soft lips on mine was like nothing I'd ever felt before. I got almost dizzy.

She could see I was startled. So what did she do? She just wrapped her arms around my neck and gave me another kiss—a real one this time. A long one.

I couldn't believe I was standing out here in the street, a couple blocks from my house, where probably all the neighbors knew me and, for all I know, were peering out their windows at us, kissing this really lovely girl. I was fourteen, for God's sakes! But for the life of me I couldn't stop. All I could do was put my arms around her waist and kiss her back.

I later learned that you shouldn't really pucker up to kiss—that's for jerks. You gotta let the kiss come to you, if you know what I mean. After that, I did a lot of practicing on my pillow, and I think I got the technique down pretty well.

So now we would come back to my place, or hers, almost every day after school. I didn't want to hang out with the other kids anymore, not even my best friends—just her. There was so much to her that I didn't know, and that I wanted to know. Where had she lived, what had she done when she was a little girl—and what was she feeling? It all became so important to me. And I told her just about everything I could possibly say about myself. Well, almost everything. . . .

You see, there was this thing about Tommy. I really couldn't tell her what good friends we were—or had been—because I knew that she would feel bad for taking me away from him. I felt bad too. He was a good kid. I can't even remember what kind of excuses I had to make as to why I couldn't come out and play with him—I mean, "too much homework" got to be pretty lame after a while. There was one time, after I'd made some really pathetic excuse, that he just walked away from my back door with his shoulders slumped down. I got this huge lump in my throat—wanted to say, "Wait, Tommy! Get your football and let's play!" But of course Anne was waiting up there in my bedroom. When I got up there, she could tell I was feeling weird, so instead of saying anything she just held me in her arms, almost like a mother. I didn't say anything either—couldn't.

This was part of the reason why I kinda liked going to her place instead of mine, even though her parents really weren't as cool about us as mine were. I think Dad was pretty proud that his son had already gotten a girlfriend, and Mom, although she sometimes had this worried look on her face (I could have told her what she was thinking: *Don't do anything foolish . . .*), liked Anne a lot and maybe thought she was a "good influence"—that she was helping me "grow up." Mom never really liked all the time I'd spent with Tommy, thinking it was a waste. Anne was sweet and soft-spoken, and she liked Mom a lot.

But her parents were not so friendly. I really don't think either of them liked the fact that their little girl already had a boyfriend—probably they just thanked their stars that I wasn't some wild-haired punk. I was always nice and polite to them. But if we went right to her house from school, I didn't have to face Tommy. Anyway, Anne had this neat attic bedroom—you could only get to it by pulling this ladder down from the second-floor ceiling. I'd never seen anything like it, and it seemed to me just the coolest thing in the world. The attic was one huge room, except for a kind of corner or alcove where her bed was.

Things went on pretty fast after that. We did a lot of kissing, in her bedroom or mine, and it wasn't long before we went to the next stage. I have to say that after a couple of kisses I was just as hard as a rock; sometimes I could hardly see straight. I wanted her so much. Sometimes I held her so tight that I must have hurt her, but she didn't say anything. Her scent—not perfume, just her—drove me crazy.

So there was one time when we were doing all this, and just by accident—it really was an accident, I'm almost certain—her hand kind of brushed my crotch. I gasped, maybe even groaned. She looked at me a little bit in surprise—maybe a little bit of fear. All I could do was look at her pleadingly. She didn't really do any-thing—I guess she wasn't certain what to do, or what she *should* do. So I reached out and clumsily tried to unbutton her blouse.

It was her turn to gasp at that. She immediately took my hand and stopped me. I felt I'd gone too far and was about to apologize, when she said, "Wait, Josh."

At that point she stood up from the sofa and very quietly and calmly unbuttoned the blouse herself. She shrugged it off, and then reached behind her to take her bra off. She let it fall from her hands and just stood there looking at me in that sad/solemn way she had.

It was the most beautiful thing I had ever seen.

I can't tell, now, whether it was her breasts or that heartbreaking look on her face that got to me. I was getting dizzy—was almost afraid I'd pass out. My mouth was all dry, and I think I just stood there gaping. My heart seemed to be thumping over my entire body. I just couldn't do anything—it was almost as if, now that I had what I had been wanting for so many weeks, I couldn't go on. I was almost scared, thinking that I'd hurt her or do something stupid or make a mess of it somehow.

But she came to my rescue. She just took my hands and placed them gently on her breasts. The feel of those soft, cushiony globes was almost too much for me. After holding them for a while, I reached out and grabbed her, and brought her chest up to my face. When my cheek made contact with one of her breasts I cried out a little. I may have shed a tear.

And then it happened. I creamed myself.

I tried to conceal it from her, just clutching her more tightly and trying to stifle my groans by pressing my mouth to her chest. But she could feel the shudders that were running through my body. She just held me gently until I became quiet. And then she did the most amazing thing.

She pried my arms off her back, quietly undid my pants, got some Kleenex and cleaned me up. I was so stunned I could only watch her. She didn't seem to have any reaction when she saw my uncovered groin. She was like a mother tending to a baby, or a girl taking care of a favorite pet.

I was still speechless—a little embarrassed, a little turned on (still), but mostly filled with this incredible feeling for her. It was like she was the only person in the whole world. My lips were so dry I had to lick them—just in time, too, for she planted a gentle kiss on them before nestling up next to me. She hadn't buttoned me up, but somehow I didn't feel embarrassed any more. I just felt wonderful.

After that, we just kept on and on. I really couldn't get enough of her, and I think she sensed that. I'm sure there were times when she really didn't want to do much of anything, but she could tell that I did, and so she would take her top off and use her hand to satisfy me. Later she used her mouth. I asked her several times if I could do anything for her. She would always say no, saying that what we were doing was just fine. But one day she took both her top and her jeans off, then took the first two fingers of my hand and placed them down there. It took me a while to figure out exactly what she wanted, and once when I was being particularly clumsy she looked at me with this almost exasperated expression—well, at least as exasperated as she could get—and I felt almost the way she must have felt when struggling with that math problem months before. But finally I got it. She did have a sort of strange way of showing her satisfaction, though—just closing her eyes and moaning very softly and shivering a bit. She would always snuggle really close to me after that.

She would never get totally naked—always kept at least her panties on, and sometimes a skirt or jeans—but I was happy to strip entirely. The funny thing was that it wasn't really that I wanted to turn her on, or turn myself on—it just seemed like the right and natural and good thing to do. I wouldn't even make much of a fuss about it, just shedding my clothes and holding her tight for a while. Sure, the touch of her skin on mine was wonderful, but there was something more. Clothes just started to seem artificial and stupid.

There was this one time when we were over at my house, in my bedroom—safely locked, of course. We were getting really hot—just feeling each other all over and kissing—it was like there was nothing else in the whole world but us. Then all of a sudden I heard something: "Hey, Josh, you there?" I couldn't believe it. It had been weeks since I'd seen Tommy, and even longer since he'd made that patented cry. He must have known by now that I was . . . otherwise occupied. I froze at the words, and Anne stopped too and looked at me, a little puzzled.

"Who is that?" she asked, a little out of breath.

I shook my head hard. "No one . . . just a kid. My neighbor."

"What do you think you should do? Do you want to see him?"

"No way!" I almost shouted. "Just forget about him."

So we tried to get back to things, but it wasn't quite the same. Then I heard Mom yell up the stairs: "Josh, Tommy wants to play."

I couldn't believe it. What was she trying to do to me? Was this her way of telling Anne and me to cool it? All I could do was yell back down: "I'm busy! Tell him I'm busy!"

That seemed to be it. Pretty soon I heard our screen door close, and after that I heard something else . . . the sound of a basketball pounding on a driveway. I knew it was Tommy. The funny thing was that I didn't hear the swish of the ball going into the basket, or even bouncing off the backboard. Just pounding, pounding, pounding on the blacktop . . . like someone's fast heartbeat.

All of a sudden I got all choked up. I grabbed Anne, pulled her to me, buried my face in her chest . . . and started crying.

Anne really didn't know what was happening—or, actually, why it was happening—but like a good little mother she just held me close, stroking the back of my head with one hand while trying to restrain my shudders as I sobbed. All these things about Tommy came into my mind . . . how we once rode our bikes like mad to the cineplex to watch a horror flick we'd been dying to see for weeks—which turned out to be screamingly awful . . . how we snuck in under the bleachers at a college football game . . . how once his little brother Dave fell in some mud and we stopped him from crying by making him recite the startling lineup of that year's Chicago Bears....

I stopped after a while. Anne used her blouse to wipe the tears from my face. We never talked about it after that.

* * * * * * *

Well, this went on for a while. I really think it may have been the best part of our "relationship." I don't want you to think it was all sex. I wish I could tell you what I felt for her. The moment I caught a glimpse of her, early in the school day, my whole world seemed to light up. I could have picked her out from a bevy of girls a mile away—there was some kind of glow about her, it seemed to me. We really didn't talk all that much, but when we did talk it was always softly, as if we were planning some kind of secret plot. I felt really lonely when she wasn't around, and after a while my guy friends even stopped kidding me about her (they of course really didn't know what we were doing, but knew we were hanging out a lot)—they could tell I really had some deep feelings for her. They couldn't understand—none of them had girlfriends—but they somehow sensed that this was something pretty serious.

When we were at her house, we had to be super-quiet, for of course her parents would have flipped if they knew what we were doing. My parents were a lot cooler, although I sure didn't tell them either. Mom just had that *Be careful* look, and Dad just kinda glowed when he saw us. But her folks were pretty uptight, even though they must have known this was more than two kids rolling in the hay. Anyway, we really hadn't done anything yet, if you know what I mean.

Well, there was one time when we were at my house and things were getting pretty hot, so I felt I had to do or say something. So I just grabbed her gently but firmly by the shoulders and looked at her. All of a sudden I found my mouth dryer than it had ever been before. I swallowed once, maybe twice, and finally croaked: "Anne, I think we should . . ."

That's all I could say. But it was enough.

She'd been pretty flushed—I never saw a girl with such pink skin—but suddenly she went sorta pale. It didn't take much to figure out what she was thinking. *I knew this day would come. . . .* She had been breathing pretty hard, but now it seemed as if she almost stopped breathing at all. That sad/solemn look came over her face, and now there was something more—worry? fear? regret? I don't know.

Anne had this way of looking down at her hands when she was upset or hurt or disturbed or whatever. She did that now. She didn't say anything for a long time. But when I said her name she broke in all of a sudden.

"Josh, I don't think I'm ready. . . ."

I had a feeling that's what she would say. I wish I could tell you what was going to my mind and my heart. I wanted her so much, not just for sex, but because I wanted to kind of fuse myself with her. I wished we could be one person. I wanted to know at every moment what she was thinking and feeling.

But now, I felt a little rotten. I knew she was scared, and I knew that I'd made her that way. But I wanted her so much. So all I could say was, "Well, then, when will you be?"

She looked up at me—it's like I'd said something she hadn't expected. I think she thought I'd say, "Why not?" letting her go on about our being too young, not mature enough, etc. etc. So after a little pause she licked her lips and said, "Soon, maybe. Pretty soon." She reached up and stroked my cheek with her hand. Usually I loved it when she did that, but this time I somehow felt it was . . . like you pet a cat when you want it to stop bothering you and curl up and go to sleep.

I looked away from her. I didn't have to say I was disappointed—she knew. She tried to get me going again, reaching her hand down to my groin, but I held it—maybe a little more tightly than I meant—and stopped her. Anyway, I wasn't in the mood anymore. But I really wasn't angry. So I just held her in my arms. For a long time.

Then she went home.

The next two days, after school, we decided we shouldn't see each other. Anyway, both of us had some catching up to do on schoolwork. The day after that was a Saturday, and we decided to make a day of it. We went to the park, playing Frisbee—she had a pretty strong arm for a girl—and just walking around. Did I mention that it was around March, and spring was about to get going? It was still a little cold, but we didn't mind. After that we went to Dairy Queen for a burger and a banana split—neither of us could ever eat a whole one, so we always split one, and it was just enough for us—and then we went back to my house.

I really didn't have to say anything. I could tell that Anne had decided that this would be the time. When we got to my room, we just held each other for a little bit, then I took my clothes off as usual, not making much of a fuss about it. She slowly took her top off, then her bra, then her jeans. So now all she was wearing was her underwear. Finally, after just a moment's hesitation, she took that off too.

It was the first time I'd ever seen her entirely naked. I won't lie to you and say it wasn't wonderful . . . but I have to say that, in my weird boy way, looking down at her crotch, I couldn't help feeling that something was . . . missing. I don't really think I was any more stimulated by seeing her naked than I was before when she was just topless. It was a funny thing.

But by this time I was pretty hot—heart pounding, head dizzy, vision almost blurry, the whole bit. I knew that it would be better for her if she was hot herself. Right now she had that same sad/solemn look on her face—which I loved, I won't deny it—but there was also something else. Not fear this time; maybe disappointment? Was I making her do something she really didn't want to do? I tried to put that out of my mind, thinking that she should get as much fun out of this as I would.

So we lay down side by side on the bed, and I kissed and stroked her, and was happy that she eventually started breathing hard and fast. For the first time I let my hand rest on her bottom, and she seemed to like that, because she snuggled closer to me and almost climbed on top of me. I then reached around to make sure she was wet, then I gently turned her over on her back. Then, almost as if she was made of eggshells and I was afraid to break them, I went on top and tried to go into her.

The moment I did so, she let out a huge gasp; her eyes popped wide open, and she almost violently threw me off. I was so stunned that I got off right away. She let out a horrible groan and held her hands to her crotch, getting into a kind of fetal position and rocking herself slowly, moaning the whole time.

I felt about as rotten as I ever had in my whole life. All I could do was stare down at her as she writhed in pain. It was as if I'd

punched her in the stomach for no reason. I couldn't do anything—
was afraid even to touch her on her shoulder or her back, for fear
that that would somehow cause her more pain. So I just sat there
looking at her.

Finally she let up a bit, lying back on the bed and relaxing. Her
eyes were closed, but her lips were still shut tight, in a way that
I'd never seen them before. I felt I should now do something, so I
reached out and stroked her shoulder and said, "Anne, I'm really
sorry. . . ."

Her eyes popped open. She looked at me with this very strange
expression. I think there was fear, shock, pain, disappointment,
embarrassment, and sadness all mingled together. I'd never seen
a face show so many emotions. I wished she'd say something, but
for a long time she was silent. Finally she said, very softly, "No,
Josh, it's O.K. I'm sorry. I messed up." It was as if she'd flubbed an
exam, or failed to hit a winning shot in a basketball game.

I really didn't know what to say now. So all I could come out
with was: "It wasn't your fault. I shouldn't have . . ."

I couldn't say any more, but she reached up her hand and almost
covered my mouth. "No, please . . ." She tried looking at me, but
she couldn't. The way her hair fell down all around her face was so
. . . lovely that I just had to reach out and hold her close to me. She
seemed to like that, and for a while that's all we did.

Then she pulled herself away and did look right at me. "Josh,
let's try again."

If she'd said "I'm really Raquel Welch in disguise" I couldn't
have been more astounded. I just said, "No, Anne, let's just forget
about it." For a few seconds I think I actually meant it—I think
I never wanted to do anything like this again, if this was what it
would do to her.

But she wouldn't let it go. "No, Josh, we have to." This almost
struck me as funny, because what she was really saying was *I have
to.* By this time, though, I was . . . how would you say, not so much
in the mood. But she fixed that pretty fast with her hand.

I really thought we should wait, but she seemed so insistent that
I went ahead. This time, she let out a gasp again, but it wasn't quite
so harsh as the one before. I wouldn't say she gritted her teeth, but
I could see that she wasn't getting much fun out of it. Her eyes

were closed, her lips were set pretty tight, and she really didn't respond much to my caressing. It was over pretty fast.

Afterwards, when I rolled over, I just lay panting on my back, and she snuggled next to me, her hand lying idly on my chest. I have to say it was the most wonderful feeling I'd ever had—not just the sex, but afterward. I felt this was the closest I'd ever get to melding myself with someone else—and, right now, Anne was the only person I'd ever wanted to do that with. I couldn't imagine doing it with anyone else. I felt wrapped in a kind of glowing cocoon of happiness, and even the dizziness I still felt was kind of nice.

I'll mention that we did it once more that time.

After that, we were at it pretty regularly. Anne told me later that those first couple of times really, really hurt, but after that she thought it was wonderful too. I won't tell you the kinds of things we did—why would you want to know that? I will say we weren't particularly adventurous—I guess we really didn't know much, but some of the things we tried didn't work very well. So we pretty well stuck to the usual.

She would almost always close her eyes while it was happening. I have to say that bothered me just a little bit—it would have turned me on if she had looked at me once in a while—but I wasn't going to say anything. She had just the faintest hint of a smile on her face—just enough to let me know she was happy.

Um, there was one time when we tried to do it outside, in the park. But that really didn't work, especially because we got to laughing so hard that we figured we'd just better stop. Still, it was kinda fun.

I didn't tell any of my guy friends what we were doing. It wasn't any of their business. Maybe they knew, or suspected, but none of them asked me. I wasn't seeing them much anyway. I suspect Anne told some of her girl friends, because after a while I saw them looking at me funny—kind of scared, but also kind of respectful or even admiring. There was this one girl, Becky Birnham—a big girl, an inch or two taller than me—who I kind of liked, mostly because she was really good in sports. (Our P.E. classes were coed.) There was a time when, just for laughs, I gave her a big bear hug—and I could feel her trembling in my arms. When I stopped she wouldn't look at me.

Anne didn't go in for "public displays of affection." She would never let me kiss her or anything like that during school. The most she would do was hold hands, and that became so natural that I stopped thinking about it. Once when we were going home to her house, she had so many books in her arms—for some strange reason she wouldn't let me help her—that we couldn't hold hands, and I just walked next to her like a dope.

Speaking of sports, there was one thing that was a bit annoying about having a girlfriend. You know how you divide up to play some team sport? The teacher—a totally bald guy named Mr. Garton—once picked me to choose my side, and one of the best athletes in our class to choose the other side. This was for soccer, I think. Now let me be honest: for all her good qualities, Anne was terrible in sports. She wouldn't even have taken P.E. if it wasn't required. But of course, I had to pick her for my side—and not only pick her, but pick her no worse than, say, fourth or fifth. Anything lower and she would feel snubbed, as if she were lumped in with the fat kids and the kids who couldn't throw to save their lives and the kids who would stumble over their feet while going out for a pass. Well, you can guess what happened. Our team got creamed.

But I forgave her pretty quickly.

Sometimes we did wonder if we had started too young. We really didn't know anyone else in our school who was doing it (although I suppose there could have been some people), and of course we weren't married or anything. But we both figured that if God had given us these feelings, He must have meant for us to act on them. It didn't make sense otherwise. Of course, we were careful: we weren't Catholic, but we kind of practiced the rhythm method. Anne seemed to know when it was O.K. to do it and when we had to do other things.

Here's something funny. We really didn't talk much about it— stuff like what we each liked or didn't like. You'd think that, after all we'd done or been through, we'd be able to say *anything* to each other. I mean, Anne sure knew me better than anyone else ever had, even more than Tommy or even my parents. I told her stuff I hadn't told anyone else. But in some weird way, there were times when I got even *more* shy with her than with others. Maybe I was afraid that she'd get hurt or embarrassed or angry, and decide never to see me again. The thought of that was so awful it made me shiver all over. Sometimes I'd ask her to do things to me, and she would just look me right in the face and say, "O.K.," and do them. I couldn't tell if she really wanted to, or was doing it just to please me. The only thing that tipped me off was that sometimes she would pause just a fraction of a second before saying "O.K." and look down at her hands. Whenever that happened I made sure not to ask her to do that thing to me again.

So we went on like this all through the summer and all through sophomore year. We weren't in very many classes together, which was kind of a relief, as I don't think I could have paid much attention to what was going on. It was understood that we'd hang out every day after class, and most of the weekends. Sometimes we gave each other a break—not because we were tired or bored, but just so that getting together would be that much more fun. And don't think it was all sex. I just liked being with her. I couldn't believe that doing nothing with someone could be so satisfying.

* * * * * * *

Well, I guess I'd better get to the next part of my story. This is going to be pretty tough.

Junior year. Halfway through high school! It was pretty exciting, because you finally crossed this invisible gulf separating you from the younger kids. Seniors may have been untouchable, but you were close enough to them that some of their glow rubbed off on you. We could actually start thinking—a little—of college, and beyond. By this time, I'd really gotten into chemistry, and was taking a lot of science classes. Anne was doing more stuff in languages, so we saw almost nothing of each other during school.

There was this new girl—Veronica Hill. Her parents had moved from Illinois—her father was a physics prof and kept wanting to find a better teaching position, so he'd changed jobs about four times in the past ten years. (She told me all this later.) I didn't think Veronica liked moving around so much—hard to make new friends, hard to get used to a new school and new town, all that stuff.

I guess I'd better describe her. She was tall—almost as tall as I was, and I was getting on five foot ten—and pretty wiry. Like a greyhound. But she had curves. A brunette who usually kept her hair tied back, although maybe that wasn't such a smart thing, because her face was a bit on the harsh side. Or maybe that's just because she tended to scowl a lot.

She was smart . . . frighteningly smart. Maybe her Dad's background helped, but she was taking a lot of the same classes as I was and was doing really well in them. And she knew it. The teachers loved her because she was so sharp—they never had to explain things to her twice. And she latched on to me because she could see that I was smart too. This time it was she and I who had long lines of kids asking us to help them with their homework. (Bill Gaines wasn't really into science—he stuck with math.)

So there was this time in study hall when *I* got stuck with something. I couldn't believe it. Organic chemistry, I think. Things just didn't make any sense, and I felt weird . . . like I'd suddenly become a failure. It almost scared me. Veronica (she was not the sort of girl who'd ever let you call her "Ronnie") came over to me— she could see I was having trouble. She asked what was going on, and I told her. When she looked down at the book to see what the problem was that was giving me fits, she looked back at me with this strange, wondering look—like she couldn't believe someone could be stumped over *this*. She gave me a smile that was almost a smirk, kneeled down by my desk, and, without saying a word, just pointed slowly to a couple things on the page. I looked at her, looked at the book, and thought furiously . . . then all of a sudden something went off in my head. I'd got it.

I almost laughed out loud—almost: if I had, I'd probably been kicked out of study hall. But I'm sure I must have had a big grin on my face. She grinned back with her sharp white teeth.

That was kind of the beginning of it. Once we went back to my house after school, because the teacher, Mr. Katz, had given a really difficult assignment that *we* (Veronica and I) were supposed to present to class the next day. It really was tough, and we worked hard at it for more than an hour. I think I was actually sweating. I know my head was spinning. Finally I threw my pencil down and said, "That's it. I'm bushed. Anyway, I think we got most of it."

Veronica looked over at me with that smirk/smile of hers. She still looked pretty fresh. "You tired, Josh?" she said.

"Yeah," I breathed, and leaned back on the sofa and closed my eyes.

The next thing I knew was that someone was pressing their lips against mine. I was so stunned my eyes popped open. There was Veronica, her mouth glued to mine, her fruity perfume wafting up all around me, and her arms almost pinning me down to the sofa. I could hardly move . . . well, O.K., maybe I really didn't want to. But she was pretty strong.

Finally she stopped and I said, "Wh-why'd you do that?"

Smirking, she just said, "You just looked kissable then."

I wasn't used to anyone talking to me that way. I got so flustered I must have turned bright red. And of course I felt awful because I'd never kissed any other girl but Anne. I'll be honest with you, though—I wasn't thinking much of her right at that moment.

After a little while I got up and made to open the door of my room so she could go home. She did the most amazing thing.

She put her hand on the door so I couldn't open it. Then she pushed both my shoulders against the door and gave me another really hard kiss. It almost hurt—in fact, it *did* hurt. I also felt a little bit of her tongue.

I tried to struggle, but somehow my heart wasn't in it. I of course didn't want to hurt a girl (although something told me it would take a lot to hurt this one), but I was just so astounded that I didn't know what to do. My arms just hung down at my sides, and I tried to avoid touching her as much as possible. But that didn't help, because she had put her whole body right up next to mine.

What she did after that was like out of some fantasy—or nightmare. Quicker than I would have thought possible, she had undone my belt, unzipped my pants, and forced my pants and underwear down to my ankles. She lifted up her own skirt, took my cock in her hand . . . and put it in her.

Her lips were still fastened to mine, and all I could do was make weird little squealing noises. I struggled, but it was no use. She'd pinned me to the door—I felt like a butterfly mounted on a piece of cork. I stood utterly still, but she took care of business by making all the motions that were needed. It was over pretty soon.

Afterward, she smoothed out her skirt and just looked at me like some sort of specimen. Let me say that I never thought her *beautiful*, but her face had this kind of curious, inquiring look on it all the time. And when she gave that smirky smile of hers, it was as if she was looking at something she found interesting but a little . . . comical.

I couldn't speak—couldn't look at her. She moved me aside, gave me another little kiss on the mouth, and said, "See you in class tomorrow," and left.

And that was the beginning of it. After that I was really like someone who'd been hypnotized. I had to follow her around, had to be with her, had to have sex with her. The funny thing is that I was never sure I even really *liked* her—but that didn't seem to make any difference. I don't think Veronica cared one way or another whether I liked her or not. I really have no idea whether she liked *me* or not.

She of course knew all about Anne—or at least something about her. She knew we'd been going out, and given how much experience she must have had, I'm sure she knew that we were "intimate"—although I could tell that she looked at Anne as if she were some kind of rabbit or mouse and she was a snake who could swallow her in a single mouthful. Veronica cared so little about Anne that she didn't think it any kind of achievement to take me away from her.

And what about me? Well, you gotta understand that Veronica wasn't someone you said no to. I couldn't stop seeing her. And the funny thing was that I could really never talk to Anne about it. Anne knew almost immediately what was happening, and she just kind of melted back into the background in school. She never confronted me about it, and I was too terrified and too ashamed to talk to her. What could I say? "I've thrown you over for someone better?" Well, Veronica really wasn't "better." I really wish I could explain what kind of hold she had over me.

We actually talked a lot more than Anne and I ever did. We made all kinds of plans. By senior year we'd determined to apply to the best schools for science, and I wanted more than anything to go to M.I.T. She applied there also, and we both got in. We talked of living together, working together as chemists or as researchers in some lab, even of getting married (although Veronica didn't seem to care much about that). Her dad really liked me, and we spent a lot of time talking about science when I was over at her house.

I'm sure her parents knew what we were doing up in her bedroom, but they didn't seem to care, because they knew we were smart and were studying hard. I don't suppose I have to mention that Veronica liked being on top. She was really a kind of animal . . . maybe like a leopard or a cheetah. She would mount me and toss her head like a wild horse, and scream when she came. (We made sure to have loud music during our sessions.) And she was even more insatiable than I was. I have no idea how many boys she had had before me, but there wasn't much she didn't know.

One time, while she was on me, she suddenly jumped off and said in that commanding voice of hers, "Go into my butt."

I looked at her quizzically. I didn't even understand what she wanted. "What . . . ?" I said.

So she had to explain it to me. I think I got kind of sick for a second, but of course I couldn't say no. So I did it. She howled even louder—almost bellowed. For just a moment I got the idea that it was like she was whipping herself. I really didn't like it, but after that I'd do it whenever she asked.

* * * * * * *

I've written most of this during summer vacation, since I was pretty much alone and had a lot of time on my hands. How come? Well, I'll tell you.

It was a couple days before graduation. The school had pretty much emptied out, and even the seniors had cleared out their lockers the week before. It was late in the day, and I was wandering the halls all by myself. Hard to realize that I'd be leaving this place, so much the center of my whole life for six years. It was an old building, and some parts of it needed a bit of work, but we all loved it. Every now and then, as I was walking along, a weird feeling came into the pit of my stomach and I shivered all over. I didn't wanna leave! What if I couldn't cut it at M.I.T.? If I had trouble in class, where would I go? My parents would be a thousand miles away. From the top of the totem pole as a proud senior, I'd be back at the bottom as a lowly freshman. Would this cycle ever end?

Anyway, I was just walking and thinking. Maybe I was even muttering to myself—I'd caught myself doing that sometimes. Then, all of a sudden, I turned a corner and saw Anne, sitting on some steps leading to the side entrance. She was by herself. I saw her from the back, but there was no mistaking her.

I thought to myself: *I'm an adult—almost—and I gotta face this.* As always, my mouth got all dry and my hands got sweaty. Another shiver passed through me. But I walked over and sat down next to her.

She didn't seem alarmed at someone else's presence next to her. She just turned her head slowly and looked at me. Some emotion passed real quick over her face, but I couldn't quite tell what it was.

Well, better get this over with.

"Hi, Anne."

"Hi, Josh."

That was a real good start. Now what? I was searching my mind for something to say when she saved me the trouble.

"Why aren't you with . . . ?" She couldn't say her name.

That sure gave me a lead. "Well, it's like this. We're kinda . . . not seeing each other anymore."

For the first time since I'd known her, Anne was so stunned that her mouth dropped open. "Why? What happened?"

I didn't know if I could even tell her. But if not her, then who? I'd told my parents, of course, but they were really no help. So, swallowing the big lump that had formed in my throat, I said: "She decided . . . she decided not to go to M.I.T. Going to Columbia instead. Said she always wanted to be in the big city. And then she said that there was no way she was going to carry on at long distance with me, and anyway she'd probably meet some guy at Columbia and settle down with him." There, I'd said it. Afterward, I let out a huge sigh that was almost a whine.

Anne was a bit confused. "But how could she change her mind now? She must have had to tell them a lot earlier. . . ."

My humiliation was complete. "Yeah, she did. She told Columbia back in April. She just didn't get around to telling me until three days ago." I didn't have to add: *And she kept fucking me all those six weeks.*

Looking at Anne, I could see all kinds of feelings go rapidly over her face. Sure, she was sorry for me. However much she may have hated me (and I had no idea whether she did or not, since we'd never talked before—and she was the sort of girl who'd never admit that anyway), she couldn't help but feel some sympathy. Did I also see just for a second—a fraction of a second—another thought? *Maybe we could* . . . But if it was there, it got wiped away at once, and all I saw were those sad/solemn eyes of hers looking at me. Looking at me a long time, without blinking. Looking at me without saying anything.

I guess it was up to me to start. "Anne, I'm really sorry for what happened. . . ."

She actually held up a hand in front of my face. "Please, Josh, you don't have to say it."

"Yes I do!" I said almost violently. "I treated you so badly. . . ." That lump in my throat was so big I couldn't say anything. I must have looked at her with this pleading expression on my face, for she finally softened a little bit—reached out and touched my cheek with one hand.

All I could do was clutch that hand and hold it to my lips. I started to cry.

She took my head and held it to her shoulder. After a long while she reached up and started to stroke my head lightly, but I could tell her heart wasn't in it. It was like something she felt she had to do.

Meanwhile, her aroma was driving me crazy. It was not perfume, it was her. I got hard right away.

She may have sensed that somehow, although she couldn't possibly have felt it. Maybe my breathing had gotten harder and faster.

She got a Kleenex and wiped my face.

I had to try one last time. "Anne, isn't there any hope for us?"

For just a second I think a look of anger—maybe even hatred—passed over her face. Then just that sad/solemn look again, which also drove me crazy—crazy with love for her. But she said: "Josh, I don't think so. . . ." I could tell what she was thinking: *You missed your chance, bud. You blew it.*

I became desperate. "Can't we even stay in touch? Just by e-mail?" Did I mention she was going to Reed College? I'm sure it was because she wanted to be as far away from me as possible. And why should I blame her?

She looked down at her hands in that way she had. "That's probably not a good idea."

"Why?" I croaked.

"It just isn't." She let out a sigh. "I guess we need to start afresh with other people." She looked at me with just the hint of a smile.

"I'm sure you'll meet someone. . . ." She didn't have to say what she was thinking: *And you're damn right that I'm going to.*

I gave up at that point. Not looking at her, I said: "O.K. Maybe that's best."

"It is."

With that, she got up and walked away.

* * * * * * *

So there I was—no Tommy, no Anne, no Veronica. I didn't do much that summer—no sports, no girls, certainly no books. Didn't want to hang out with my other friends—they were all leaving for colleges nowhere near me, so I knew I'd never see them very often, if ever.

I think there was one time when I went out to the back yard and threw a tennis ball against the side of the garage.

CASSANDRA'S PLAN

1.

Cassandra Phillips
May 27, 1996, 8:14 p.m.

The bar stank. Why do people drink American beer? Why do people drink beer? I hate places like this. And I wouldn't even be here if David hadn't . . . Oh, fuck him. Fuck him for what he's making me do—for making me what I've become.

And where the bloody hell is Justin? Always late, the little shit. And why on earth did he have me meet him in this tweedy hole? He knows I hate being south of 14th Street. As if there's any chance of David seeing us . . . and what if he did? What he's doing is a lot worse.

Here he is at last. Look at that shy-but-eager-puppy look on his face. There are some people whose faces you'd like to remold out of sheer mercy. He sits down in front of me.

"Gee, Cassandra, it was nice of you to come all the way down here. I just didn't want David to—"

"Yes, yes, I know," I interrupt. "He won't. He never comes down here. Neither do I."

"I really like this place," says Justin. "And do you know, almost right next door is this really neat old tavern? Actually, it's not a tavern anymore, but it used to be. Fraunces' Tavern—not *Frances*, Fraunces. Samuel Fraunces was a black guy—can you believe it, a black guy owning a tavern in the eighteenth century—and that place hasn't changed much in two centuries. I think maybe the wainscoting is—"

"Justin, I'm not a tourist. I don't care about that goddamn tavern. Nor this one."

His teeth come together with a click. "Oh, I'm sorry . . . we could go somewhere else maybe. I know a place—"

I close my eyes and breathe deeply. Very softly: "I don't want to go anywhere else, Justin. Let's just do it here, okay?"

"Okay." Chastened-but-still-eager-puppy look.

"Do you want to buy me a drink?"

He gets more eager. "Sure! What would you like?"

"Scotch on the rocks."

He calls the waitress over—or tries to. She takes a while recognizing Justin's spasmodically half-raised hand as anything but a mild epileptic fit. Finally she comes by.

"Scotch on the rocks for the lady and . . . um, I guess a tom collins for me."

The waitress goes away without a word.

"You know," Justin says, "it's already pretty hot. Gee, New York just doesn't get any spring. From winter right into summer just like that!" He claps his hands together; he winces a little, as if the impact was more violent than he had expected. "I love tom collinses, only I really should have asked her to put vodka instead of gin in it. That makes it a vodka collins, doesn't it? Do you think I should call her—?"

"Justin, shut up."

Teeth click together again.

"Justin, you know that I want you to do something for me."

"Sure, Cassandra. I'd really like to. It's really an honor for me to do something for—"

"Shut up. I want you to do something you may not want to do. But I really need you to do it, Justin. I really do. I don't have anyone else to turn to." It nauseates me, but I try to look earnest and pleading.

"You just name it, Cassandra. I'll do anything . . ."

The waitress comes by with the drinks. I wait until she's gone. No one else is close by, and anyway the tavern is so noisy that conversations two tables away can't be heard.

I reach into my handbag. There is a big, heavy object wrapped in a newspaper. *New York Post*. I knew it was good for something.

"Take this, Justin."

"What is it?" He takes it from me. "Gee, it's heavy, Cassandra. What is it?" He begins to open it.

"Don't do that."

I whisper it between my teeth, reaching over to stop his hands from unwrapping the parcel.

"What is it?" He takes to whispering himself, so softly that I can barely hear him in the noise of the place.

"It's a gun. I got it at a pawnshop on East 14th Street."

The eager-puppy look finally gives way. He's a scared and confused little puppy now.

"What . . ."

"I want you to kill my husband."

2.

Cassandra Phillips
May 27, 1996, 8:23 p.m.

"Gee, Cassandra, are you crazy? Why . . . ?" He can't even finish.

"I just want to, Justin. Do I have to tell you every little thing?"

"Cassie"—I hate people who call me Cassie—"I think you might want to tell me this little thing. I just don't get it. Why? And why me?"

I sigh heavily. For once Justin isn't going to do what I tell him just because I say so. I suppose I owe him some sort of explanation.

"Why? Because David is fucking around—and I mean that literally—with that little bitch Lauren, his 'old flame'! And why you? Because you're the only friend I've got who'll do it. Okay? Is that enough?"

He is trying to digest all this, and it seems to be taking him a while, though it seems pretty simple to me. Finally he decides to take one thing at a time.

"How do you know that he's . . . um, I mean, about David and Lauren? You didn't actually see them, did you?"

"I saw them with hands clasped and gazing soulfully at each other at Café Europa," I spit back at him. "God knows how long it's been going on. Maybe weeks, months—years, for all I know. I don't think he ever stopped loving her. Christ, he's known her since she was a child. Anyway, Justin, our marriage is over—and it would be over even without this." Suddenly I'm very tired and don't want to talk any more.

"But, but"—he's actually blubbering—"why don't you just leave him? Wouldn't that be better?"

I can't believe I'm hearing this. *"Better?* Oh, you want me just to walk away from this and let David and Little Miss Bitch waltz into the sunset? No way, Justin. I don't work like that. He's wronged me. I don't take this kind of treatment from anybody. Not from anybody!"

My anger seems to have stunned or intimidated him. I think he's afraid to speak—afraid that I'll chew his head off. I probably would, too.

"But why me? How'm I supposed to . . . ?"

I realize that a different tack is in order. I talk to him soothingly, softly stroking his hands, which are still clutching the newspaper-wrapped object.

"Justin, you have to do this for me. For me, Justin. I know how you've felt about me, and I've always respected those feelings. We've kept in touch all this time, haven't we? I don't forget my friends and my . . . lovers." I have trouble getting the word out. "And who knows? After this thing is over, maybe we could . . ." I really can't go on. I'm about to retch.

His eyes grow large as if he's discovered the relativity theory before Einstein did. He opens his mouth slowly; a little strand of saliva runs vertically between his lips, and I want to slap the side of his head to dislodge it.

"You mean . . . you mean we could . . . ?"

"Yes, maybe, who knows?" I'd better turn this in a different direction. "But we can think about that later. Will you do this for me?"

He looks at my hands, still stroking his. I think he's really looking at the newspaper and thinking of what's in it.

"I always like to please you, Cassandra. You know I'll do whatever you want." It doesn't sound as if he's really agreeing to things; his tone suggests a "but" coming up.

"Good; then that's settled," I say before the "but" can come out. "And here's something to help you a little."

I slap a fat envelope on the table between us. He doesn't have to look hard to realize what's in it.

"Just to cover any incidental expenses, okay?" I'm starting to get up.

"Wait . . . I mean, how am I supposed to . . . ?"

I sit back down. Keeping my gorge down, I stroke his cheek. "We'll worry about that later. Some opportunity will present itself. We'll stay in touch. I haven't worked anything out, but we'll think of something. Won't we?"

"I guess so." His voice is very small. He looks as if he's going to cry.

I get up again. He grabs my arm almost viciously. "But wait! What if I get caught? What do I say to the police?"

Here's my trump card. "You won't get caught, Justin. That's why we have to think this over. And if you do"—I look him right in the eye—"you tell them that I put you up to it. So if you get caught, we go down together."

He looks at me almost reverently, as if I'm a Giotto Madonna that's walked out of a picture.

"But we won't get caught. Will we, Justin?"

3.

Lauren Oxley
May 23, 1996, 5:27 p.m.

"It was nice of you to come, David."

"You know I'm always glad to see you, Lauren."

"Yes. I know." I look away from him a bit.

"I'm sorry I had to ask you to meet me here," he goes on. "You sounded so frazzled, so I didn't want to wait, but I had to meet my agent earlier today, uptown." He doesn't seem to want to look at me either.

Café Europa is already pretty full. I look across the street at Carnegie Hall and sigh. This is the closest I'll ever be to that place.

I turn back to look at him because he's starting to make more small talk. It's not like him to do that. "Are you still at NYU?"

"Yes. Still there." I don't want to get into that discussion again.

He doesn't either, so he says nothing. But then he goes on: "Are you doing okay? Is New York treating you well?"

I've never heard him so trite. "I'm fine," I say a little tiredly. I try to steer the conversation in the direction I want it to go. It's hard, I don't even know if I have the gumption to do it, not with him, anyway. . . . But who else can I turn to?

But he's jumped the gun on me. "You know, Lauren, it always struck me as funny that you chose to remain here in the city. I didn't think New York was really the place for you." Then, as if suddenly realizing what he's saying—or rather, what the subtext of what he's saying might be—he adds quickly: "I mean, I love having you around, and I wish we could get together more often, but you know, with Cassandra and all . . ." He looks totally miserable.

I really don't want to go on about this, but I figure I might as well settle this thing before moving on. "David, I did try to get out. Remember? Maybe you don't—I don't think we were much in touch then. Three years ago I went back home for the summer— NYU was really nice about it, they gave me three months off and hired a temp—but it didn't work."

"You went back to your parents?" he said with incredulity. I don't wonder.

"Yes, I went back to my parents. Where else was I going to go?" As his look of amazement—mixed, it seems, with a kind of sympathetic horror—persists, I add: "Oh, that part was okay. They've forgiven us . . . well, maybe not you, but they forgave me. I'm their only child, after all.

"It wasn't that. It was just . . ." I look around the place trying to find some inspiration for the words I want. I don't see anything except men in suits, well-dressed women with Lord & Taylor or Bloomingdale's bags, and efficiently discreet waitresses everywhere. Thank God ours has chosen not to bother us after putting a pot of tea down in front of us. "It just wasn't the same. I couldn't go back—I've changed too much. I changed without even knowing it. It was awful . . . so provincial and—and small-town. You know, I thought that's the way I was." I laugh abruptly. "Well, that's right, at least. It's the way I was."

David has been nodding at intervals. I think he's changed even more than I have.

This has to stop. I don't want to talk about this. I shake my head vigorously, maybe a little frantically, as if there's a bee entangled in my tresses.

"David, I'm in a jam." There. It's out. Part of it.

His intense look turns to a kind of hesitant fear. "Jam? How? Why?"

"Look, it's kind of a long story, okay? Well, maybe not—maybe a very short story. I'm not going to go into details."

I take a deep breath. "You remember a guy at Columbia named Jud Wynn?" I say no more.

David expects me to go on, thinking that it was a rhetorical question, or a question that I myself would answer. I don't. I want him to answer it.

He racks his brains. "Wynn? That scumbag? I haven't thought about him for years. Just as well, too. What could he possibly want with you?"

"He both has something and wants something." David seems to be losing patience, and I don't blame him: this is not coming out very easily.

"All right, look, David, I'll tell you. I did a really stupid thing in college. Beginning of my junior year. After we . . ." I bite my tongue. Don't get into that. Don't. Not now.

"I posed nude for a porn magazine."

There. It's out.

David's expression of expectation mingled with fear is frozen on his face. It's like he didn't hear me, or that I suddenly started speaking in a language he didn't know.

"Wh . . . what did you say?"

"You heard me, didn't you? I don't need to say it again." I look down at the tea. Neither of us has taken any of it. It's quite cold.

"Why . . . did you do that?" he says very quietly.

"Oh, God, David, don't ask me that!" I say it so loudly that, even in the clamor of the place, several heads turn. "I just did. I was stupid. I didn't really know what I was doing. I thought it was a way of . . . rebelling, maybe. Being my own person. Getting away from my parents." How could I forget that horrible summer I spent at home after sophomore year? I wasn't going to say, "Also to get away from you." I don't suppose he would appreciate that.

"Anyway," I go on rapidly, "somehow Jud got the negatives. He's in the porn business now, you know."

"No, I didn't know. How do *you* know?"

"Because"—I hiss this very softly but very firmly so that no more heads turn—"he called me up and said he had the fucking negatives, that's how! And now he wants me to work in a porn movie or he'll turn the pictures over to my parents!"

I'm starting to shake. I've been leaning forward, almost in David's face, but now I slowly sit back in my chair. I don't look at him.

"Oh, my God." He sounds sick.

"Yeah. It's bad. Real bad." I look up. "David, I can't hurt my parents like that. I've hurt them enough already." Shouldn't I have said "We hurt them enough already"? Let it pass. "You've got to help me."

"How? I mean . . . how? What . . . ?" He's blubbering. "What can I do?"

"Can't you talk to him? Do something to get the negatives back? Just see if you can talk him out of it! Maybe . . ."—I really don't like to say this, but I have to—". . . maybe give him some money."

He ignores that for now. "Well, what's to stop him from getting a copy of the magazine and showing it to your folks?"

I shake my head. "That was a fly-by-night rag that probably didn't circulate for more than a month or two. I mean, it wasn't *Penthouse* or anything. You'll never have heard of it. It was sixteen years ago, God knows. But I have to get those negatives away from him."

I hate to play this kind of emotional blackmail, but I have to. I grab both his arms, which have been clutching the edges of the table, and look right into his eyes. "David, please. . . . For all the things we've been through over the past twenty-odd years— I must still mean something to you, don't I? You still care for me?"

First he avoids my eyes, then he looks back at me. "Lauren, of course you mean something to me. More than I can say. More than you can even know. . . ." He looks away again.

"Then you'll do it?" I hate the eagerness and pleading in my voice.

"Well . . . yes, I mean . . . I'll do what I can. I'm not sure what the upshot will be. What if this guy won't listen? He was already lowlife back in school. Now he must be a real sleazeball."

I fish in my purse. "Just try. It's all I ask." I hand him a slip of paper. "Here's his number. Just call him up and see what you can do." He takes the paper grudgingly, as if it might be poisoned.

"God, David, you don't know how much better I feel. Even though nothing may come of this, at least it good to know I have a friend." I mean all that.

"You're more than a friend, Lauren. You always will be."

He bends forward and gives me a long kiss on the lips. It's the first time in sixteen years that he's kissed me like that. I don't expect it. I can't even say anything.

He gets up hastily, as if he knows he's done something he shouldn't have. "Sweetie, I have to get home. I'll be in touch, okay? I promise."

He throws some money down and leaves.

He hasn't called me "sweetie" in sixteen years, either.

4.

Cassandra Phillips

I wish I knew how my marriage went wrong.

Sure, fifteen years is a long time to be married, and maybe people grow a little bored with each other, a little tired of being together all the time. I've tried to give David his space. What does he want from me? I'm still attractive. Certainly he found me so when I first met him.

Cassandra Connolly
April 3, 1980, 5:22 p.m.

God, if I ever step into Butler Library again it'll be because I own the place. A big rectangular block of marble with the names of big-shot Greek and Latin writers—all men, naturally—chiseled on top; huge long windows with gratings that open creakily and infinitesimally, as if reluctant to let in any fresh air that might actually blow some of the dust away from books nobody reads; a bafflingly labyrinthine layout whereby you reach the book stacks by sidling through a narrow slit at the side of the circulation desk, and then you discover that, even though you're on the *third* floor, you're on the *sixth* level of the stacks. . . .

But those stacks are the worst. Shelves piled high to the ceiling with musty books, with barely enough room between them for one person to pass, let alone two. . . . And the dark! Every time you want to enter a shelf you have to turn a little timer mechanism that feebly illuminates—if you're lucky and the overhead lights aren't broken—the aisle while you dash in and get the book you want. If you stay there too long, the light snaps off without warning—and you're in the dark again with books ready to fall upon your ears. What's going on? Doesn't Columbia University, of all places, have enough money to avoid this kind of piddling energy saving?

Every so often there are signs posted up saying that there has been some sexual assault or "attempted" sexual assault—which presumably means that the poor chump couldn't get it up or finish the job—and that people (meaning women) should be extra vigilant. . . . Doesn't occur to anyone to post guards there—no, that's too much money (just like it's too much money to keep the lights on all the time); we just have to be vigilant.

Well, that's fine with me. Somebody's balls will get shot off if they try to do something to me.

Here's this guy in the PS3500 shelf, trying to pull down something just out of his reach. I look at my little slip of scrap paper. I need PS3505. I scan the numbers—PS3501 (Sherwood Anderson), PS3503 (Pearl S. Buck—God spare us). . . . I get closer and closer to where he's standing. He doesn't notice me at first, he's so intent on reaching that book. Finally I come up right next to him. He's standing in front of the books I need. In fact, he's reaching for the very shelf I want. Only then do I notice that he already has a half-dozen books piled up on the floor, and he's just snapped up the one that has eluded him.

"Hey! You can't take all the Cains!"

He almost jumps out of his skin. "Ssshhh—this is a library . . ."

"Don't shush me. You can't take all those books. I want them."

Some little snot-faced girl comes over to the head of the shelf. "Would you please mind . . ."

"Oh, fuck off, you stupid cow."

She seems struck by lightning. After a second she whirls away.

I turn back to him, grudgingly whispering. "Look, guy, you really can't take all those books. I—"

"But I have to write a paper on Cain."

"So do I."

He looks at me curiously. "You're in Tough Guy Writers of the Thirties?"

"Yeah." I finally recognize him. "So are you."

"Yeah, I am. What's your name?"

For some reason I don't know whether I should tell him. "Cassandra. What's yours?"

"David. David Phillips."

I scour my memory some more. "Don't you write for the *Spectator*? Stories. They're pretty good."

Dim as the light is, I can see that he's blushing. Blushing! Imagine anyone blushing nowadays.

"Thanks. I . . . I didn't know anyone read them."

I'm sure he's not that dumb; just nervous. "Well, if they're printed in the paper, I guess people would read them."

"Yeah, I guess so. . . ." He can't look me in the eye.

Suddenly he picks up all the James M. Cain books. He almost throws them at me in handing them over. "Here, you can take these. I can write about somebody else. Hammett, maybe . . ."

"Yeah. He only wrote four books."

"Four novels. He wrote a bunch of short stories."

"Oh, they don't count." There is a little silence. "Thanks, David. I really didn't mean to force you to give these up. Maybe we can split them up. . . ."

"No, no, you take them. I want you to have them."

"It's very nice of you." Another little silence. "You want to get some coffee or something?"

I can't believe it. He's blushing again.

"Sure . . . I guess so . . . I mean, if you want to. . . ."

I look at him straight in the face, with a tight smile. "If you don't want to, it's okay." I turn to go.

"No!" He almost shouts it; then he claps a hand over his mouth. "I mean . . . it's just that . . ."

"What?" I wait patiently.

"I'm already going out with someone. . . ."

This is so quaint I can't believe it. "David, I'm not trying to seduce you. I don't care whether you're going out with someone. Go out with her all you want. I just thought you might want to have a little chat over coffee."

He gives me a crooked smile. Very appealing. "Okay. I didn't mean to offend you."

"You didn't. Come on, let's go."

We check the books out—his Hammett novels all fit into one omnibus volume, while I have seven or eight Cain books for my trouble—and he magnanimously carries mine for me. He's a little shy in offering to do so—the women's movement has got men so confused they don't know whether doing things like this might be patronizing—and he's also a little shy, not to say clumsy, holding open the incredibly heavy door leading out of the building.

We go to the West End. The coffee comes incredibly fast, slammed down by a waitress who darts away before we can trouble her for anything else. David puts liberal amounts of milk and sugar in his coffee, paying a great deal of attention to it. I see nothing but the top of his head.

"So, where are you from?" I ask.

He looks up and stares right in my eyes. "Kokomo, Indiana." He says it with a certain pride.

"A Midwestern boy? How charming. I knew you weren't from around here."

"How could you tell?"

"Your accent."

His eyes cloud over and he looks as if he's afraid to speak again. "Do I have it bad?"

"No, no, I didn't mean that. It's just that you don't have a New York or Eastern accent. Anyone can tell you're not from around here, but that's cool."

He sighs in relief, as if I've just freed him from a trip to the guillotine. "Yeah, those Indiana farmers"—he puts on an exaggerated accent (or is it exaggerated?)—"speak reeeel funny. It's awful." He pauses. "Where are you from?" it finally occurs to him to ask.

"Upper East Side."

He has to think about that a little, even though as a junior he must by now know what that means. "A lifelong New Yorker, eh?"

"Eh."

My hint of sarcasm abashes him. I feel a little guilty. "Sometimes I think I want to get away from New York—but I just can't imagine where else I would go. There's no other place like this, is there? Maybe London. Have you been there?"

"No," he says in a small voice.

"You ought to go. It's wonderful."

He mumbles agreement but says nothing. His coffee is almost finished.

"So what's your girlfriend like?" I say this just to say something. I can't think of any other topic of conversation.

But he perks right up. He looks me right in the eye and says enthusiastically: "Oh, she's great! Her name's Lauren. I've known her since grade school."

"She's from Kokomo, Indiana, too?"

"Yes." He starts the word eagerly but then trails off, as if he's ashamed to have to admit it.

"That's nice. Is she in our class?"

He's a little confused. "In our Tough Guy Writers class? No, of course not . . ."

"No, I mean is she a junior?"

He seems about to slap his forehead, but refrains. "Oh. I'm sorry. No, she's a sophomore."

I smile—kindly, I hope. "And she followed you here all the way from Indiana? That's sweet." I mean it. It is.

"Yeah, isn't it?" His eyes get dreamy. "I mean, I'm sure she wanted to come to Columbia because it's a great school"—maybe he thinks that as a New Yorker I have some need to defend the prestige of my town—"but I guess my being here didn't hurt." He grins sheepishly.

"No, I'm sure it didn't." I finish my coffee. "Are you going to get married?"

He looks a little confused. "Gee, I don't know. We haven't talked much about it. . . ."

"Is it what *you* want?"

Now he's confused and embarrassed. "I don't really know. I guess so. After we finish college."

I feel a change of gears may be useful. "You want to be a writer, I suppose?" That sounds vaguely condescending, but he doesn't take it that way.

"Yeah! I sure do. I mean, if I can manage it. . . ."

"Why shouldn't you manage it? You write well. Damn well."

He's blushing again—so hard that he can't speak, even to say thank you. He looks into his empty coffee cup. I figure I'd better help him out.

"What do you want to write? Stories? Novels?"

"Yes, sure, both. I tried writing some novels in high school, but they were pretty bad."

"You wrote novels in high school?" I'm moderately impressed.

"Well, I finished one and got half through another before I discarded it. They were really bad. Detective novels."

"You threw them away?" I'm half outraged.

"Sure. They weren't worth anything—nothing in them that could be preserved. Take my word for it. I don't think I'm up to writing novels yet. I need to get more short stories done first." He sounds in total command of himself; no shyness now.

"That's good. Keep at it." I start to rise. "Let me see your stuff sometime. I'd like to read it."

He gazes up at me. "Would you? Really?"

"Yes, really." I pat him on the shoulder and leave.

5.

Cassandra Connolly
April 26, 1980, 11:42 p.m.

"David, I'm stuck. I just don't know what to say." I throw my pen down in disgust.

He gets up from the typewriter and walks over to the couch where I'm sitting. Books are piled up in a heap around me; some lying open on their fronts, some on their backs, some with little slips of paper stuck in them like cheap bookmarks. All of them say Cain. I can't stand the sight of them.

David sees one of the open books. "You shouldn't write in library books," he says softly.

I can't believe what I'm hearing. "David, that's not helping."

He's chastened. "No, it isn't. I'm sorry." He flips through a sheaf of typed pages in his hands. "But this is really good so far. You don't have much more to go."

I take the pages from him and leaf through them. Something strikes me as odd. "You've made a mistake." I point to a word.

He looks sheepish. Even more softly he says: "Well, no, Cassandra, that's how it's spelled."

I look at the word, then up at him, then back at the word. I don't have the energy to look it up in the dictionary. He must be right—he's the writer.

"I guess you've fixed up my grammar, too, haven't you?"

His sheepish look remains, but turns into a boyish grin. "Well, yeah, a little—but I do it automatically, without thinking about it."

I'm supposed to be comforted by that?

"Okay. Fine." Let's change the subject. "But how do I finish this off?"

He sits down next to me. "I think all you have to do is to get some overall idea of what Cain's novels are all about—the unifying theme, you know? Maybe—"

"But what the fuck *is* the unifying theme, dammit?" I almost shout.

He freezes, his mouth hanging open.

"I'm sorry, David, I didn't mean that. I'm just so tired of this thing. I wish it were over. Jesus, I've killed myself over this paper. I'm really not very good at this."

I push the typed pages away; I can't stand to look at them. Then I look up at him.

"I'm being selfish, aren't I? You've helped me a lot. I'm sorry I've kept you away from Lauren so long. Who else would waste a Sunday evening waiting for some stupid girl to finish writing a page so he can type it for her? I can't write, and I can't type. Not much use, am I?"

He puts his arm around me—like a brother, I suspect. "Oh, don't be silly. There are lots of other things in the world besides writing and typing." He pauses a moment, doubting whether he should say what he wants to say. Finally it comes out:

"You know, Cassandra, maybe I could finish it up for you. You only need about a page or two more." He looks at his feet, as if ashamed of the suggestion.

"How could you do that? You haven't read the books!" I think his idea is sweet but crazy.

"Oh, I can just infer it from what you've written. The conclusion is really already there; maybe you just can't see it."

"Maybe." I look at him skeptically. "Oh, go ahead if you want to. I just can't write any more."

He almost rushes back to the typewriter, where there is still a sheet about two-thirds filled. He starts rattling away—pretty damn fast, it seems to me, for someone who is presumably composing off the top of his head. I start picking up all the books and piling them up on the floor next to the couch. The room is very small, and David's bed, couch, and desk take up about all the space in it. Still, it's a lot neater than my room back on East 68th Street.

In about twenty minutes he's finished. He's typed about two and a half pages. I can't believe it, and I start reading from where I left off, just to make sure he hasn't typed gibberish.

It isn't. It's pretty good. In fact, it's damn good.

I look at him. I feel something very strange. I feel tears in my eyes. Christ, I haven't cried since I was in junior high.

"Thanks, David," I say in a small voice. "This is a lot better than I could have done."

"Oh, I don't think it is. You could have done it."

He's sitting next to me, but seems to be trying not to touch me. I change that pretty fast. I throw my arms around his neck and kiss him on the lips. For a long time.

When I let go, it's like he's gasping for breath. I thought it was women who did that.

He has this totally astounded look on his face. It's especially funny because there's lipstick smeared diagonally across his lips.

I smile at him. "I'm sorry if that bothered you."

"No, no," he stammers. "It's just . . . I just wasn't expecting it. It was sweet of you."

"Do you want more?"

"Oh, Cassandra, we'd better not. . . ." I know he's thinking of Lauren. I'll put an end to that.

"I think we'd better."

I kiss him again, hard, and slowly take his left hand, which is gripping my shoulder a little spasmodically, and move it to my breast. At first he shies away from it as if it's electrified. I put it back, forcing him to hold it for several seconds. I'm still kissing him, so he can't speak, but he's trying to mumble something. All that comes out, though, is a kind of moan.

Finally he unglues his lips from mine and says, "Please . . ." In response I push him backwards so that he is half lying on his back on the couch, his feet dangling over the edge. I'm on top of him, and his left hand is now sandwiched between my breast and his chest. I take his other hand and place it directly on my bum. He moans again; it's almost a whine.

I rub my crotch against his. I can feel him getting hard. I know I have him.

Eventually we move to the bed.

After it's over he just lies there, dazed. I rest my head on his chest; its soft hairs both cushion me and tickle my nose. He smells nice. It's not cologne or aftershave or anything; it's just him.

He is gingerly stroking my head. He seems hesitant or ashamed even to do that, but feels he has to do something. I turn my head so that my face is looking right at his.

"Was that nice?"

He has this scared look on his face. "Yes, of course it was. It was wonderful. But I don't think we should have . . ."

"Why not?"

"Well, well, because—"

"I know, I know," I cut him off. "Because you're going out with Lauren. Do you sleep with her?"

He looks even more scared. "Well, of course I do, sometimes . . ."

"Sometimes? Not often? Doesn't she like it?"

"No, I mean . . . sure she does . . . But we've been pretty busy. A lot of work at the end of the semester."

"Don't I know it." I smile, and he finally smiles back. But he still has a scared look in his eyes.

"Listen, David, just relax. We don't have to do this again if you don't want to. And I didn't do it to reward you for your help. That's vulgar. I did it because I like you. A lot. But we can be just friends if you want."

He looks a little more reassured. "Okay. Okay, sure, fine."

I lie there on his chest a little longer. Neither of us speaks. His heart is still beating pretty fast.

I turn my head again to face him. "Can I stay here tonight?"

The scared look again, but not as scared as before. "Gee, I guess so. I mean, it's pretty late . . ."

"Isn't it." A little silence. I reach for his member. "Do you want some more?"

It's like I suggested we fly to the moon in a Studebaker. "Well, sure, I guess . . ."

"Good." With my tongue I paint a wet line from his nipple to his crotch.

6.

Lauren Oxley
May 22, 1980, 2:37 p.m.

"Listen, Lauren, we have to talk."

I don't like the sound of this. David's usually pretty serious—that's one of the things I like about him, he's not a goofy jerk like so many other college guys—but he has a kind of scared look in his eyes that I've never seen before.

I sit down on the edge of the bed. His dorm room is so small that there's no room for anything except a very narrow bed (not narrow enough for two, though!), a ratty couch, and a long desk with his typewriter and more papers and books on it than I've ever seen anywhere else. They're all pretty neat, though. I wonder how he does it.

"What is it, David? What's wrong? You look upset."

He turns away to stare out the window. Then he looks at his feet. It's not like him not to want to look at me.

"We've known each other a long time, haven't we, Lauren?"

"Yes," I say, a little guardedly. "Since junior high."

"I remember the first time I saw you," he says in a hurry. "My family had just come from Illinois, and I was petrified. Eighth grade in a new school, a new town, a new state! Who knows what would happen? We were in the auditorium, the whole school was. I was sitting toward the back, trying not to call the least attention to myself. You were sitting several rows up, talking to a lot of people—I guess you already knew everybody, since they were your grade-school chums—and for some reason you turned around and looked right at me. At first your face was blank, and then very slowly you smiled. That's all. Didn't say anything. You just smiled and turned back around.

"I'll always remember that smile, as long as I live."

It seems like a speech he's rehearsed. I don't think it is: David sounds like that a lot.

"I remember that, too, David." I'm trying to prompt him.

He suddenly gets up from the bed. There's very little room to walk around, but he manages it.

"David, please tell me what's on your mind. You've never been like this before."

He wheels around and says loudly: "I've met someone else!"

I don't understand what he's said. I literally don't understand what he's said.

"What?" I wish my voice didn't sound so small and cracked.

"I've met someone else," he says more quietly. It's as if he can't say anything more. I have a mad conception that we'll be saying the same things over and over again for the rest of time ("I've met someone else." "What?" "I've met someone else." "What?").

I feel dizzy. There's a roaring in my ears. I don't think I can move, even though I either want to run out of the place or punch him in the chest—not because I'm angry or hurt (that hasn't hit yet), but because I want to make him say something more. Anything more. Anything to help me understand.

"Who is it?" I finally manage.

It's like he wasn't expecting the question. He waves his hand a little spasmodically. "It doesn't matter. You don't know her. She's in my class. I mean, I'm taking a class with her, but she's also a junior, like me." He's babbling again.

I look up at him. "You're telling me this and I'm not supposed to care who she is?"

He seems to lose patience. "Lauren, her name's Cassandra Connolly. Is that what you want to know?"

I say very quietly: "I want to know why you're doing this."

He looks frantically all around the room—at everything but me. He's not used to this kind of situation. He's used to being in charge of his life. He always has been.

"Lauren, I just . . . I just fell for her, that's all. I love her. I love you too," he adds hastily, "I still love you, sweetie."

"Please don't call me that." I'm starting to shiver all over; can't seem to stop. The ringing in my ears is getting worse.

"I'm sorry, Lauren. I'm sorry."

I look up at him again. "That's all you can say? After seven years of knowing me, and five years of sleeping with me, that's all you can say?"

He sits down heavily on the bed, but looks out the window. "What else am I supposed to say? What can anyone say at a time like this? You've been wonderful."

"So it's over. It's all over. Just like that?"

He still doesn't look at me. "I guess so," he says in a small voice.

I just sit there. I seem to have stopped shaking, but now I feel tears running down my cheeks. I don't even know how they got there—it's like they just started without my having anything to do with it.

"You remember the first time we slept together?" I don't know why I'm saying this, it'll just make it hurt more, but I can't stop. "You snuck out of your parents' house, and we met in my back yard, and we tiptoed up to my bedroom in the attic—God, I never had another room like that, the whole attic just for me—and we lay there all night in each other's arms. It was so cold, unusually cold for October, and the heat was somehow not getting up to the attic, but we kept each other warm, all night. My parents didn't even know you were there. God, if they did, they'd have killed us both—or at least felt we were instruments of the Devil." I'm just babbling now. "You remember how much I cried when you left for college. And I vowed I'd do my best and get good grades and follow you. And you said yes, you wanted that, and you wrote me every week, almost, and we called a lot, and you came home for Thanksgiving and Christmas and Spring Break. The big city hadn't changed you a bit."

I was out of breath. He still wasn't looking at me.

"That summer before I came out here was the best, wasn't it? I miss Indiana, don't you? We rode all around on our bicycles, and sometimes we'd get lost on purpose just so we could have the fun of finding our way back again, sometimes it took hours and hours, and we'd stop at some little gas station out in the middle of nowhere and get something to drink and cuddle, and it was so hot and we were sweaty, but it didn't seem to matter, it was just nice to be close . . ." I can't go on. It's like I've swallowed a meatball and it's lodged in my throat. My cheeks are all wet, as if I've held my face up to a shower, and drops are falling on my blouse.

"Please stop," he says in a small, choked voice. He turns to look at me. Tears are on his cheeks too. I'm a little stunned. I've never seen him cry before. Not when that bully Frank McCurdy knocked him down on the sidewalk and kicked him; not when he failed to win a short story contest at Purdue University; not when his mother almost died being hit by a car.

"So what do you want to do?" I manage to whisper.

"I don't know." He's looking at his feet again.

An idea occurs to me. "Maybe we can talk it over this summer? I'm not going to try to win you back, David, but maybe we could just spend some time together and see—"

"Lauren, I'm not going back home this summer."

Again it's like I can't understand what he's saying. "Not going back? But where will you go after the semester?" I have wild visions of him being a derelict in the gutter somewhere around Times Square.

"I'm staying with Cassandra and her parents. They have a place on the Upper East Side."

"Oh." I don't know what else to say.

"But listen"—he throws out his arm at me suddenly, almost as if he's going to attack me, and grabs my wrist—"let's . . ."

I pull my wrist away violently. "Please don't touch me."

"Oh, Lauren . . ." He comes closer.

"Please don't touch me!" It comes out as a scream. I stand up. I'm shaking again.

He gets up too. "Can't we stay friends? We've known each other so long. . . ."

I can't believe what I'm hearing. "You want to be . . ." I can't even go on.

"Please . . ." He holds out his arms pleadingly.

"Fuck you!"

The words seem to echo in the room. He stands stock still. So do I. It's like we're in suspended animation.

"Fuck you," I say more quietly.

I turn around and walk out.

7.

David Phillips

I wish I knew how our marriage went wrong.

Maybe it was a mistake from the beginning. I was just swept off my feet—didn't really know what I was doing. Cassandra and I are not well matched; I don't even know what she ever saw in me. She seems to have wanted me as some kind of prize. Maybe she just wanted to hurt Lauren, although she didn't know her very well and didn't even seem to care about her.

Things seemed to go wrong from the start. What could I have been thinking of?

June 3, 1980, 5:43 p.m.

"David, these are my parents, Mr. and Mrs. Connolly."

My whole arm seems stiff as iron, but I extend it and shake hands with both the people standing before me. In all honesty, they seem pretty nondescript: the woman of medium build (Cassandra is taller), with salt-and-pepper hair and bland face; the man a little stout, with a pasty kind of complexion that fleetingly makes me ashamed for the entire white race. Only their clothes would distinguish them on the street: as little as I'm interested in clothing, I can tell that what they have on wouldn't be found in those discount stores on 14th Street.

I must make sure not to say anything stupid. Nothing like "Gee what a nice place you got here." Of course, the place is nice: so nice that I can hardly take it all in. Renaissance paintings on the wall—the real thing, you betcha, no reproductions. Vases that look delicate as origami. Furniture that could have come from Versailles. God, I hope I don't break anything while I'm here.

There's an awkward little silence, as if everyone expects me to start the conversation going. I don't want to start a conversation; I don't even want to know these people. With my eyes I plead for Cassandra to help me, but someone else comes to the rescue.

A reed-thin, elderly, sober man in a coat and tails walks in silent as a cat. Cassandra turns her head, and a big smile bursts out over her face—she almost looks like a little girl. My heart feels as if somebody's squeezed it hard. I realize that at this moment I love her very much.

Cassandra cries out: "Oh, Jenyns, it's you!" She runs over to him and gives him a little peck on the cheek. He endures it gravely and with monumental patience, as if he expects everyone to know that this is just the slightest bit undignified.

She turns to me. "This is Jenyns, the butler." Somehow I have trouble believing my ears. I think she had mentioned him before, but it all struck me as so unreal and Wodehousean that I must not have taken it seriously. But there he is. A real, live butler.

I can't even begin to think what my parents in Indiana would say right now.

Mr. Connolly asks if we would like drinks. Everyone names a different drink; I mention something, forgetting it the moment I do so. Jenyns nods shortly and glides away.

We all sit down in the living room. Cassandra sits next to me on the couch, and actually puts her arm halfway around me. It comforts and relieves me more than I can say. Her parents are still looking fixedly at me: smiling a little, but clearly giving me the once-over. I wonder how I stack up in comparison to the men and boys who may have been in this position before. I don't know exactly how many there were, but from Cassandra's guarded hints I'm sure there have been several.

The drinks come. We sip. Still no one speaks. Cassandra looks at me with a peculiar, mischievous twinkle in her eye. I think I must look petrified.

Finally Mrs. Connolly speaks up. "So, David, Cassandra tells me you wish to be a writer."

"Yes, ma'am." Should I have called her "ma'am"?

"Mother, he doesn't *wish* to be a writer—he *is* a writer!" Cassandra cries vehemently. "He's already had a story accepted for *Ploughshares*."

The parents look at me blankly. I'm sure they've never heard of *Ploughshares*. If they know I'm from Indiana, they probably think it's a farming journal.

"That's very nice, dear," Mrs. Connolly says, looking at me as if I've just done a flawless somersault. "But can one make a living by it?"

I shrug. "It depends. There are lots of things one can do—fiction, articles, reviews, journalism. I might try them all; I've done several already."

The parents seem grudgingly impressed.

Mr. Connolly takes a different tack. "So, David, I hope your parents don't mind our hijacking you this summer." He chuckles at his own joke.

"No, sir. I guess they've seen enough of me the last two summers. I'm glad to be here. And very grateful, too."

Maybe I shouldn't have said that. The parents seem to take no notice of that last sentence, and Cassandra frowns at me sharply. Maybe I'm being too humble and effusive.

After our drinks are over, Cassandra leaps up and pulls me up as well. "We want to freshen up before dinner, okay? We'll see you later."

We wind through a series of labyrinthine corridors until we reach a closed door, which Cassandra opens violently and slams shut almost before I'm inside. It is as gaudily furnished as the rest of the place. She flops down on the bed so hard that it groans.

"Oh, God," she says, "I'll be so glad when they're gone!"

I sit down next to her. "They seem like nice people."

She stares at me with a mixture of disbelief and disgust. She doesn't look like a little girl anymore. "You try living with them."

"But you still do live with them."

She sits up, propping herself stiffly on her arms. "Of course I do. You think I'd live in one of those ratty little dorms for undergraduates? I'm not stupid. I like comfort." She lies back on the bed and rolls around a little, like a sleek and contented cat.

Now that I'm alone with her I feel a little less uneasy. I lie down beside her and force her on top of me. She cries out a little in surprise, but she's smiling. I pin her legs with my own, locking my arms around her waist. She takes tufts of my hair on either side of my head, looks right into my eyes, and says:

"What did you have in mind, sir?"

I suddenly get apprehensive. "Can they hear?" I whisper.

"Oh, don't be ridiculous! Of course they can't."

I would feel more comfortable if we were on a different floor from her parents, the way it was with . . .

Don't think about that. But it's too late.

I'm suddenly very tired. I let go of her and gently pull her hands away from my hair. At first she doesn't want to let go, but when she sees that I'm no longer playing she releases me.

"What's the matter?" she says sharply.

"Nothing." I can't look at her face. "Nothing. It's just . . . just been a long day."

She's peering intently at me. She's still lying on top of me, her arms stiffly propping her up. She lets herself down gently, resting her head on my chest. "David, this is going to be a wonderful summer, isn't it?" She's not going to take no for an answer, so I say "Yes." And at that moment I believe it.

8.

Cassandra Connolly
July 30, 1980, 4:27 p.m.

It's hard not to be a little antsy when you know your parents are going to leave you alone with your boyfriend for a month.

My parents aren't the most observant people in the world, but they could tell. No doubt I blundered a bit by actually being nice to them.

Less than two days to go. God! These last two months have seemed like ages. David too has been pretty antsy—but maybe not for the same reasons I've been.

Mother and Father come up to me. They both have this pursed look on their faces: aside from their gender, they might be identical twins. Maybe that's what happens when you're married too long.

"Dear, come and sit for a moment," Mother says.

There's no way I can escape this. Might as well get it over with. But really, they should know better than to try this on me. It won't work.

"You know we're leaving for Newport soon," she goes on.

"Yes, Mother." Does that sound dutiful enough?

"You'll have the place to yourselves, you know."

"Yes. I know."

"You will be all right, won't you?" Jesus Christ, Mother, why can't you just come out and say it? *You won't get into any trouble, will you?* This subterfuge is so damned stupid.

"We'll be fine, Mother."

She peers at my face, but the effort of penetrating its blandness seems to prove too much for her, and she leans back heavily on the sofa. This gives Father an opportunity to pitch in.

"We like your boy, Cassandra . . ."

My boy? Have I given birth to him? Haven't I been seeing "boys" for six or seven years now? Well, now that you mention it, those loathsome prep-schoolers really were "boys."

There's an unspoken "but" in Father's voice. I know a kicker is going to come presently, but Father tries to do a conversational end run.

"You're very fond of him, aren't you, Cassandra?"

I look at him and wonder why more children don't kill their parents. "Yes, I'm very fond of him, Father."

I'm not going to give them any slack.

"Then you're serious about him?" Mother blurts out.

"Yes, of course. And he's serious about me. Can't you tell?"

Her eyes say it all: *Yes, unfortunately we can tell.* But what she actually says is:

"Do you think you might marry him?"

I stare right into her eyes and say: "Yes. I think that's very likely."

"Has he mentioned it?"

I lose patience. "Oh, Mother, we've only known each other for four months! But surely you can see how close we are. David means more to me than any other—" (bloody hell, I almost say "boy") "—man I've ever met. He's wonderful." I can't say any more, I'm so knotted up inside.

And now Mother finally comes out with the remark I've been expecting to hear from the beginning. "But, dear, is he really our sort?"

I leap up from the couch. I want to throw something.

"Oh, God, Mother, what is our 'sort'? Washed-out little shits like Marlin Schumaker?" (Dad predictably mutters, "Watch your language, dear.") "You really didn't want me to tie the knot with him, did you? Just because his parents are your bridge partners?" ("That's not it at all," Mother mutters, not quite under her breath.) "Jesus, can't I start making my own decisions for once? I'll be twenty-one next month . . ."

I'm out of steam. I'm standing there, breathing heavily and looking down ferociously at them. They just sit there placidly. Their mouths are getting that pursed expression again.

"Cassandra," Dad starts in, "I think we've given you a pretty long leash." What am I, a dog? "We don't interfere in your affairs. We've helped you whenever you've needed it"—oh, God, don't bring up that time in high school when Frank Wendelstadt knocked me up—"and always stood by you. We just want to look out for your best interests."

There ought to be a law stipulating that if you use a certain number of platitudes in one speech, you should be taken out and shot.

But confrontation isn't going to get anywhere. My parents are like the Tar Baby: the more you struggle with them, the more entangled you get in their meshes.

I can't speak a word to Father, but maybe Mother will understand a little better. "Mother," I say very quietly, "David and I are very well suited to each other. We need to get to know each other a little better, and that's what this next month will be for. It'll be a little like a trial marriage, don't you think?"

"Yes, dear," she says, "that's very nice. But . . ." She can't look at me when she says this. "But what sort of prospects does that young man have?"

"Oh, Mother, what the f—" I bite my tongue. "What does that matter? I don't think we'll starve, do you? Anyway, he's just about the best writer I've ever met, and he's going to go far."

Father intrudes. "You know we'll always provide for you, Cassandra. We have no one else, you know." You make it sound like I'm a last resort—a process of elimination. You shit.

"Thank you, Father," I manage to choke out. "We won't let you down." I'm almost on the point of bursting out in a fit of crazed laughter. This must be a bad '50s movie or something.

They seem to have heard what they wanted to hear. They both get up heavily and simultaneously—rather like a flock of birds who, on some mysterious signal, suddenly fly out of a tree in droves. Father places a heavy hand on my shoulder, and Mother actually pats me on the cheek. Yes, she does.

I can't take much more of this. I give them a kind of sickly smile and stalk out.

Please, David, where are you? Get me away from this. . . .

9.

Lauren Oxley
September 19, 1980, 4:47 p.m.

Vanessa accosts me at the subway entrance.

"Are you coming to the lecture tonight?"

"No, Vanessa." I don't think I want to hear about "Wolf Whistles as Mental Rape" tonight, not where I'm going. "I have a—an errand to run."

She looks at me blankly for a while. "What . . ." She begins to realize that I don't want to talk about it. "Well, see you later, I guess."

"See you."

I get on the 1 train. Even though it's a rickety local—every metal surface covered with multi-colored graffiti, except the ads, strangely enough, as if out of a weird sense of respect for commerce—the Times Square stop comes faster than I expect. I almost miss it in stumbling out: since I'm one of the last to leave, the people who want to get on are already starting their relentless stalking into the car. I don't want to touch these people, but I force myself to elbow my way through them and on to the platform.

The address is hard to find, because there are no numbers on any of the doors. I can't imagine it would be one of the endless row of sleazy movie theatres, playing either porn or action films. Does he work above one of the peep show emporiums or X-rated video stores? I see a lot of lowlife—men and women both—and a single policeman who doesn't seem to be doing anything, even though what looks to me like a pick-up or a drug deal is going on about ten feet from him. Maybe he'll only intervene if there's a murder or something.

A dim, faded number—made, it seems, of red tape affixed to the wall—is barely discernible above a warped wooden door. There's an Indian guy standing in front of it. I walk up to him and try to go around him and through the door, beyond which I see a flight of stairs leading up. He halts me by gruffly putting his hand on my chest—almost on my breast.

"Where do you think you are going, miss?" he says in a very pronounced Indian accent.

"I . . . I'm here to see Mister Weaver," I manage to stammer.

He looks at me keenly for a moment, then seems to lose all interest in me. "Up the stairs," he says with a gesture of his head.

I open the door at the top of the stairs. It's only a kind of tiny lobby that has two other doors in two of its three walls. Neither is marked in any way. I almost want to go back down and ask the Indian which door it is, but I'm afraid to—maybe he'll hit me for being so stupid.

I try one of the doors. It's locked. I guess it's the other one.

A room not much bigger than the lobby has a desk with a man behind it. There are various porn magazines scattered over the desk, and pictures—cut out from the magazines, apparently—pasted crookedly on the walls. There's no other furniture in the room.

The man looks up at me. He doesn't seem much interested in me either. He seems to expect me to say something, but I don't know what to say. All of a sudden my heart is beating really fast, and I don't think I could speak if my life depended on it.

Finally he says: "Yeah?"

I have to take a few deep breaths before I can say: "Are you . . . are you Mister Weaver?"

"Yeah. Who're you?"

"Lauren Oxley." Suddenly my name sounds ridiculous, as if I'd made it up on the spot. "I have an appointment. . . ."

He moves some of the magazines away and comes upon a clipboard with what looks like a single sheet of paper attached to it.

"Oh, yeah." He looks at his watch. "You're early."

"I'm sorry. . . . Should I—?"

"That's fine," he interrupts. "You know why you're here?"

I'm not sure I understand the question. "Well, I answered your ad and you said to come by now. . . ."

He finally looks right at me—he hadn't done that before. "I'm saying, do you know what you're expected to do?" He speaks very slowly and deliberately, as if to a somewhat slow-witted child.

"Well, you wanted to . . . to—"

He cuts me off again. "How old are you? Are you over eighteen?"

"Yes, I'm twenty. Well, I will be in a week. . . ."

"Do you have proof of that?"

I wasn't expecting that. I look hastily through my handbag. "Well, I don't think so. . . ."

"No driver's license? Passport?"

"I don't drive. . . ." I continue scouring my purse. I guess credit cards won't do. But not very many people under eighteen get credit cards, do they? "Listen, I can go back and get my pass—"

"Fuck it. Are you willing to sign this?"

He passes a sheet of paper to me. It was exactly under the sheet that had his appointment schedule on the clipboard, so I didn't see it.

"What is it? Should I read it?"

A crooked smile from the side of his mouth. "I think that might be a good idea. When you sign it you certify that you're over eighteen and that any photos we take of you are our property, to use as we like. You get a flat fee. You have a problem with any of that?"

I try to hear him while reading the contract at the same time. The effort makes me dizzy. "No, I guess not. But I don't want my real name being used. Is that okay?"

"Yeah, sure, we'll come up with a name." He pauses a moment, then looks at me with almost a kindly expression.

"You ever done this before?"

"Well, no."

"You sure you want to? Don't sign that paper if you don't want to."

"I *do* want to. I really do. . . ."

"Why?"

I don't expect that question—none of these questions, really. I thought we would just go ahead and do it and get it over with. "Well, I just want to make some more money, I guess. My parents can't—don't give me much."

"Do you work? You have a job?"

"No, I'm a student. Barnard."

Another crooked smile. "Barnard? I thought they were all feminists up there."

"No, well, I'm not . . . I mean, I kind of am, but I don't go too far. . . ." I realize I'm babbling, so I shut up.

"Well, if you really want to do this, then sign."

I have to bend over his desk to sign the contract. He doesn't even give me a pen, so I fish one out of my handbag. I sign.

"Okay." He takes the paper back and puts it in a drawer—just stuffs it in without putting it in a file folder or anything. "Take your clothes off."

"What?" I can't believe I'm hearing this. I can't believe I'm doing this. "Right here? Now?"

"Yes. Here. Now."

"Why? I've already signed the paper. . . ."

"I want to see how you're built. I guess you didn't read the part in the contract where it says I don't have to use you if I don't find you suitable. So please"—the word seems to come hard out of his mouth—"take your clothes off." As I still do nothing, he seems to get peeved, as if I'm a disobedient schoolgirl: "You don't have to worry. I'm not going to do a damn thing to you. I just have to assess my wares."

Well, I guess that makes me feel a lot better, doesn't it?

I unbutton my blouse, then unzip my skirt. I have to remove my shoes in order to get my pantyhose off, and it's all pretty difficult to do without even a chair to sit on. I'm down to my bra and panties, and my hands suddenly start to tremble. I don't think I can do this.

"Go on, hurry up!" Mr. Weaver almost shouts. "I have another girl coming in twenty minutes."

I take off the rest of my clothes.

I think I look okay. Real blonde hair—not that mousy blonde that makes it hard to tell whether you're a blonde or a brunette—slim waist, freckles over part of my face and over my shoulders (do men like that? does it turn them on because it makes me look underage?), firm round breasts, a pretty heavy blond (not dark) bush. I wonder if he wants it shaved or trimmed.

He looks at me with a furrowed brow. I get the feeling he doesn't like me, but maybe it's just his way of concentrating. He's doing his job, and I guess he wants to do it right.

"Turn around."

I turn around. I almost giggle, feeling like some sort of model. I'm facing a blank wall. At least there are no pictures pasted there. I try to focus on a crack that goes diagonally from the northwest corner almost to the floor. I wonder if my buttocks are shaking.

"Okay. Put your clothes back on."

I do so in such a hurry that I almost rip my pantyhose to shreds and break the zipper on my skirt.

"What now?" I manage to say. I wonder if I have a fever, my face feels so hot.

"The shoot's at 8 p.m. on Tuesday. Is that all right?"

"Yeah, sure. Where? Here?"

"No. Not here." He scribbles something on a piece of paper. "Here. Be there next Tuesday. Eight o'clock."

I take the paper and leave without a word.

10.

Lauren Oxley
September 23, 1980, 8:20 p.m.

"Here. Take this."

Weaver has just handed me a dildo.

"What am I supposed to do with it?"

He looks at me as if I'm a slow-witted kindergartener. "What does a girl usually do with a dildo?"

I get all red. Maybe that'll look more appealing to the camera. I'm lying on some satin pillows, wearing a kind of Middle Eastern costume that reveals all the parts that the camera seems to think worthy of interest. The corset or whatever it is pushes my breasts up so that they almost touch my chin. And they're not that big, even.

"Mr. Weaver, I'm a little dry. . . ."

I'm sure he was prepared for that. He throws me some K-Y jelly that he happens to have in his pocket. "Here. Use this."

I use it. Then I start stroking myself with the dildo. I feel absolutely nothing.

Weaver: "You gotta look a little bit more like you're enjoying it, okay? How about it?"

The cameraman—he's the only other person in the room—hasn't taken any pictures of me yet in this costume or in this position, although there have already been plenty of me taking off my clothes one by one, lying on my back, my stomach, on my side, and once standing up and looking down between my legs, so that my breasts seem to hang like ripe fruit. Now he has me arrange my hair differently—so that I look like a different girl, I suppose—and dress up in this costume.

I moan a little bit. I start feeling something—not turned on, because this dildo's cold as ice, but a kind of irritating abrasion, as if I'm rubbing myself with sandpaper.

"Stick the dildo in your cunt."

Weaver is saying this with absolutely no emotion. I guess there's some mercy in that. I mean, he's not slobbering. It's just a job to him.

I stick it in—too fast, for I'm not ready and it hurts. I cry out.

"Just go slow, doll. No rush."

"Okay."

After a little bit of this, Weaver says: "Do you want to stick that thing in your ass?"

I'm speechless for a moment. "Oh, God, Mr. Weaver, it's too big . . . it'll kill me. . . ."

"Okay, okay, skip it." I think that's very nice of him until he says: "It's not in your contract, anyway."

A little more of this, and then we stop.

"You can get dressed now."

In order to get dressed, I first have to take off the stupid costume. But why should I be embarrassed at being seen naked by these two men? They've already seen everything I have to offer. I take the costume off blandly and put on my own clothes.

"What now?" I ask.

Weaver reaches into his pocket and pulls out an envelope. "Here."

It's full of money. "Cash?" I say in some surprise.

"Sure, what did you expect?" He chuckles. "Tax-free, doll."

There's something in that, I suppose.

As I'm about to go he takes my arm—not gruffly, that's not the way he is.

"Listen, doll . . ."

"You can try using my name, Mr. Weaver. I use yours."

"Right. . . . Listen, Lauren, do you want to do any more of this? You're really pretty good."

I look him in the eyes, trying to read his expression. It's as bland as always. "What do you mean? Do what? More photographs?"

"Sure. But maybe with someone else. A guy, maybe . . ."

I'm not sure I'm hearing this. "I won't fuck someone in front of a camera, Mr. Weaver! I just won't!"

My tone of voice finally gets an emotional response from him. He winces a little and puts his both hands in front of him. "No, no, nothing like that. You won't actually have to fuck. For photographs, you just pretend. Nobody'll know the difference."

I suddenly feel incredibly weary. I just want to get out of here. "Listen, Weaver"—if he doesn't want to use my last name, I won't use any "Mister"—"I'll think about it. Okay? I'll think about it."

"Okay. Fine. Maybe I'll hear from you."

"Maybe. Maybe not."

11.

Lauren Oxley
October 1, 1980, 8:14 p.m.

"Hey, baby doll. Why don't you give me a little help?"

A guy sticks a cock at half-mast in my face.

I look at Weaver, half in anger and half in pleading, but say nothing.

Weaver: "She doesn't do that, Joe. Just get it up yourself."

Joe looks at Weaver as if he's said something offensive about his mother. "You gotta be kidding. I've just come from a shoot where I had to do three come shots in two hours, and now this little girl can't give me a little head to get me up again? Do you know who I am?"

Weaver, in tones of disgusted weariness: "Yeah, I know who you are. But Lauren doesn't do that kind of thing. She's not a porn actress, she's just a college student. And this is photography, not video. You don't touch her parts, she doesn't touch yours, okay? Got that?"

Joe looks at Weaver, then at me, then at Weaver again. "What kind of set-up is this? I've never heard of such a thing—"

"You're hearing it now, guy. Let's go."

I'm lying there naked, and Joe is standing nearby, also naked; but he's now so disgusted with me that he doesn't even look at me while trying to get hard. Instead, he turns around and closes his eyes while pumping himself. Maybe he's remembering the shoot earlier in the day. I guess three come shots is quite an achievement for one session.

When he's at about a forty-five degree angle Weaver says it's good enough and let's get started. He wants me to get on my knees in front of Joe, take his cock in my hand (but letting the camera see the circumcised head), and pretend to be licking it.

"Why do I have to be on my knees? Isn't that kind of—"

"Our audience likes that," is all Weaver says. I bet they do. Poor saps.

"You don't mind touching my thing, do you, doll?" says Joe sarcastically.

"No, I don't mind. But don't call me doll."

The next shot is supposed to be Joe licking my pussy. I'm totally dry. I say so to Weaver.

"How about K-Y jelly?" volunteers Joe.

"No, that doesn't look right." Weaver ponders the problem as if he's trying to solve a differential equation. Then his face lights up (you can almost see the light bulb over his head going on), and he goes to a cupboard—we're in the kitchen of somebody's apartment, a real apartment where somebody actually lives, not a set—and gets some cooking oil. He hands it to me.

"Put a few drops of this on your cunt. Not too much."

"You gotta be kidding!" Joe cries out. "That stuff tastes awful!"

Weaver turns blandly and a little scornfully to him. "I don't give a fuck. And you're not going to taste it anyway. No touching, remember?"

"Oh, yeah." Joe looks almost sheepish.

I pour a little on. It seems to work well enough.

"All right, now pretend you're gonna fuck her," says Weaver.

I'm supposed to climb onto the kitchen cabinets and lie down flat on my back, with my feet hanging over the edge. I guess the audience likes that position, too. Joe stands in front of me, holding his cock about a half-inch from my pussy. Don't get any closer, asshole.

The photographer is going to shoot over Joe's shoulder. Weaver stands behind him to gauge what the shot will look like.

"Spread your lips a little, Lauren."

I don't think he's referring to my mouth.

After a little break Weaver takes me over to a corner—it's funny how I no longer give a damn whether I'm naked or not—and asks me something. I just shrug my shoulders. "Sure, why not?"

We now go to the living room. I lie down on some pillows—on my back, of course. Joe straddles me across my stomach. He takes one breast in each of his hands and moves his cock back and forth between them. The camera clicks like a spastic cricket.

And now for the climax. Joe is kind of losing his hardness, so we'd better act fast. Weaver takes a little dishwashing detergent and spreads some drops of it over my stomach and breasts. Then he applies a few drops to Joe's cock, where it slowly drips off. Joe adopts a look of almost painful ecstasy, opening his mouth wide and shutting his eyes tight. The camera clicks a bunch of times before all the dishwashing liquid falls from his cock.

"Okay. Good work." Weaver wraps things up, I put my clothes on, Joe puts his clothes on while glaring a little resentfully at me.

Weaver shoves an envelope into my hand. Just as I am about to go, he takes my arm gently and says, "Listen, Lauren . . ."

12.

Lauren Oxley
October 13, 1980, 8:17 p.m.

"Hi. I'm Marge."

"I'm Lauren."

"Pleased to make your acquaintance."

I don't even know what to say to that, so I don't say anything.

Marge is a flaming redhead with big hair. In fact, a lot of her parts are pretty big, although she's not fat by any means. She seems a good bit older than me—maybe late thirties—but it's so hard to tell with people in this industry.

I look over to Weaver and say: "Shall we start? I don't want to stay too late."

He looks up from his clipboard and gives me a sharp glance before his face returns to utter blandness. "Yeah, sure. Get undressed. And put these on."

He hands me a pair of fishnet stockings and a garter belt. Marge, who's already practically undressed, is supposed to wear the same kind of corset—maybe the very same corset—I had on last time: one that pushes up her breasts and leaves her pussy uncovered.

I take my clothes off and put the other stuff on. I apply some K-Y jelly, then hand it to Marge. She shakes her head: "I don't need it, doll."

I look at her for a moment, then shrug.

God only knows why straight men get turned on by two pretty women getting it on. What can there be in it for them? Just voyeurism, I suppose. Two beauties for the price of one, even if it's just to watch. No doubt they dream of joining in.

The first setup seems to me pretty bizarre, but I guess Weaver knows his business. While Marge lies on some cushions with her legs splayed, I have to take one of my breasts in my hand and rub her crotch with it. I don't see any way of doing this except by placing my head under one bent knee, and even then it's not a very good fit. But I somehow manage to start rubbing my nipple against her clit. The camera clicks. I've hardly even noticed the photographer standing there. He's just a prop.

After a while Marge starts to moan. She's getting wet, too. This isn't any jelly, any oil. It's her.

Now I get into a somewhat more orthodox position. I lie flat on my back while Marge squats over my face. The photographer seems to get directly behind Marge's asshole to take the shot. My tongue is working on her pussy, and she's actually dripping—dripping all over my chin and nose. It's clear liquid, but I suspect the photograph can pick up the shiny wetness on my face.

All of a sudden the photographer jumps up. "Fuck!" There's something wrong with his camera. "The goddamn film's jammed." While he's trying to fix his machine without ruining the pictures he's already taken, I find myself frozen in my position, my tongue pasted to Marge's crotch. Am I supposed to stay this way, like some pornographic Canova sculpture, while the guy gets his camera working, or is there going to be a break in the action? Marge's moans tell me she wants me to continue, but I don't give her the pleasure. I put my tongue back in my mouth.

The photographer picks up another camera; says he can probably salvage the earlier pictures, so at least we don't have to do that ridiculous pose again.

Marge then licks my pussy with gusto, although I don't seem to get very wet. She sticks a finger or two in my vagina every so often, something I find rather irritating although I don't suppose I can tell her that. Weaver would probably chew my head off anyway. Marge turns me over so that I'm lying on my stomach; I don't recall this as part of the sequence of shoots, but am too bored and tired to resist. At one point she forces my cheeks as wide apart as possible with her hands and fixes her tongue to my asshole, freezing so that the camera can take a good shot.

Now Weaver gives us an object about two feet long—a two-headed dildo. Circumcised rubber penis at either end. It's jet black, maybe to give our prospective viewers the titillation of fantasizing about interracial sex. But with just two women and a long dildo, that seems beyond my powers of imagination.

We stick each end of the dildo into ourselves, our knees bent and legs somewhat intertwined, our hands stretched back to support ourselves. We are in an exactly symmetrical position, like obscene bookends. Marge has stuck the dildo in a lot farther than I have.

Some sort of climax is approaching. Marge is working the dildo furiously into herself; every time she thrusts it in it comes out of me a bit, and every time she pulls it out it makes its way rather painfully into me. All of a sudden she pulls it out of both of us—it makes a weird sucking noise—and nods rather frantically to Weaver. He shouts "Now!" and I do what I've been told to do. I fling myself face down toward her crotch and lick her clit, making sure that I'm over to one side so that the photographer—whose camera is now about two inches from my nose—can have a good view.

Marge starts crying out rhythmically. Then a long drawn-out groan, almost a scream. A thick white liquid begins oozing out of her cunt. I'm stunned; I've never seen such a thing. I have some wild notion that she's hemorrhaging, or having a fit of some kind. I'm frozen, transfixed by the white pool that's collecting on one of the cushions.

Weaver almost shrieks at me: "Keep licking, Lauren! Don't stop now!"

I continue as ordered. Finally Marge's pussy stops pumping out the ooze. She seems totally spent. So is the photographer—out of film.

As we get up to put our clothes on, Marge comes over to me. She has a kind of dreamy, goofy smile on her face. "You were good, kid."

I look at her in genuine admiration and say: "Nothing to you, babe."

She just chuckles.

"By the way," I add, quietly so that the others can't hear, "I'm not a lesbian, you know."

Marge looks me right in the face and says: "Neither am I. But it's fun anyway, isn't it?"

A little later Weaver takes me over to one side. He looks me up and down—not as if he's giving me the once-over, but (incredibly) to see if I'm all right. I'm okay.

"That was good, Lauren. You're getting better all the time." He pulls the usual envelope out of his pocket—it's fatter than the previous ones.

"Thanks." I'm thanking him for the money, not for the compliment—if that's what it is.

"You think you'll be ready for men next time?"

"Weaver, if I can do this, surely I can do anything."

"It's a lot different with men." He looks genuinely concerned. "Really different."

"I know that." I'm really tired now. I just want to go home.

"Okay. As long as you know."

13.

Lauren Oxley
October 22, 1980, 9: 31 p.m.

Times Square Station. I know it so well now that I feel like a bored commuter. But this time I'm shaking—I'm so clumsy that I almost stab myself in the groin with the turnstile. Wouldn't that be funny? Porn actress injured on the way to work. I wonder if I would get workmen's compensation.

Another dimly numbered door, another flight of steps up, a man sitting at the top of the stairs on a stool reading the *Daily News*. I'm about to tell him who I am when he nods with incredible boredom and waves me in to a door. Maybe he recognizes me from some of my pictures.

Weaver is inside, with two other men, a woman, and two—count 'em, two—photographers. I'm moving up in the world.

I nod a little nervously to Weaver. He actually forces a little smile that seems somehow embarrassed. None of the others takes the least interest in me.

Weaver introduces me. The two men are Jim and John, the woman is Flo. I have some faint hope of trying to make friends with her, but she is less interested in me than the men are. Jealous? She must be well into her thirties, she looks so tired and bored.

We go over the planned shots. I'm getting more and more nervous as we do so. Weaver tells everyone to take their clothes off, but before I can do so he pulls me over.

"Lauren, you really ready for this? You can still back out if you want to."

I stare at him in confusion. "How? I signed the contract. . . ."

"You signed it with me. No one else is involved. I can just tear it up." He pauses and looks at me, almost benevolently. "You look a little nervous. Are you absolutely sure?"

I look back at him, wondering what's really going through his mind. I breathe heavily and say, "Yes, I'm sure. I . . . I need the money."

He shrugs, still a little uncomfortable. "Okay. Then let's go."

We're naked. I get down on my knees in my usual position and take Jim's (or is it John's?) cock in my hand. One photographer squats next to me, pointing his camera directly at the guy's member. The other photographer stands as close behind me as he can without touching me; in fact, he spreads his legs so that he can get directly over me. The camera must be aimed right at the top of my head.

I put Jim's cock in my mouth.

It smells awful and doesn't taste very good either. I close my eyes so that I don't have to see what I'm doing. It gets hard pretty fast, which is a relief. Weaver tells me to lick the tip with my tongue. I do it. He tells me to take one of Jim's balls in my mouth and hold it there while the camera clicks. I do that.

I wonder crazily what would happen if I were to bite down hard. Would I get slapped around? Would they kill me? Or just kick me out without giving me my money?

Next shoot. Flo has hardened John's cock by this time. Neither she nor I are wet, but there's always K-Y jelly to the rescue. This time, lo and behold, I'm actually on top. Jim lies on the floor and I slowly place his cock in my pussy. It doesn't go. I feel pain. I'm too tight.

"Weaver, I can't do this right now. I can't." I think I'm about to cry. I get no sympathy from the others, who are all looking at me as if I'm either crazy or stupid.

Weaver says, "Okay. Okay. Jim, try to loosen her up, will you?"

I lie on my back on the floor and spread my legs. Jim lies down on his stomach, his face over my pussy. He begins licking me.

His tongue feels like sandpaper. Like a cat's. I close my eyes again. Maybe people will think I'm sighing in ecstasy. I wrap my legs around Jim's head—for a moment I want to asphyxiate him with my thighs—but Weaver says I have to keep my legs spread. Gotta have good camera shots of my cunt, I suppose.

My heart's beating faster. I actually start feeling a little wet. On Weaver's instructions, Jim sticks first one finger, then two fingers into my vagina while continuing to lick me. He moves them in and out. They're getting very wet. I'm opening up.

Weaver: "Okay. Go in her."

Jim climbs up on top of me. He keeps his arms stiff on either side of me while guiding his cock in. It's like he's going to do pushups over me. He's not even looking at my face, he's looking at his cock.

One photographer is behind my head. The other is at my feet, squatting down. He tells Jim to spread his legs a bit for a better view. As Jim does so, my legs spread even wider until I think I'm going to strain a groin muscle or a hamstring.

It's all so weird. Jim pumps me for a while, then stops to let the camera click. I guess it has a slow shutter speed. Wouldn't want to get a fuzzy image, not after all this hard work. At one point the photographer at my feet puts his camera about two inches from my cock-engorged pussy and snaps. No zoom lens, I suppose.

Jim pulls out of me wetly. There can't be any breaks, because the men will get soft. Now John rubs some K-Y on his cock, squats

in front of me, and goes right in. Flo is somewhat awkwardly trying to lick his balls or his asshole or something. Jim kneels down
next to my head and sticks his cock in my face. It smells of my
pussy. I open my mouth and he stuffs it in.

Not a word is being said this whole time. I wonder if anyone is
enjoying any of this. I don't hear any sighs or moans or grunts of
pleasure. I hear nothing except the cameras clicking.

Now Jim pulls his cock out of my mouth and walks away, stroking himself so that he remains hard. His work isn't over. John is
still inside me, pumping away but stopping every now and then
for the camera. Flo gets up and walks over to my head. She squats
over it.

I lick her pussy.

Or rather, I start doing so, stopping every so often with my
tongue on her clit or her lips or even deep inside her vagina so that
the camera can do its work. She's actually rather wet, and it's not
just the jelly. She doesn't taste as good as I do.

Looking up from behind her bottom, I notice that she and John
are kissing and he is fondling her breasts. I think for a moment
that poor Jim must feel left out, but I've forgotten how Weaver the
choreographer has arranged things. Jim comes over now. Flo and
John stop kissing, and Flo instantly takes Jim's cock in her mouth.
John is still in me. We all freeze for the camera.

We uncouple. I roll over on my hands and knees. John gets
on his knees and goes back in me from behind, Jim squats down
in front of me as I take his cock in my mouth, and Flo—quite an
acrobat—arranges herself under me and flicks her tongue at Jim's
balls.

Things are heating up. John is pumping me more and more furiously, making slapping sounds as his thighs hit my bottom. He
doesn't seem to stop for the camera. I hear him grunting heavily.
Weaver is just standing there, looking more at the photographers
than at us.

Suddenly John comes out of me—so fast that I gasp at the
vacancy in my cunt. Then he does something strange. He holds
his hand tight around his cock, grimacing fiercely. I think I even
hear his teeth gnashing. Meanwhile one photographer, who had
been behind him, goes as fast as he can to one side of us, almost

stumbling over my feet. Once he is in position, John releases his hand from his cock.

It spurts. I feel warm liquid all over my bottom. John is making rough growling noises, almost screaming. Both cameras are clicking furiously. I'm so distracted by what's happening that I take Jim's cock out of my mouth and try to look around.

Weaver shouts: "Don't stop, for Christ's sake! Keep at it!"

I stick Jim's cock back in my mouth, working on it almost maniacally. Although John retreats to a corner of the room, no one bothers to wipe me up, and I feel a trickle of moisture trailing down my thigh.

Now Jim is starting to moan and grunt. He looks up to Weaver and nods. There is a flurry of bodies changing position, as Jim stands up and faces Flo and me, both of whom are on our knees in front of him. Our mouths are open. Jim is pumping himself with his hand harder and harder.

My eyes are closed tight, so I'm not prepared for the hot, salty liquid that lands right on my tongue. More liquid falls on my chin, my nose, my forehead, even my hair. A few drops dribble off my chin and land on my breasts, as if I'm a messy little girl who can't eat properly.

Finally the flow of liquid stops. But my eyes are still shut fast. I'm afraid to open them. I start shaking all over. I have to swallow the liquid that went in my mouth; it's too far in for me to spit it out.

All of a sudden I cry out and get to my feet, knocking Jim's cock—which I now see is still in front of my face, dripping a little—out of the way. I glancingly notice that there's no liquid on Flo's face or body.

I run over to Weaver. God knows I must be desperate to hope for any sympathy from him. I start sobbing and shaking, burying my face in his shoulder and actually putting my arms around him. He seems stunned, but slowly places his arms around me and strokes my head, like a father comforting a young daughter who's skinned her knee. For a while he doesn't seem to know what to say, but finally he starts crooning softly, as if he's afraid to be overheard: "It's all right, babe. Take it easy. It's all right."

I don't seem to be able to stop shaking. It's like I have epilepsy. There's not a sound coming from anyone else in the room, although

I seem to hear the photographers dismantling their cameras and putting them away. Someone has lit up a cigarette.

Finally Weaver gets impatient. He takes me by the shoulders and gives me a little shake. "Snap out of it, Lauren. It's over. You were fine. Just stop now and get dressed."

I look at him. He has a stern, irritated expression on his face, but somehow I also see a little sympathy. I wonder if he has a daughter.

He gives me a towel for me to wipe myself off. There's no shower in this place—it seems like an actual set, however primitive, not somebody's apartment. I walk over to where I had dumped my clothes. The others are almost fully dressed already. Flo says to me in the most exaggerated New York accent I've ever heard, "You were good, kid. You were good." The men say nothing to me; don't look at me.

Everyone leaves except Weaver and I. He looks at me with a kind of shy hesitancy. "Are you all right now?"

"Yeah. I'm fine." I'm so tired. I just want to go home.

Weaver seems about ready to say something more when I cut him off. "No, Weaver. I'm finished. No more. I don't want to do any more. It's over. Just give me my money and I won't bother you again."

He hands me a very fat envelope, which I stuff into my purse; I don't even want to look at it. He is still hanging around indecisively, as if he's trying to work up the gumption to say something to me. Finally he does.

"Lauren, you could be a real star in this field. You're fresh, sexy, hot. You're really good. I can get you a lot more money if you want to do some videos—"

"No, Weaver! I said no!" I feel I'm about to start shaking again, but manage to control myself.

He seems to realize it's no good pressing me. He hangs his head in disappointment, as if his favorite football team has just lost a big game. Then he looks me right in the eye and says: "If you change your mind, you know where to reach me."

I walk out without a word.

14.

David Phillips
June 25, 1981, 8:27 p.m.

I don't think I've seen this many people under one roof in my life. Nor this many white ties and tails. Nor this much food, this much liquor, this much jewelry, this much everything.

Mike Sullivan walks over to me.

"Gee, this is some bash, isn't it?"

"Yes, it is."

He's holding a champagne glass in his hand. "Where's the wife? You can call her that now, can't you?" He digs me in the elbow.

I push him away, smiling. "God, I don't even know if I could find her in this mass of people."

"Sure you can," says Mike. "She's just the one with the huge white dress with the twenty-foot-long train." He scans the room. "Yeah, there she is," pointing almost to the opposite corner of the hall.

"Mm." I can't think of anything more to say.

He looks at me, smiling a little tentatively, then takes another swig of his drink.

"Looks like you're really set for life now, aren't you?" he says.

"Looks like it."

He peers at me curiously. "What gives? You never have to work a day in your life, unlike us *hoi polloi*. You can spend all your time writing. Isn't that what you want to do, man?"

"Sure it is. Sure it is."

There is another little uncomfortable silence.

I have to fill it up somehow. "Gee, Mike, it was really good of you to come out here for the wedding. Man, I need some familiar faces right now, aside from my parents." I look at them in a kind of protective anxiety, but they're sitting as quietly as they have through the whole ceremony. I hope other people don't think they're as dowdy as I think they look.

"Hey, man, it was easy. After all, you bought the ticket."

"I didn't buy the ticket," I say quietly.

"Well, you know what I mean," he blubbers. "Your wedding-party bought the ticket. Real nice of them."

"Yes, it was." It's probably the last time they'll ever buy a round-trip ticket from Indianapolis to New York.

Another silence. Now Mike takes it into his head to fill it up by saying:

"I don't see Lauren here."

I turn to him as if he's just said he's the grandson of Jack the Ripper. "Are you crazy, man? I have a little more tact than that."

"You didn't invite her?"

"Of course not! Do you think she'd accept?"

"No I guess not." After a pause: "She knows about it, I suppose?"

"Sure she does."

"How's she doing?"

I shrug my shoulders. I can't look at him. "I don't know. I haven't seen much of her—lately."

"She has another year to go, doesn't she?"

"Yeah."

"Then what?"

Now I look at him. "Then what? How should I know? I have no idea what she'll do." I'm almost shouting it, although hardly anyone can hear with all the other racket going on.

It's Mike's turn to look away.

"I don't think," I say, a little more quietly, "that she'll go back to Indiana. She may stay here."

"Stay here?" he says in some surprise. "In New York?"

"Yes. In New York."

It seems to take him some moments to digest the idea. "Lauren in New York. Man, that's weird. You, I can understand. But Lauren . . . she's such a small-town girl."

"I know," I say. "It does seem strange. But there's plenty of stuff for her to do here. She's bright, talented, and there are lots of jobs available."

"I guess so," he says, not quite convinced.

"Gee, man," I say impulsively, "I wish you were here to look after her. I worry about her sometimes."

"David, she's grown up now. She doesn't need looking after. She can take care of herself. Even in New York."

"Yeah, I guess so." I look at my feet again.

All of a sudden Cassandra comes wafting up. I'd hardly noticed she was in the vicinity.

She has a huge smile on her face. "Well, isn't this nice? Two old high-school chums chewing the fat. Is that what you do in Indiana?"

"I've never done it," I say.

"Neither have I," says Mike.

Cassandra looks at us both for a moment, her smile frozen, not sure whether she's been made fun of. But she quickly puts it out of her mind.

"Well, boys, are you having a good time?"

"Swell," says Mike impulsively, as I wince.

"Good." She actually pats him on the cheek. "We're so glad you came."

She turns to me. "David, I have some people I want you to meet."

Before I can control myself I say: "What? More?"

She looks at me hard, but still smiling—probably for Mike's benefit.

"Yes, more, sweetheart," she says quietly. "They're old friends of my parents, and they're very anxious to meet you. David, you know that you're really the star of this show."

"Am I?"

"Yes, you are." She turns to Mike with a regal swerve of her head while taking my arm. "You'll excuse us, I hope?"

"Sure," he says.

We go off.

15.

Justin Federlein
May 31, 1996, 8:42 p.m.

The phone rings. I don't want to answer. I know who it is.

But I have to answer. I'm too scared not to.

"Justin? He's just left. Heading south on Fifth Avenue."

I try to stall. "Where's he going, do you think?"

"God knows where the fuck he's going. Maybe to fuck that little bitch Lauren. He certainly isn't fucking me much lately." She stops, as if she knows she shouldn't have said that. "Anyway, take a cab—follow him. It's already dark. You know what to do."

Don't I.

I have to do what she says. She doesn't take no for an answer.

I grab various things—including that heavy object still wrapped in newspaper—and leave my apartment. I don't take anything from that fat envelope; don't even want to touch it, look at it, know it's there.

This whole thing seems ridiculous and crazy. How am I supposed to find him? What if he darts down some subway entrance before I have a chance to get up there? What if he stays along well-lighted streets or just sits in a café? I know what Cassandra has told me about where to do the job—she's catechized me like some schoolboy, till her harsh, droning voice seems to fill my head and drum out every other thought in it—but what if there's no opportunity? She doesn't tolerate failure.

I tell the cab driver to go to 65th and Fifth, hoping that David will be somewhere around there. If he's beyond that point, I'll just tell the driver to keep on heading south. I feel like a detective in a bad movie.

The cabbie makes unpleasantly fast time zooming up Lexington Avenue. He drives so that he makes all the lights just as they are turning green, swerving recklessly to the right or the left to avoid other taxis letting out slow, old people with canes, trucks double-parked and unloading goods (at this time of night?), and the occasional ambulance or fire truck to whom no one pays attention in spite of their wailing sirens. The cabbie's a Sikh, with full beard and tightly wrapped turban. I sit scrunched up in a corner of the cab, so that he can't get a good look at me in the rearview mirror.

The corner of 65th and Fifth looms up. I see no one familiar there. The cabbie asks me, in a thick and nearly incomprehensible accent, which corner I want to be let off at; I gesture him to go forward, and he looks at me as if I can't understand English. I tell him to go slow; he shrugs, knowing it will mean more time on his meter.

As we work our way through the traffic lunacy of Grand Army Plaza at the southeast corner of Central Park, I finally spot David walking on the west side of Fifth Avenue at 57th Street. I shout "Here!" abruptly, and the driver puts on the brake so fast that I slam into the back seat. He looks at me again: not only am I stupid, but I may have damaged his cab. No, guy, it's fine. I appease him with a big tip and scramble out.

I'm on the east side of the street. Plenty of people still here. Some, maybe most, are probably tourists. It's already pretty hot—seems so to me, anyway—and people are taking the opportunity to wear as little as possible after being bundled up during the long winter. Parked cars on both sides of the street impede my view, but they also impede his, I guess. Not that he seems very intent on anything except walking boldly ahead.

It's weird. I probably haven't laid eyes on David in over a decade—we don't exactly run in the same social circles—but he doesn't look a bit different. Come to think of it, he doesn't look much different from when I knew him at Columbia. Knew him? Can't say I ever did. I was just one of Cassandra's many hangers-on, begging for a little dollop of her attention whenever she could spare the time. She usually couldn't.

What is it about Cassandra that gets me? It's like she's some sort of snake-charmer. Why has that incident more than ten years ago become the defining moment in my life? Well, big guy, what great things have you done since? Can't think of much.

She's so tough, mean, sharp-tongued. Like a harpy. I thought I didn't like women like that—they scare me. Is that it? Is it just fear that's making me obey her every word like a robot? What other reason can there be? Why else am I walking down Fifth Avenue carrying a Barnes & Noble tote bag with a gun in it, waiting to blast her husband to smithereens?

And where the hell is he going? He's the one walking like a robot—scarcely seeing where he's going, hardly moving to get out of the way of people approaching him (but then, that's how all New Yorkers walk), walking real stiff with eyes wide open. Now we're in the Grand Central Terminal area, and for one crazy instant I wonder if he's just going to leap on a train going somewhere—anywhere. Maybe back to Indiana. Oh, sorry—you can't get there from here. Gotta go to Penn Station.

Suddenly David veers west on 42nd Street. I didn't think he was going to the Public Library, which is closed anyway. The big marble building looms darkly, but Bryant Park, behind it, is lit up and full of people. I don't see any chance of doing what I have to do.

Past Sixth Avenue, then Broadway, then Seventh Avenue. He's looking around, as if trying to find a number. This is no idle constitutional. But I can't believe what Cassandra said—surely Lauren doesn't live around here. I can't imagine anyone but lowlife living around here.

I'm right behind David now, on the north side of the street. This area certainly has changed in the last fifteen years—a lot of the porno joints driven out, although they've merely gone elsewhere, all over the city. Several even in Soho, with an emphasis on gay stuff.

Suddenly David stops abruptly. I do too, and some guy nearly runs into me from behind—he'd been walking too close and has to veer around me at the last instant, cursing at me as if it was my fault. Look, pal, I want to say to him, do you know what I have in this bag? But I know I can't say it, and he probably wouldn't believe me anyway.

David goes through a door that's lying ajar. Christ, what do I do? Follow him? He's obviously meeting somebody. But who? Why? Am I supposed to blow both him and his friend (companion? partner?) away too? I inch toward the door, and as I come upon it I see it leads almost immediately to a flight of steps going up. At the top is some real young, thin guy—either Latino or East Indian, it's hard to tell—sitting on a stool looking incredibly bored. David's not in sight; must already have gone by.

I hang around irresolutely at the door, wondering if I'll be mistaken for a male whore. Not many porno joints left, but the ones that are still here seem to have jacked up the neon to make up for their lost compatriots. A number of dark-skinned guys are standing on the street trying to hustle the usual number of sailors and tourists—"Live girls, check it out!"—while businesswomen working late walk as briskly as possible so they can get to Port Authority without having to see or hear anything.

I'm standing with my back to the door and the flight of steps. Suddenly I hear a rapid tramping down the stairs. Turning, I'm horrified to see David there. I almost leap into the next open door, which turns out to be a porno video arcade, where the guy sitting on a stool in front looks suspiciously at my bag and then at me.

It's like he thinks me an idiot for not forking over a few dollars for some tokens to use in the private booths, where I hear nameless grunts coming either from the videos being played or from the guys watching them. I hand over a dollar, get four tokens, then turn around just quick enough to see David hail a taxi and get in it.

Oh, Jesus. I feel covered with sweat. The guy on the stool is pointing in the direction of the booths, but I just drop the tokens on the floor and walk out like a zombie. The cab with David in it has already turned on to Eighth Avenue and is heading north.

I feel more horrified than if I'd pulled the trigger. I've failed. Cassandra's not going to like that.

I'd better call her. She's not expecting her husband to come back alive, and when he walks in the door maybe she'll think it's a ghost. Probably not; she's too hard-nosed for that. She'll know what happened. But I'd better tell her first.

All the phones on the street seem taken, so I dash into Port Authority and find a vacant one. I call. One ring. maybe even half a ring. Then:

"Yes?"

The harshness and greedy anticipation in that voice terrify and sicken me. I hold the phone away from my ear. I don't know if I can speak.

"Yes? Who is this? Justin? Answer me, for Christ's sake!"

I try to say her name, but I start stuttering on the very first consonant, so that it sounds like I'm choking.

"Who the fuck is this?"

"It's me!" I shout. "J-j-j-Justin."

There's a pause. Then, very softly:

"What happened, Justin?"

Can I say it? She'll flay me whether I say it or not. Suddenly I'm so tired that I just want to drop the phone, curl up in a little ball, and go to sleep right here on the floor.

"Nothing happened, Cassandra."

"What?"

The word bores through my brain like a gunshot. It still seems to be bouncing around in my cranium when I say: "Cassandra, I just didn't have a chance! He was never by himself! People all around! Bright lights everywhere. Busy street." I want to laugh like a lunatic. I suddenly sound like Bob Dole. Nothing but sentence fragments. No verbs. Like this.

As there is still no answer—scarcely even any sound of breathing—I speak just to fill up the silence. "Look, maybe there'll be another time. I'll try again. Next time I'm sure it'll work!"

Just a snarl at the other end: "It'd better, Justin." Then a loud click.

I stand there looking at the receiver of the phone, wondering if I should just beat myself over the head with it till my skull cracks open.

16.

Lauren Oxley
July 14, 1984, 10:47 p.m.

"Would you like to come up for a drink?"

Jake seems hesitant. It's like he's almost afraid to get out of the taxi. He must be the first shy man I've ever met in New York. Except for David, that is, and he doesn't count.

"Sure, I guess so." He hastily pays the cab driver and scrambles clumsily out.

"It's still early," I say. "I just thought we could talk a little more. That restaurant was so noisy."

I shouldn't have said that. He takes it the wrong way. "Oh, Lauren, I'm sorry for taking you there. I didn't know it'd be like that. It's just that I really like the food . . ."

I turn to him and smile as warmly as I can. "I know, Jake. The food was really good. It was great. It was just a little noisy."

He retreats into silence as I take his hand and lead him into the building.

My place is on the third floor and there's no elevator. It's your typical New York shoebox apartment. Two rooms, each of which are probably smaller than the bathroom in my parents' house in Indiana. I don't even know how I ended up here. The Village gets pretty noisy on weekends, too.

I sit him down on the couch and ask him what he wants. I hope to God he doesn't say a diet Coke, and I'm relieved to find he wants a little whiskey. He must have noticed the bottles on the cabinet in the kitchen—which, by the way, is also the living room.

I pour him one and pour one for myself.

I remember back a month ago, when I got his letter in the mail, responding to my personal ad. It was sweet. But then, he didn't have much competition. He didn't come out and say he wanted to fuck me, didn't say how much money he had (or how he had *no* money because he was divorced and paying alimony and child support and God knows what else), didn't say that I'd be doing myself a favor by seeing him, didn't say how many beautiful women he'd gone out with in the past, and didn't say he just wanted to be friends.

He's still shy, but he was really shy when we first met. It was a coffee shop—Dean & DeLuca, on University Place. It was nice of him to have come all the way from the Upper West Side to my area, since all I had to do was walk up from my office at NYU. I think he knew I lived down here, and I'm sure he wasn't fishing for an invitation to go back here after that first date. He probably would have been petrified at the idea. Amazing to find an otherwise fairly normal man in his late twenties in New York being so shy.

I sit down next to him, although leaving a little gap on the couch so he doesn't feel uncomfortable. "I've had a very nice time tonight," I say.

"So have I," he says, sipping his drink daintily.

"You know, I haven't seen very many men lately. And certainly not more than once."

"No, I haven't either." Then he almost blubbers in confusion. "I mean—I mean I haven't seen many women either." He looks fixedly at his drink.

I have to smile. I want to throw my arms around him, he's so cute, but I'm afraid he'll have a heart attack. I hope he drinks up; maybe that will calm him down a bit.

I wish I could just tell him that I really don't expect him to seduce me right on the spot. If it happens, fine; if not, maybe next time. I hope there will be plenty of next times.

I move just a little closer—almost imperceptibly so. I place my hand on his arm. "Jake, you're a real sweetheart. I feel very comfortable with you."

"And I do with you." He looks at me out of the corner of his eye. It's probably the best he can manage right now.

"I'm surprised someone hasn't snapped you up."

He looks back at his drink. "Oh, I'm not much. I told you about Jennie, didn't I?"

"Yes, you did. We all go through bad things like that." I haven't told him about David—not the whole story, anyway. And I certainly haven't told him about some other things.

His drink is finished. I take it out of his hand and put it on the floor. I put mine down too. I guess it's now or never.

I take his face in my hands and kiss him gently on the lips. He squirms a little at first, then is still. But his arms still hang at his sides.

I stop kissing him and look right at him, smiling. "That was sweet. You're sweet. Do you want some more?"

He looks a little scared, but nods eagerly.

I kiss him some more. Finally his hands go around me, still rather hesitatingly. He places his hands on my back so that they don't make even the least contact with my bra, even through my dress. What a sweetie.

I don't really know how I'm supposed to let him know how I want him to continue. I have my arms wrapped tightly around his neck, and after a long kiss I nestle my head on his shoulder, every now and then softly kissing his neck. But his hands just kind of knead my back as if he's giving me a massage.

I figure I have to take the bull by the horns. I say: "Please unzip me."

He looks at me as if he didn't understand what I said, so I say again, "Please."

He fumbles at the zipper and finally gets it to go down. I have to release my arms from around his neck to let the dress fall to my waist. I look right at him and say softly: "Take my bra off."

It seems to take him forever to undo the hooks, and his face gets almost contorted with concentration, but finally he manages it. I slip out of the bra.

He looks down at my breasts in a kind of reverential wonderment. I stand up and let the dress fall to my feet.

I hope I can go through with this. I don't want to ruin it. This is the closest I've come in a long time.

I sit back down on the couch and say, "Let's make you more comfortable." I take his sport jacket off, then his polo shirt—it's a little damp from sweat. He doesn't have much chest hair, and he seems very pale, but it sets off his dark hair nicely. Now the test.

"Please stand up, sweetie," I say.

He does so a little mechanically. He's looking down at me, alternately at my face and at my breasts. My panties are still on, but takes a peek there also—almost covertly, as he if doesn't want me to notice, but I do. I always do. I don't know how men can think we don't notice.

I start unbuckling his belt. My hands shake a little, but I clench my teeth and the shaking stops. Then I undo his pants—first a button at the top, then the zipper. They fall to his ankles. He's hard.

I bring his briefs down to his ankles.

Oh, no! Please, no! Please don't let this happen—not to me, not to Jake, he's such a sweetheart. But it's happening.

I try to take his cock in my mouth, but I'm now trembling so much I can't even see it clearly. I can't touch it. I try to force myself, but I just can't do it. I utter a kind of strangled cry and fling myself away to the end of the couch.

He's standing there, clothes at his feet, his cock hanging in mid-air, with a look of dazed confusion on his face. He can't even say anything except, "What . . . what . . . ?"

I leap up and throw my arms around him—from the side, so I don't touch his cock. "Oh, Jake, please, I'm sorry, I'm sorry, please forgive me. . . ." I'm crying and sobbing now, and can hardly breathe.

He's still so confused that he can't even put his arms around me. It's like he's torn between trying to comfort me and concealing his nakedness, which now seems to embarrass him horribly. Finally he puts one arm around me; with his other hand he covers his member, which is rapidly wilting.

"What's the matter?" he manages to say. "Did I do something...?"

"No, no, it's not you," I almost cough between sobs. "Not you. Me. Me!"

That doesn't seem to help him, and his look of confusion returns. "But why? What . . . ?"

"Oh, God, I just can't explain it!" I shriek as I fly out of the room and rush into my bedroom, slamming the door.

I'm lying there crying on the bed. I can hear him putting his clothes on. Then silence for a time. Finally a timid knock on my door. "Lauren? Are you all right? Maybe I'd better go. . . ."

"Wait."

I hastily fish out a robe from the closet and tie it around me. My hands are still shaking, but I grasp the knob and walk out of the room.

He's fully dressed and looking at the floor. He seems itching to get to the front door and bolt out of the place. I have to try to do something.

"Jake . . . sweetie . . . I'm really sorry. I just got an attack of nerves or something. I don't know what came over me. You're such a nice man. Please forgive me. Okay?"

He still looks at the floor but says, "Okay." A momentary pause. "I'd better go."

"Please, let's talk in a day or two. I want to see you again."

"Okay." I know he doesn't mean it.

He walks out, closing the door quietly.

I'm know I'll never hear from him again.

17.

Cassandra Phillips
September 29, 1984, 7:14 p.m.

"Darling, are you ready?"

"Not just yet." He sounds a little testy.

I walk into the dressing room. He's fiddling with the bow tie. "Darling, why don't you just get Jenyns to put that on you?"

He glares at me. Really, he's such a child sometimes.

I glare right back at him, although I'm smiling. "Shall I get him?"

He stops fiddling. "Sure," he says, a little petulantly.

Jenyns—who always manages these affairs from behind the scenes—comes in without my having to call him: he's like that. He immediately ties the bow tie just right. I look at both men, realizing I love them both in very different ways.

"Come on, dear, we'll be late." I take his arm.

The ballroom is already filled. It seems the tradition of being fashionably late is giving way. And why not? The main event is going to come early: those Brazilian dancers we hired need to leave by ten, for some reason.

As we arrive, I place David in the company of my old friends the Warwicks and say, "Darling, I have to check something. I'll be back in two shakes."

I leave him and go to the band that's setting up. I can't exactly tell who the leader is—they're all dressed pretty much the same, in very colorful loose-fitting outfits—but just speak to someone at random. "Do you think you can start at 8:30?"

Someone I wasn't speaking to turns around and nods. "Yeah, lady. Is okay."

"Fine. And the dancers . . ."

"They're coming too. Getting dressed. Don't you worry."

"All right. I won't."

I go back to David. I pull him away from the Warwicks and head to our table. Of course, we're right in the front row of the big circle of tables on the dance floor. We're going to have a good view. And we should—we paid enough for this shindig.

Right at 8:30 the dancers rush into the floor in a big flourish. They look wonderful. The women have flared skirts and loose blouses, the men baggy, loose-fitting pants and shirts that balloon out when they whirl around. It's all an enchanting splash of color.

For the next hour and a half they regale the guests with divine dancing: in pairs, in a quartet, and sometimes all eight together in complex but always breathtakingly rapid and acrobatic maneuvers. They're really good. The band is pretty good, too—maybe more loud than they are good. But it all creates an unbelievably exhilarating intoxication—more so than the drinks I keep having. I'm itching to get out on to that floor.

Finally the dancers finish and rush away to a thunderous applause. The musicians leave too, more's the pity, and are replaced by a rather more sedate four-piece band. But the moment they start I leap up from the table and grab David's arm. "Come on, darling, let's dance!"

He holds back like a shy schoolboy. "No, darling, not just yet...."

I look fixedly at him. "David, we're the hosts of this thing. We have to take the lead. My parents aren't going to start; *we* have to."

With rather bad grace he gets up and accompanies me on to the floor. This is the cue for several other couples to come out, which seems to put David a little more at his ease. The tempo of the dance number is a little slow for my taste, but at this point I don't care: I just want to move.

David steps on my toes every so often, but otherwise he does pretty well. He's learning, slowly. He'd do better if he'd just put a little more effort into it and not be scared. He seems so afraid of making a fool of himself, but you can't have that attitude when you're dancing.

I decide to give him a rest after the second number, even though I just want to keep on. He's already sweating, however. We sit down and order more drinks—non-alcoholic this time. I look around the room. Everyone seems to be having a good time.

After a couple more numbers, I hear a song I've been waiting all evening to hear: "Summer Breeze." How we all loved that song when we were teenagers! Those lovely lyrics—didn't make much sense, but they had pretty words like "jasmine" in them.

I leap up and cry out, "Oh, David, 'Summer Breeze'! Come on, let's dance!"

He holds back again in a reprise of his schoolboy routine. God, this is getting really tiresome. What's the matter with him? Can't he feel the rhythm in that song? How can anyone not want to just get up and dance?

I repeat: "David, come on! I want to dance!"

But he looks as if he's glued to the chair. He has this weird, frightened look on his face. What a baby he is! He manages to croak: "Cassandra, please ... please go with someone else. I can't.... Please, dance with someone else."

I don't believe what I'm hearing. I look down at him to try to figure out what he could possibly be thinking, but his head is now bowed and he won't look at me. He's hopeless. Well, I'm not going to waste time arguing while the number is playing. I scan the room and find my old high-school friend John Paton, sitting there with his lump of a wife, Marion. She doesn't like dancing, either. John's a sap, but he's at least a good dancer. I look one last time at David, realize he's not going to budge, then go to John.

I don't even want to think about the rest of the evening. David says next to nothing to me; can scarcely stand to look at me. By the time we're in the taxi I'm blazing with anger. He's ruined the evening!—or at least he could have made it a lot better if he didn't sit there and sulk like a two-year-old. Okay, so David doesn't like dancing much—but it's only because he hasn't really tried it. He never puts any effort into it, he's always so scared. Scared to make a fool of himself. But you can't think that way if you're going to dance. You just have to let yourself go—get comfortable with your body. The only kind of dancing David's good at is the horizontal kind.

He's such a child sometimes. Never wants to try new things, just stuck in his rut, banging away on that typewriter all day. Oh, he does damn good work and I'm proud of him, but he needs to be a little more well-rounded. I try to get him to come out of his shell, but he's so recalcitrant. He doesn't seem to realize that I have his best interests at heart. It's been a good marriage, and I do love him, and I'm sure he loves me; but there's something not quite right.

I just wish held take my advice sometimes.

18.

David Phillips
September 29, 1984, 7:14 p.m.

"Darling, are you ready?"

God, how that irritates me. Why is she so impatient? "Not just yet."

She stalks into the dressing room while I'm trying to knot this stupid bow tie. Why do people ever wear bow ties, anyway?

I know what's coming: "Darling, why don't you just get Jenyns to put that on you?"

I glare at her. She can be such a bitch sometimes.

She has this superior smirk on her face. "Shall I get him?"

I give up the tie as a hopeless proposition. "Sure."

Jenyns appears as if by magic. Maybe he was listening in the hallway. He immediately ties the bow tie just right, as I stand in front of him like a little boy. I try to avoid looking into his eyes. Cassandra stands gazing like a benevolent mother at both of us.

"Come on, dear, we'll be late." I rather wish we would be, but she takes my arm and marches off.

The ballroom already seems to have an appalling number of people in it. How are they all going to fit? A bunch of musicians are setting up off to one side. It's a weird mix: electric guitars, xylophone, marimba, and various wooden percussion instruments whose names I don't even know. Well, at least my actual participation may be postponed for a while.

Cassandra guides me to a small knot of people talking to themselves. I scarcely remember who they are. They greet Cassandra warmly but look at me as if they don't quite know what I'm doing there next to her.

To my alarm she lets go of my arm and says, "Darling, I have to check something. I'll be back in two shakes."

I give her this almost yearning look not to leave me, but she doesn't notice. So I'm left with these people. I look at each one in turn, trying to dredge up some memory of who they are.

An elderly man grips my hand and says, "How are you, David?"

"I'm fine." What else can I say?

"Looking after our Cassandra, I hope?"

"As best I can."

"That's all anyone can do, isn't it?"

"I guess so."

After that scintillating exchange he turns back to his own people and begins talking softly to the elderly lady next to him. No one else makes any effort to talk to me.

Finally Cassandra comes back and rescues me. I never thought I'd be so relieved to see her. She leads me to a table in the front row of a big circle of tables on the dance floor. Her parents have already sat down in the table next to ours; I nod to them with attempted cordiality, and they nod back—dutifully, it seems.

The dancers rush on at about 8:30—eight of them, four men and four women. Their costumes are superb. They immediately begin a variety of dances—extraordinarily complex ones, it seems to me. I haven't the faintest idea how people learn all the steps and whirls and other motions required by these numbers. It's not something I would want to do, but I'm overwhelmed by their expertise. They're really good.

The band I could have done without. It's not that they aren't good—but they're so damn noisy that I get a headache after half an hour. During the very brief breaks between numbers I still seem to hear the chords and drums throbbing in my head. I'm getting a little dizzy—thanks in no small part to the abundant drinks and the rather skimpy solid food being served at this affair.

Cassandra is wriggling rhythmically in her chair. She hardly gives me a glance; in fact, she seems hypnotized by the dancers. After they leave at ten to tremendous applause, another band—a more orthodox one—takes the place of the Latin musicians. At once Cassandra tugs my sleeve and cries, "Come on, darling, let's dance!"

I'm petrified at the thought of dancing in that huge space all by ourselves. I've told Cassandra repeatedly that I'm not a dancer, that I don't like dancing, but she doesn't listen. I don't know whether she feels that going to dance parties—or, as here, putting them on—is necessary to maintain her social standing; but whatever it is, I wish she'd somehow leave me out of it.

She's not going to take no for an answer. "David, we're the hosts of this thing. We have to take the lead. My parents aren't going to start; *we* have to."

I seem to have no choice, so I get up and go out on to the floor. Maybe if I delay a little, other couples will come out and join us. I'm relieved to see they're doing just that. I'm also grateful that the tempo of the number is slow—at least slower than the tarantella-rhythm of that Brazilian stuff.

As I expected, I'm a klutz and step on Cassandra's toes every so often; after a while I even stop saying "Sorry." By the second number I'm so wrought up that I seem to be sweating at every pore. I look pleadingly at her after the second number, and she decides to give me a reprieve and sit down. Some drinks—non-alcoholic this time, thank God—are placed in front of us. Cassandra looks around the room rather regally, as if surveying her domain.

Several numbers are played—a rather bland pop (or should that be pap?) medley. Then a number is struck up—I was dreading this. It's "Summer Breeze."

A nice song, certainly, even in this washed-out arrangement. Cassandra jumps up, crying out, "Oh, David, 'Summer Breeze'! Come on, let's dance!"

I hold back—really hold back this time. I can't go out on to that floor.

She looks at me as if I've lobotomized myself. "David, come on! I want to dance!"

I manage to squeeze the words out of my throat. "Cassandra, please . . . please go with someone else. I can't. . . . Please, dance with someone else."

She continues to glare at me in mingled confusion and derision. I feel totally wretched. Finally she realizes she's not going to get her way this time. She looks around the room and seizes upon someone else—I should know him, but I've forgotten his name too. She gives me one more barbed parting glance and goes out on the floor with the guy.

How can I tell her that "Summer Breeze" was my prom song? That I took Lauren to that prom (the only prom she ever went to, since she didn't want to go to her senior prom without me), and that we danced every number? If you want to call clutching each other tightly and moving a few paces here and there dancing.

The rest of the evening is a disaster. Cassandra says next to nothing to me; scarcely even looks at me. The same scenario persists in the taxi ride back home. She's really angry, but she doesn't seem to give the least thought about me. Even aside from the "Summer Breeze" débâcle, I don't think she realizes what she made me endure this whole evening. She knows I don't like dancing; so why does she take me to these things and deliberately humiliate me? Don't my feelings matter to her in the least? What does she want from me? What did she ever want from me? She just wants me to be her ornament, the sober guy in the tux and bow tie whom she can introduce to all her friends and say, "This is my husband, David, the writer." It doesn't seem to matter to her that, when she does that, these same people just look at me blankly, dutifully impressed, as if I'm a prize pig at a state fair.

It's been a good marriage, I suppose. I do love her, and I guess she loves me; but there's something not quite right.

I just wish she'd leave me alone sometimes.

19.

Justin Federlein
August 17, 1985, 4:48 p.m.

I don't believe it. It's Cassandra. She's stepping out of her Ferrari and walking right toward me.

"Hi, Justin. I was just in the neighborhood and thought I'd stop by."

My tongue is dry—and not only because it's so damn hot today. I can barely say: "Gee, Cassandra, it's nice of you to come. I haven't seen you in months." I try not to make that sound like a whine.

"Yes, I know. I'm sorry. I've been very busy."

She looks at the paintings—my paintings—hanging on the side of the building. She looks at them for a long time, saying nothing. "They're good, Justin."

I stare at her as if she's just crowned me king of Sumeria. "Thank— I'm glad you think so."

"Have you been displaying long in Soho?"

"Oh, yeah. Years, really. Off and on. We have a little colony here, and we put up our work every Saturday." I sweep my arm around, although she probably can't tell the artists from the few spectators we have. Everyone seems to be looking at her—and her car—curiously and maybe resentfully. I think some of them don't believe she's really my friend.

"Do you sell a lot?"

I shrug. "No, not a lot. Sometimes. I don't really care."

She looks at me incredulously. "You don't care? Don't you want to make some money? Do you have any other job?"

"Well, I work part-time in one of the warehouses. And I work now and then for a moving company. That's it. I don't need much. And every so often I sell a painting. So I'm doing okay." I hope I don't sound too defensive.

She's still looking at me, but moving closer to my pictures. She comes up to one of them.

"This one's really nice. The use of color is superb. What do you call it?"

"I don't call it anything. Titles can be so limiting. It's just a bunch of reeds by the ocean that I saw once at sunset near Sheepshead Bay."

"No title, huh? Well, it's damn good." She is now about half a foot from the painting. "What would you sell this for?"

I look away from her. I'm feeling more and more embarrassed. My friends are either staring right at us or making a point of looking away. "Oh, Cassandra, you don't have to buy it."

"Justin, I want to. I like it. I like it a lot. What are you charging for it?"

She's obviously not going to give up. She never does. "Oh, maybe six hundred."

"Six hundred dollars?" I'm afraid I've offended her by asking too much when she says immediately: "That's crazy! It's worth a lot more than that! I'll give you a thousand for it."

This is getting to be more and more like a dream. I don't even know why she's here; she never paid much attention to me in college, and afterwards we would run into each other—mostly by accident—maybe three or four times a year. We don't exactly move in the same circles.

"Justin, come on, please make up your mind. It's so bloody hot out here. I want to buy this painting. Are you selling it?"

I guess she really wants it, although I can't imagine why. It's not that good. "Sure, if you want it."

"Good. That's settled. I can write you a check right now."

I start to take the picture down, then stop. "It's getting kind of late; I need to pack up my stuff and take it back to my place. I may have a frame there if you want one. . . ."

"I don't think I do—I'll get my own frame, if you don't mind—but I can help you take your 'stuff,' as you call it, back. We can put it in my car. Okay?"

"Okay."

Some of my friends are smirking as they see us load up her Ferrari with my paintings. They bid me a very curt farewell as we drive off.

The streets in lower Manhattan are so confusing that I have to guide Cassandra very slowly—and she doesn't like driving slowly. But I don't live far away. We get there in five or six minutes.

"This is where you live?" she says with a kind of mingled disbelief and scorn.

"Yes." I don't see any point trying to defend myself.

The building is an old warehouse that has been converted into apartments. I live on the fourth floor, and have to use a freight elevator—which I operate myself—to get up. It's not very clean. The lower floors are still being used for storage.

We bring all the paintings—except the one she has bought, which she puts in her trunk—up to my place. It's a one-room apartment with a tiny kitchen alcove. There's not much furniture there, especially since I need to make as much room as possible for my art supplies.

"Jesus, Justin, it's so hot in here. I'm drenched already."

"Sorry. I don't have air conditioning." I turn on the fan, which I've placed in the one window in the place.

She sits down on a ratty easy chair which I picked up from a used furniture store on Varick Street. As she sits, some of the foam is pushed out of it and floats in the breeze. She looks around, but there isn't much to see. So she turns and looks at me.

"Well, let's take care of business first." She fishes out her checkbook from her handbag and writes out a check with something of a flourish on the arm of the chair. She hands it to me.

"Thanks." I stuff it into my pocket. I don't want to look at it.

"Justin, do you have anything to drink? I'm so parched."

"I keep some cold water in the fridge." I almost run in the direction of the kitchen alcove to get it. "Is that okay?"

She looks at me a little pityingly. "Well, to be honest, I was hoping for some alcohol."

I stop in my tracks. "Oh. Sorry. I don't have any." I look at my feet.

"You don't drink?"

"Oh, I do. Sometimes. It's just . . . just that I don't have any right now." I perk up. "But I can get some real quick. There's a liquor store about two blocks from here—"

"Never mind, Justin. The water will be fine."

I feel like a total failure. I get the water, but am almost ashamed to hand it to her. But she reaches out for it eagerly as I come close to her. Her hand brushes mine for a second.

"So, Justin, are you happy with your life?" She always was one for getting right to the point.

I squirm a little. "Sure. I like my painting, and I can get by doing this and that. . . ."

"But what do you want to do in the future? No offense, Justin, but you can't just live like this all the time."

I feel like a rabbit being cornered by a fox. "Well, I think I'm doing okay. . . . There's not much money in painting unless you get really big."

She presses on. "Well, why can't you get really big? You have the talent, I think. Can't you display your things other than on a wall on Soho? How about the galleries here?"

I shake my head, half in resignation and half in disgust. "The galleries here are all run by cliques. They have their friends, and if you're not one of them, then you're nothing. They won't like my work—it's not avant-garde enough for them. I may have to start outside New York—way outside. Like the South or the West. If I get into galleries there, then the snotty New York ones might consider me."

I think this is the most number of consecutive sentences I've ever spoken to Cassandra.

She looks at me with a kind of grudging respect, almost wonderment. "Are you doing that?"

"What?"

"Getting into galleries in the South or wherever. Are you trying?"

"Sure. I'm sending my slides all over. I have some prospects here and there." I feel I'm slowly getting control of things.

"That's good. That's good." She's smiling; it's as if she almost respects me.

Suddenly she leaps up from the chair—the water was finished long ago—and goes to stand right in front of the fan. "Oh, God, Justin, it's just so hot. Anybody'd be crazy to stay in New York in August. I wish I'd gone with my parents to . . ." She cuts herself off, almost as if she's biting her tongue.

Standing in front of the window, the fan making her dress cling to her, she says: "Hey, this is some view."

The window faces south, so that you can see the towers of the World Trade Center looming on the right and Battery Park and the

Statue of Liberty almost straight ahead. Tourists would love it, I guess. I've never been to the Statue of Liberty.

I walk up so that I'm pretty close behind her—closer than I've been to her in years. I can smell perfume mixed with her sweat. Even her sweat smells nice.

She takes the neck of her dress and pulls it out, bending over a bit so that the air from the fan can reach there. My heart leaps into my throat as I see she's not wearing a bra. I've never seen her breasts before.

She doesn't notice my glance immediately; but then, when she straightens up and turns around, she seems a little startled to find me standing so close. I didn't really mean to, it just happened that way. She first looks at me blankly, then starts to smile slowly.

"It's hot, isn't it?" she says softly.

"Yes." It's all I can say, and it sounds like a groan.

Without warning she puts her arms around me. I can feel her dress cling to my T-shirt. I can feel her breasts against my chest. I can feel her sweat.

"Justin, you sweet boy," she says, then kisses me hard.

I'm dizzy—not from heat. "Cassandra, what—" I manage to say after she stops kissing me. "What do you—?"

"Don't say anything." She steps back from me for a moment and, before I can even comprehend what's happened, in a single motion she unzips her dress and steps out of it. She has nothing but panties on.

I'm already so hard that I'm ready to burst. I can't believe this is happening. Things like this don't happen to me. She pushes me gently back, so that I have to walk backward. An obstruction hits my knees. It's my bed. I fall back on it.

She's standing over me, looking down at me, smiling. In a flash her panties are off. I can't move or speak.

She wastes no time. She unzips my jeans and pulls them, along with my briefs, as far down as they will go. They're now around my ankles. My cock is standing straight up. She seems impressed— not at its size, but probably at the speed with which it has risen to attention. She takes it in her hand.

She puts her mouth over it.

I can't believe this is happening. I just can't. Should I tell her how long I've dreamed of this—how many times, from the moment I saw her in a class sophomore year, I've pounded myself to climax just thinking about her? How sick I felt attending her wedding? How grateful I was that she would even be my friend? And now this. . . .

Oh, no! Please, no! She's only licked me a few times, but I feel that familiar explosion coming from my balls up to my cock. Oh, God, not now!

But I can't stop. I come while her tongue is licking the top of my shaft. Her face is bespattered; some of it goes into her mouth.

I'm horrified, but I still can't move. I'm afraid she's going to yell at me, kick me, maybe kill me. But all she does, after being momentarily taken aback, is to take a Kleenex from the floor (I have no end table) and wipe her face daintily with it.

"You naughty boy," she says, smiling.

I smile so hard that I start to laugh. She laughs with me. I see her sharp, straight, white teeth.

"I'm sorry," I say. "I didn't mean that to happen." I reach to put my pants back on, but she stops me.

She looks me right in the face with a kind of amused outrage. "We're not done yet, are we? Don't you want some more?"

I'm stunned by what I'm hearing. This really isn't happening to me. "Ye-ye-yes, I guess so." I feel like a fool—a child.

"You guess so? You better be sure, Justin." With that, she climbs up on the bed and tugs off my T-shirt. My pants are still around my ankles, because my shoes are still on, but I manage to kick both of them off somehow. It seems to take forever.

We start again. More slowly this time.

When it's over, she rests her head on my chest; I wonder if my chest hairs are tickling her nose, but she doesn't seem to mind. We say nothing, but after a while she turns her head and looks right at me, saying:

"Justin, this was really great, but we can't do this any more, okay? We've done it, and it's over. Okay?"

"Yeah, sure." I never expected anything else.

"You can handle that?"

"Of course."

"And you won't tell anyone? I *am* married, after all."

"No, of course I won't. What sort of person do you think I am?"

"You're a sweet person, Justin. Very sweet." She rests her head on my chest again. I lie back, totally spent. I drift off to sleep.

When I wake up she's gone.

20.

Lauren Oxley
March 18, 1986, 5:12 p.m.

"Hi, Lauren. It's good to see you again."

"Good to see you, too, David."

"It's been a while. Hasn't it? Almost a year."

"Yes, I suppose so. I've been really busy."

"That's good, I guess." He stops abruptly, then, as if to fill up the silence: "That's good."

I look up at him over my coffee. "I'm sorry I haven't called. You know I feel funny about calling you at home. You could have called."

"I know. I should have. I've been pretty busy too."

"Writing?"

"Yeah. Writing."

He's not drinking his coffee, just stirring it around.

"Why did you want to see me, David?" I say after a long silence.

"Do we have to have a reason? You're my oldest friend—my best friend, too, I guess."

"What about Mike?"

His face clouds over. "I'm not in touch with Mike much anymore. He doesn't like writing letters. In fact, I haven't really heard from him in three or four years."

"Really?" I'm rather dumbfounded. "You were so inseparable in high school." Except when I was there.

"I know. That was a long time ago." He looks up from his coffee, but not at me. He stares out the window of the coffee shop. "A long time ago."

I try to make a go of it. "Well, it's nice to see you again. It really is."

"It's nice of you to see me." Now he does look right at me. "Lauren, I'm really glad we've become friends again. You don't know how much it means to me."

"Oh, that's okay." I hope he doesn't get weepy. I don't think I could deal with that.

But he's not finished. "Those three years you wouldn't speak to me were the longest of my life—they really were, Lauren! I felt awful."

"You had . . . your wife." I can't seem to say her name.

"Yeah, sure, I did." He looks back at his coffee. He hasn't drunk any of it; it must be cold by now.

"And still do."

"Still do."

He sighs heavily, then says in an unexpectedly loud voice: "And how about you? Are you seeing anyone?"

I know this is his way of trying to turn the tables, but I'm too tired to resist. "No, not just now. I don't seem much interested."

"Not interested? You, a lovely, bright young woman like you? There must be lots of men banging at your door—"

"I said I wasn't interested, okay?" I don't mean to say it so loud, but I can't help it.

He realizes that this is a subject not worth pursuing, so he shuts up. For one fleeting instant I hate him. But then it's gone.

"How's your job?" he asks.

"Okay."

"You're still at the same place? The physics department at NYU?"

"Yes."

"Gee, physics . . . I never thought you'd get into physics."

"Oh, David, you don't need to know anything about physics to be the secretary of the department. It's easy."

"You've been doing that for years, haven't you?"

"Yes."

"Ever since . . ."

"Yes. Ever since I left Barnard."

He actually takes a sip of the coffee, but finds it stone cold. He grimaces and puts the cup back down. Gently he says:

"Are you satisfied with that? Is that what you want to do for the rest of your life?"

I'm sure he doesn't mean it to sound sarcastic, but it does. "No, David, it's not what I want to do for the rest of my life. But it's fine for now. It doesn't take any effort."

"Maybe you could take classes and learn some other skill. . . ."

"Maybe."

I guess I shouldn't be so short with him, but he's now sounding really patronizing. What's he done with his life, anyway? But I do feel a little guilty, so I say:

"I'm sorry, David. I'm just a little tired."

He doesn't respond immediately. Then he looks me in the face and says: "Lauren, you had so many dreams. Maybe we all did, and maybe a lot of those dreams were crazy, but you weren't like this. There were so many things you wanted to do in life. What happened to your singing? You were such a good singer. . . ."

"I wasn't that good."

"Sure you were!" he says with a mixture of enthusiasm and scolding. "I heard you that Easter back home in the church choir. That Fauré solo you did was superb! You had a magnificent voice! Still do, probably."

"I don't sing much now." I wish this conversation were over.

"Why not take lessons?"

"Lessons are expensive."

"Couldn't you get a discount with someone who teaches at NYU? You're staff there, after all." He sounds almost frantic.

"David, it doesn't work that way. Private lessons are private lessons. There's no discount."

Almost sheepishly he says: "I could give you some money. A gift, not a loan. You never have to pay it back. I'd just like to hear you sing again."

I look up at him. He has that same boyish eagerness on his face that he's had ever since I've known him, but now there's a tinge of something else—a kind of fear or guilt or agitation or something— that makes him look like a gorgon.

I put my hand over his. "That's really sweet, David, but I just don't think I want to do that. I don't want singing lessons, and I don't want your money." As he looks away from me I add: "But it's very nice of you to offer. There's no one like you, David."

I hope I'm not seeing tears well up in his eyes. I don't want to see that.

He gets up abruptly. "I . . . I guess I'd better go home. Dinner will be ready soon."

I get up too. "It was good to see you again, David."

"Yeah. Good to see you too, Lauren."

"Can we stay in touch a little more now?"

"Yes. Yes, of course. We'll do that."

Will we? I wonder.

21.

David Phillips
August 12, 1989, 2:16 p.m.

It seems heartless to say so, but it astounds me that there are tears in Cassandra's eyes.

I've never seen such a big funeral. It's almost as well attended as our wedding. Different crowd entirely, of course—scarcely anyone under fifty. Either the Connollys were very well known or a lot of people in this set feel the social necessity to make an appearance.

I should try to console Cassandra, but I'm still trying to take in the fact that she's so wrought up. Oh, sure, her parents' death couldn't have been pleasant—they had trouble even finding the bodies after their yacht capsized in Rhode Island Sound—and the suddenness of it was startling. But still . . .

Cassandra hated her parents so much.

Well, maybe not hated. But she did seem to take a perverse delight in tweaking their noses. Bringing me over to spend that summer with them so many years ago was one of her more brilliant tactics—she seemed, at any rate, pretty delighted with the result.

We've hardly had anything to do with them for the last eight years—Cassandra saw to that. They didn't complain too much when she demanded that we get a place of our own after we were married; I'm sure they would have preferred us to stay with them, but maybe they realized they couldn't expect that. And the place on East 85th Street was certainly more than anyone could have asked for. They didn't go there much, however.

Here's Jenyns. He's the only one who doesn't seem unruffled by things—not even sweating in this incredible heat. But wait—am I doing him a disservice? Are his eyes actually rimmed with red? His jaw seems tight too. Cassandra comes up to him and actually throws her arms around him, sobbing. It's like he's her uncle or something. Maybe he is, in a way.

The ceremony proceeds with appalling formality. I'm becoming a little dizzy—from the heat, from the droning of the preacher, from the rustling of all this expensive mourning attire, from the fact that Cassandra is actually clinging to my arm in a kind of desperation. I can't convince myself that this is really happening.

I think back to yesterday. Four of us in a little room—one that I didn't even know existed—back at her parents' place on East 68th Street. Cassandra, Jenyns, some lawyer whose name I have already forgotten, and me. That fellow droned pretty much like this cleric up there.

"Miss . . . Mrs. Phillips"—he seems to have a little difficulty with that—"may I ask what disposition you intend to make of this residence?"

Without hesitation Cassandra says: "Why, we'll live here, of course!"

I turn to look at her in amazement. "Wh-what are you saying?" I sound like a scared little boy.

She looks me right in the face. "David, this place has been in our family for three generations. Do you think we're just going to give it up?"

She seems to expect me to respond, but there's nothing to say. Meanwhile the lawyer looks at her with a certain placid satisfaction.

He tells Jenyns about a pretty substantial legacy he has been left, and asks if he wishes to continue service or to retire. "The former," is all he says. Cassandra places her hand on his arm and actually gives him a little peck on the cheek.

"That's settled, then," she says, looking around as if daring anyone to contradict her.

I don't take up the matter with her until a few hours later, when we are back in our place.

"Cassandra, maybe we could have come to this decision jointly? Don't I have a say in things?"

She gives me a look as if I'm an especially slow preschooler. "Darling, there was no decision to make! You want me just to sell that brownstone that Connollys have lived in for a hundred years? David, it's our home."

I look at her querulously. "But somehow I thought you didn't like the place. God knows you were in a hurry to get out after we were married."

She turns away. Not even she can come out and say what she's thinking. *It's not that I didn't like the place—only some of the people in it.*

Well, I guess maybe it'll be for the better. Certainly that other place has more room. I may need a blueprint to find my way around it, though. I don't remember it very well from my stay nine years ago, and anyway I spent most of my time then in Cassandra's bedroom.

Maybe there's a room there where Cassandra can't find me.

22.

David Phillips
March 22, 1991, 5:43 p.m.

I delete the file.

It isn't quite as satisfying as ripping the sheet out of the typewriter, crumpling up the paper into a little ball, and hurling it into the wastebasket, but it serves the same purpose. More ecological, too, since I hadn't bothered to print out the wretched mess of hash.

I get up from the computer. The blank black screen seems somehow more ominous-looking than the virgin white of a sheet of paper in a typewriter. And that damned little flickering cursor at the top corner of the screen: waiting in impatience for me to begin writing something—anything; winking at me as if it knows some secret about me that I don't know myself; laughing at me for my impotence.

God, I sound like a bad novelist. Which is, I guess, what I am.

The door opens. I hear Cassandra's resolutely cheery voice. "David, dear, I'm home! Are you in the study?"

For one crazy instant I don't want to answer; want to hide in the closet so that she can't find me. But it's useless. "Yes, I'm in here."

She stalks in, throwing off her fur wrap—a little warm for that, isn't it?—and marching up to me. She gives me a little peck on the cheek. (What happened to the kisses on the lips we gave each other every time we went out or came back?) I'm standing by the computer. She looks at me, then at the blank screen, then back at me. She has a wary look on her face, as if I'm somehow trying to trick her.

"Guess you're taking a break, eh?"

"Eh."

She chooses to ignore that bit of sarcasm. "Well, I guess you've gotten a lot done before. You haven't stayed in the whole day, have you?"

"No, I haven't stayed in the whole day. I took a little walk earlier. And no, I haven't gotten much work done."

She sits down on the couch next to the desk. She says nothing, just looks up at me with a kind of glance an entomologist might give to a new species of insect.

"What's the matter, babe? Is the novel stuck?"

I almost want to do violence to her. "No, the *novel* isn't stuck. *I'm* stuck. The novel isn't anything. It isn't going anywhere. It may never go anywhere." I sit down heavily at the opposite end of the couch from where she is sitting. I feel suddenly exhausted.

She moves a little closer to me. "Babe, you were so confident about this one. So excited! What happened?"

"I don't know what happened. It's just like all the others. The other four novels that I actually finished. They really don't go anywhere, either."

She gets suddenly angry—not at me, though. "Well, why doesn't your fucking agent do something with them? Maybe you should dump him and get someone else."

"I'm surprised he hasn't dumped me. I don't bring him any money. Writing reviews for the *Voice* and landing a story once in a blue moon isn't exactly the most lucrative job in the world."

I get up and walk about the room. It's a big room. When people are at the opposite ends of it you almost have to shout to be heard, but somehow I say in a whisper, "Maybe I'm just no good, Cassandra."

Soft as that is, she's heard. Maybe she was expecting it.

She leaps up from the couch and stalks over to me. I wonder whether she'll slap me in the face, as if I've insulted her. But she only hisses: "David Phillips, don't you dare say that! Don't ever say that!" She wheels around, almost as if looking for something to hit or throw. "Look, you have a book published and a bunch of short stories and articles and reviews, and you're only thirty-two. That's pretty good, isn't it?"

I laugh shortly. "A critical study of James M. Cain doesn't exactly make me God's gift to literature. Especially when it's only sold about two thousand copies."

"Well, why the hell didn't you take it to a trade house instead of a university press? Those places only sell to libraries!"

"No one else would take it, sweetheart. Don't you remember how many publishers we tried?"

"Oh . . ." She spins around again like a top. I have a momentary fear that she's going to run amok.

But she settles down. "Look, guy, you're good and you know it. I know it. I wouldn't have married you if you weren't. I don't marry losers." She seems to expect some response from me, but what response can I give? I say nothing. "Maybe you just need to get away for a while. You want to go somewhere? Newport? Maybe London?"

I sigh in weariness. "No. You know I can never write in those places. I don't feel at home there."

"Well, then, where the fuck *do* you feel at home? Clearly not here!"

I try to calm her down. "I didn't say that. I like it here. It's nice. You're nice. You're wonderful."

Suddenly, in a quiet voice, she says: "Well, you could try showing it sometime."

I say, also quietly: "I do try. You could too."

We stare at each other. I feel as if I should be taking her in my arms, but something prevents me. I don't know what. She doesn't seem to be making any overtures, either. Does she always expect me to?

The moment is lost. Now there's just bitterness and irritation left. An embrace would be a mockery now.

"Look, Cassandra, I'll try again. I'll keep trying. You know I don't give up."

"Yes, I know that." She's speaking about as quietly as I've ever heard her. Now she seems about to say something that she's almost scared to say. Imagine Cassandra being scared of anything!

"Maybe, David, you could just try being a critic. You're good at that. There's nothing wrong being a critic. Take a break from novels for a while. Write a book of criticism, a biography, something like that."

I know better than to verbalize the subtext: *You're a failure as a novelist. Give it up.* "Yeah, you may be right. Maybe I'll do that."

"Good." She's perky again. She actually pats my cheek.

"I'll tell Ethel to start getting dinner ready, okay?"

"Okay."

She walks out. I go back to the computer. I turn it off. Still a black screen, but at least no flickering cursor.

23.

Cassandra Phillips
February 12, 1994, 9:42 p.m.

David doesn't touch me any more.

Here I am, sitting on the couch, and he walks in and sits down in the easy chair. There's only space for one there. He gives me this embarrassed smile but says nothing.

This has gone on for a long time.

Oh, I don't just mean we don't have sex. Christ, I can't remember the last time that happened. But he literally doesn't even want to come in contact with me. It's like I have some contagious disease—or he does.

Is there such a thing as being married too long? God knows I couldn't conceive of my parents having sex for the last ten or fifteen years of their lives. The way they flew off the handle at my little indiscretions in high school and college, you'd think they had me via test tube.

But we're only thirty-six, for God's sake. Fourteen and a half years of marriage, and it's come to this.

Those first few years were good; damn good. Not just the sex—everything. I took David to places he'd never been to—Europe, Egypt, even India. He said he'd work it all into his writing someday. He had a lot of hope then.

But it didn't happen. His novels got rejected, and he took it hard. God, what does he expect?—Few people make it the first time. He was still only a boy then. Christ, most other writers would give their right arms to be in his position: doing whatever he wants all day, not having to worry about money, everything provided for him.

Somewhere along the way he forgot to be grateful to me.

Then he actually gets into little conniption fits whenever we have to go to a formal function. He'd be a lot less uncomfortable if he just worried less about not making a *faux pas*. Not everyone knows he's from Indiana.

He'd better not be thinking of that girl . . . what's her name, Lauren? I wonder where she is. I was stunned to hear she was staying in the city—I was sure she'd flee back to her cornfields after college. Maybe she has by now. But he's probably forgotten all about her. It was a long time ago.

He rustles the paper he's reading. Somehow I thought he'd already looked at it this morning.

He doesn't even talk to me any more.

"Anything interesting happen in the world today, dear?" I venture.

"No, not much," he mutters, the paper shielding the entire upper part of his body.

"Would you like to go out for dinner tomorrow?"

He turns a page. I'm sure the noise of it hides a sigh of irritation. "Yes, if you wish, dear."

What do you wish, David? What do you want?

I'm not going to take the blame for this. I've done a lot for him—more than most women would. I'm not clingy, I'm not flighty, I'm not a spendthrift (well, maybe I am—but it's my money), I'm not very demanding. And he found me pretty damn attractive once. I'm *still* pretty damn attractive, if only he'd notice.

Have I made a mistake? Is this whole marriage a mistake? *No, dammit!* I want to slap myself in the face. Don't say things like that, bitch. I won him and I'm going to keep him. He knows me—my body, my mind, my whole being—better than anyone ever has. I've never let anybody get this close to me—not my parents, not my friends, no one. He's not going to run off to somebody else, after all that. He's mine.

What did Elaine say the other day?

We're sitting down at a coffee shop near Bloomingdale's. Shopping was exhausting, and we needed a break. Coffee, croissants, cake, the works. Too bad there's no booze here.

I can't believe she married that sap Henry Lockerbee. Maybe she didn't have much of a choice—she was unpleasingly plump even in prep school. And I guess one could do worse than an investment banker, although she has plenty of dough of her own. Her parents will still give her anything. But Henry . . . I shudder even to think of him.

But I have to ask politely: "How are things between you and Henry?"

She shrugs, looks off in the distance. "Okay. Nothing special." She feels she has to say dutifully: "He's a good man."

I want to shake her and say, *Cut the crap!* But before I have a chance to say anything, she pipes back: "And you and David? Are you doing well?"

"Yeah. Okay."

She's not going to let that go by—she's always one for turning the tables on you, just so you won't pry open her own problems. "That doesn't sound very good. You sure there's nothing wrong?"

I frown at her and sigh. "Oh, Elaine, it's pretty much the same as usual." I can help myself from saying: "It's not like what it was."

"Oh, it never is." Oh, shut up, Little Miss Psychologist! Who are you to lecture me?

"Why isn't it? Why can't it be?" I say, more loudly than I intend. "Why have things gotten so boring? Is that how they are with you?" How's that for turning the tables?

She's pretty shrewd. "Oh, things are fine. I still love him. And he loves me."

"Jesus, Elaine, David and I love each other too! That's not it, you know it isn't!" I'm so mad I can't go on.

She looks around conspiratorially, then cranes over and whispers: "Maybe you should try one of those 'Better Sex' videos."

I laugh in her face.

"You must be joking, Elaine! Are you out of your mind? Don't tell me you've tried them . . ."

She turns bright red. "Well, no, of course not . . . I'm too embarrassed to order them. I thought you might get one and I'd borrow it—"

"Oh, so sex with Henry isn't so good, huh?" I say quite loudly.

"Cassandra, shush!" She slaps my hand petulantly; I'm sure she wishes she'd done that to my face.

"Elaine," I say tiredly, "you know it isn't just sex. The romance has gone. The spark that we had has gone out. We seem like brother and sister now—or no, we seem like roommates. That's it—just roommates in some big apartment. It's like a bunch of college students in some large sublet, who go off one by one so that only we two are left. Don't you see that?"

"Yes, I see it." She's looking down into her cup.

"We don't touch, we don't fuck"—she colors again at that—"we don't talk, he can hardly get through a meal with me, he doesn't want to go anywhere with me, and he seems to mope around the house all day." I take a breath. "Aside from that, things are fine!"

She smiles at that out of the side of her mouth, but she's still looking at the cup.

"So what's there to do?" she whispers. "Should we . . . ? I mean, will you . . . divorce him?" That word comes hard.

"No, I won't fucking divorce him!" There's no need to tell her the thought that's in my head: *I won't give him the satisfaction.*

"What are *you* going to do?" I say, almost shoving my nose into her face.

She leans backward, almost in horror. "What do you mean? I ... we aren't going to do anything. Henry and I are fine. Fine!"

I know what it is. She's terrified of being alone. She doesn't want to crawl back to her parents and admit her marriage was a failure. She's about my age, but she looks a hell of a lot older. She'll have trouble finding someone else, and she knows it.

We talk about other things until we finish our snack and go our own ways.

David gets up, puts the paper down, and without a word or glance goes back to his study. He'll probably stay there until I go to sleep, then he'll tiptoe in and crawl into his side of the bed without trying to wake me. But I'll know. I always do.

The only mercy of the situation is that I know he's not fooling around.

24.

David Phillips
November 24, 1994, 3:22 p.m.

Dad is sitting in the easy chair looking intently at the TV screen. There's a football game going on—Detroit Loins against somebody or other. The Lions always play on Thanksgiving. It's about the only exposure they get, I suppose. The game is almost over; Dad seems very keen on the outcome. There'll be another game after this one—always two on Thanksgiving—and he'll watch that one too.

Mother, of course, is in the kitchen. The aroma wafting from there is already almost intoxicating, although the meal won't be ready for another hour or two. I can just see her through the door of the den. She looks totally at home. She's like a general, giving orders to an array of battalions for some incredibly complex maneuver; and she knows it will all work out like clockwork. Nothing goes wrong when Mother's in the kitchen.

I decide to join her there. The outcome of the game was long ago decided, although I don't know or care who's winning. I sit down a little heavily in a chair. The table in front of me is already covered with sweet potatoes, mashed potatoes, broccoli, and the succulent crust of the pumpkin pie. That crust is just waiting to encircle the filling.

Mom looks over at me abruptly and with some startlement: she was so intent on her work that she didn't see me come in. But she gives me a big smile, wipes her hands on her apron, and looks about for something to shove into my mouth, as if there were no other reason for my coming in here. I just smile and wave her off gently, taking up a broccoli spear just for show.

She is still beaming at me. "David, it was so good of you to come out here!" I have a feeling she wants to take both my cheeks and pinch them.

"Mom, I love to come back here. You know that."

Her smile remains, but her eyes cloud over. "Yes, I know that. I just wish you'd make it here more often."

I look down at the table groaning with food. For an instant I feel a little sick. "I'm pretty busy, Mom."

She turns her head at an angle. "Dear, it's not as if you're working . . ." A momentary flicker of horror passes over her face at the *faux pas*. "I mean, it's not as if you have a job that keeps you at a desk working overtime or anything. . . . You could do your writing here, can't you? We'd leave you alone."

"Yes, I know you would. It's just . . ." I feel overwhelmed at the attempt to explain. I'm not even sure what there is to explain anyway.

Mom feels she has to take up the slack of the conversation, but she does it in a way I don't care for. "It's too bad Cassandra couldn't come out. We'd love to see her."

"Yes, I know. She's . . ." This is certainly something I don't want to explain. Surely Mom and Dad haven't forgotten the time early in our marriage when we came here for a couple of weeks? God, what a nightmare that was!

But I see that Mom *has* remembered. She is presumably about to change the subject when Dad walks heavily in. I'm rather surprised to see him, but he says that the game is over and the next game won't start until four. The pre-game show is boring.

He sits down next to me. He claps me on the shoulder. "Good to have you here, son." That's about the extent of the emotion he'll ever express.

I don't mean that maliciously. As I look at his warm, open face, a little puffy with age and eating too well, I wonder why there can't be more people like him. Maybe there are; they just don't seem to move in the circles I move in now.

He's retired now, thank God. He sold the drugstore for a good price, and he and Mom can look forward to a comfortable retirement. They don't need me to provide for them. Not that Cassandra or her parents would care to do that anyway.

Mother resumes speaking. "David"—she's not looking at me, she's stirring something on the stove—"you know, we'd like to see a grandchild before we're too much older." I knew this would come up sometime during my visit here, but I didn't think she'd throw it at me quite this soon.

"Mom, believe me, we're trying. . . ." I have to lie on this one. I can't tell her about Cassandra's views on the subject. Thank Heaven Mother hasn't had the courage to raise the issue with Cassandra herself, so that she's never heard Cassandra say in that barbed tone of hers that children will ruin her figure and that she doesn't have the patience to raise them, etc., etc.

Anyway, the idea of Cassandra as a mother fills me with a kind of shuddering terror.

Mother considers my remark and decides to say nothing. Even she is not so naive as to think that thirteen years of "trying" with nothing to show for it is just bad luck. She says instead:

"You know, I hope you keep in touch with Lauren now and then. She's such a nice girl."

This is going from bad to worse. Dad has removed his hand from my shoulder and is looking fixedly at the food on the table. He doesn't say much, and he doesn't even seem to feel much sometimes, but he knows me a lot better than Mom does. He knows what things I don't want to talk about. But Mother either doesn't know or feels she has to force me to talk about them.

"I do stay in touch with Lauren. She's pretty busy too."

"Everybody's busy in New York, I suppose," she says, not looking at me but at her cooking.

"Yes, they are."

"Then it must be a pretty awful place to live. Everyone running around like tops spinning on a game board." She seems proud of that simile.

"It can be a strain sometimes. But there are lots of other good things about it."

She doesn't want to hear that, so she just gives a little scoff of disbelief and takes the bubbling pot off the stove.

Presently it's time to eat. We all sit in front of the TV, each of us with our own little folding tray. It's so small that we can barely accommodate all the food that goes on it. We just watch the game, even Mother, even though she doesn't like or understand football. She's learnt enough, though, not to ask potentially stupid or irritating questions about what's going on.

I wish I knew what I was doing here. Why did I come back? Oh, sure, it's nice to see the folks, especially when they refuse to come to New York, and I really ought to come back here more often—at least once a year—before they get too much older. But at this exact moment I haven't a clue why I'm here or what I hope to accomplish. It all seems so totally futile. Going back up to my bedroom makes me feel as if the last seventeen years had never happened: the room hasn't changed one iota since the time I left to go to college, except that Mother has gradually filled the corners with a variety of objects that they don't use anymore and that really ought to be thrown away. I even once found one of my old term papers from junior high in a closet.

I can't sleep in that bed, though. I've insisted on taking the guest room. I'm sure Mom and Dad know why; they're not stupid.

I have to laugh thinking of the time they tried to make peace with Lauren's parents, saying that two young people who love each other shouldn't have needless obstacles put in their path. Her parents simply looked on with outraged horror and marched out of the place. I don't imagine they've spoken to each other ever since, certainly not after what I did later.

I look at my plate of food. The sick feeling has returned, but I take no notice and start shoveling the food into my mouth. Maybe if I eat enough I'll get so heavy that I can sleep through the next three days. Imagine actually being eager to get back to New York. And now I can't even imagine how I could ever have felt eager to come here.

25.

Lauren Oxley
June 19, 1995, 7:33 p.m.

Friday night. Another stellar week of secretarial duties behind me. Dinner—pasta with meat sauce—finished. Dishes washed. Nothing on TV; don't have cable. Have already told the girls I don't want to go out with them tonight.

The apartment diagonally across from me is already getting noisy with a party. It'll go on all evening, well into the night, I'm sure. I share one wall with them—my bedroom wall, unluckily enough. No use pounding; that never works.

The personal ads in the *New York Review of Books*, *New York* magazine, and the *New York Press* have turned up nothing. Maybe I'm getting more particular, although God knows why I should be after all the prior failures. Maybe I'm just losing interest.

It's so funny. People from out of town say, "Gosh, Lauren, there are so many men in New York! You must have them lining up outside your door!" Oh, there are men all right; but people don't seem to realize that the bigger the city, the harder it is to meet anyone. What are you supposed to do? Grab a briefcase-toting businessman on the street (once you've noticed there's no ring on his finger—you get pretty good at that), and say, "Hey, guy, are you nice, employed, straight, and not a serial rapist? If so, how'd you like to get married and have my kids?"

And then there's the problem of being an immigrant . . . God knows I still feel like one, even though I've lived here for eighteen years. Immigrant from the Midwest? Don't laugh. I still seem to have some trace of an Indiana accent, which makes some people look at me as a kind of quaint sideshow attraction and makes others wonder which wrong turn I took from my cornfield. Are New Yorkers cosmopolitan? No, they're pretty provincial. Just like the folks in Indiana.

I don't want to do this, but I can't help myself. I think back at my involvement with David. I've been thinking of that—and of him—a lot lately.

I don't blame him for what happened. Leaving me was his choice; I had no hold on him. I was just a chump for reacting the way I did; I've been reacting for fourteen years.

I wonder, though. . . . Would I have been so devoted to him if, back in high school, my parents—soul-saving evangelicals that they were, and are—hadn't been so horrified at finding that we had "had carnal knowledge of each other" and tried to prevent us from seeing each other? It didn't work, of course; my parents weren't exactly jailors. After a couple of months they gave it up, although their continuing disapproval of David must have fed my emotions at least a little. That's how you are at that age.

(David's parents, cheerful agnostics that they were, didn't seem to have a problem with occasional double occupancy in his bedroom.)

But what's the use? What's the use of dredging up the past? No use—except that one who has no future doesn't have much else to do.

I go to my bedroom. I open the bottom drawer of my dresser. God, I really shouldn't do this—not this early, anyway. It's scarcely even dark outside. For one mad moment I wonder whether I should put on some kind of show for the noisy partygoers across the way;

but I start to shudder at the mere idea of it. I draw the shade and fall heavily on my bed, vibrator in hand.

I close my eyes so that I can fantasize better. Sometimes it takes a great effort, and sometimes it's not even possible. Let's see what happens this time. I slowly unbutton my blouse, then unzip my skirt. I've already taken my stockings off. I rub the vibrator—not turned on yet—over my breasts, still encased in my bra. The vibrator is a little cold, even though it's been buried in my woolen sweater. I place it between my thighs to warm it up while I reach around and unclip my bra. I think of all the men—not all that many, actually—who have had so much trouble with that procedure. Really pretty simple once you get used to it.

I roll over on my stomach and take my panties off. I'm not really very wet yet, but no jelly for me—never use that stuff. I finally turn the vibrator on; it makes a sound like an electric razor. Doesn't matter; I'm used to it, and it doesn't interfere with my fantasies.

Getting on my back, I place it between the lips of my pussy and rub it gently there. I start feeling a little wet. I grab one breast with my other hand and knead it. I wonder suddenly if this sort of thing makes one sag. I don't know, and don't care very much.

I decide to take the vibrator on my chest and squeeze my breasts around it. Mistake. I start shuddering uncontrollably. I have to turn the damn thing off, fling it away from me, and hug my knees to my chest to stop shaking. After several minutes I finally do.

I open my eyes and look at the vibrator, looking a little forlorn at the corner of the bed. I don't know if I want to go on. The party next door is getting louder; a lot of laughing. I feel wetness between my legs, but also at the corners of my eyes. I'd better finish; what would be the point of stopping now?

I take up the vibrator, turn it on, and rub myself vigorously with it. I stick it in my cunt, although I don't really like this action all that much; but I'm pretty wide now, and feel it's something I should do. If I were with a real man, he wouldn't just want to rub his thing on me. But I take it out pretty quickly—too fast, for it makes an unpleasant sucking sound—and start rubbing again. I'm shuddering, moaning, almost grunting. I'm so worked up I don't notice the tears falling down my cheeks until one of them enters my mouth and gives me a start with its salty taste.

I open my eyes, suddenly confused. I don't know where I am or what I am doing. I look down at myself—at my hand holding this smooth plastic object that's buzzing like an angry bee. It's as if somebody else is doing all this. It's as if I'm somebody else. I'm almost about to stop when an explosion goes off simultaneously in my mind and my cunt.

I cry out. I throw the thing in my hand away from me; it clatters somewhere on the other side of the tiny room. I'm shuddering uncontrollably. I try to grab the wall, but there's nothing to hang on to. I have to close my eyes—I'm getting dizzy.

The shuddering is still going on—this has nothing to do with my climax, which is long over. Grabbing my knees doesn't seem to help any. It's like I'm having an epileptic fit. God, please stop! My heart is pounding as if it's going to burst out of my chest—it's like there's a little gremlin inside of me rattling the bones of my rib cage. I put one hand, then both hands, on my chest as if that might help, but it doesn't; I only flatten one breast painfully.

Jesus, I think I'm going to die. . . . Maybe it's better if I do. I try taking deep breaths, but at first I can't even breathe—an intake of breath makes a weird noise like a cotton blouse being ripped apart, and it feels like sandpaper in my throat. But finally I start breathing a little more regularly, and then more and more deeply.

After a few minutes I find I'm still shaking a little, but only in my hands. I'm lying on my back, and I place my hands under my bottom to stop the shaking, but it doesn't seem to help very much. I just try to relax—make myself feel boneless. I feel drenched; sweat is probably glistening all over my body, and if there were anyone to see—

Shut the fuck up. Don't say that.

I roll over on my side and bury my face in the pillow. I lie there for a while. It seems to have gotten dark all of a sudden. I haven't noticed the party noises for a while, but now I hear them again in a blare—as if someone suddenly turned on a radio just to shatter the silence. I don't dare close the window: that wouldn't help much anyway, and I'd suffocate in here without any air conditioning.

I get up in a kind of drugged trance and walk—still naked—into the other room. I hastily draw the shade there. I sit at the kitchen table; I think of fixing myself a cup of herbal tea, but the amount of effort that would take seems to overwhelm me. There's some ginger ale in the fridge, so I drink some of that.

I look around this grubby apartment and feel suddenly disgusted. I feel like a hamster in a cage that hasn't been cleaned lately. But the idea of going out fills me with a weird sort of horror. It's only a quarter after eight, and that somehow appalls me.

There's this little kernel of an idea that's lodged deep inside my brain. I don't want it to grow any larger, but it does. My hands start to shake again, so I grip the cold, half-empty glass, but that doesn't seem to help much; it only makes the shaking go up my arms into my shoulders.

Fuck this.

I reach behind me and thrust open a kitchen cabinet. I fish around utensils I almost never use, stupid little magnetized ornaments that people put on their refrigerators, and a confused assortment of bobby pins and paper clips. Yes, it's there. A tiny, ragged slip of paper. It's quite old, and the crease down the middle is so sharp it almost cuts my finger.

I open it up and place it before me. It's been creased so long that it immediately folds back. I have to bend it backward for it to stay open.

I stare at the ten numbers before me. Without moving my head I slowly extend my arm and grab the phone hanging on the wall. I'm still looking at the numbers; am fixated by them.

Now I'm fixated by the number pad of the telephone. It's all lit up, as if impatient to be used. My hands start to shake again, but I suspect I can't do anything about that now.

Suddenly I dial the last seven digits of that number. The phone emits a tune that's almost recognizable.

I hear the phone at the other end of the line ringing once. Ringing twice. Then it's picked up. Oh, God, maybe it'll just be an answering machine. Or maybe it'll be someone else altogether.

But it isn't.

"Yeah, Weav—"

That's all I hear before I slam the phone down, rush into the other room, and spend the rest of the evening sobbing on my bed.

26.

David Phillips
June 16, 1995, 2:32 p.m.

I initially have difficulty finding the doorbell, since the bells don't seem to be arranged very logically. Finally I locate 1E. I press it.

Almost instantly a voice chirps: "Who is it?"

"David." I didn't see any reason to use a false name; I hadn't given my last name, anyway, and I'm sure she wouldn't have cared.

A buzzer goes off. I open the door and go in.

Now I'm beginning to remember. The door is immediately to the left after the short corridor. The door is slightly ajar, but I knock anyway. It opens.

"Hi!"

From speaking to Diane on the phone, I found her bright, well-educated, and sympathetic. But her resolute cheerfulness is already getting to be annoying. She's new; her predecessor I did not find entirely satisfactory.

But Diane is by no means young. Although shapely, she has telltale wrinkles around the eyes that show that she's probably close to forty, maybe older. I don't know why that should concern me. It doesn't, really.

We make idle chit-chat about the weather—what an early summer we're having, how nice it's cool in this little place, and on and on. The conversation seems rather unreal. No doubt she's trying to put me at my ease. Am I nervous? I don't seem to be; I feel actually rather flat and empty. But maybe I'm a little on edge; just because she's new.

While she's talking about something or other—I don't even know what—I pull out my wallet and hand her some bills. She immediately shuts up, counts the money quickly and expertly, and looks right in my eyes, saying: "So you want the full treatment?"

I just nod.

We begin talking off our clothes. She's naked in less time than it takes me to get my shirt and tie off. She's clearly experienced; must have come from some other establishment. Of course, she wasn't wearing much to begin with.

The room is incredibly small. A studio apartment, clearly, with barely enough room for a couch (where I dump my clothes), a tiny kitchen, a tiny bathroom, a few closets, and the main attraction—a long table-like bed with a thin sheet on it, such as one might find in a hospital examining room.

I know the procedure, even though she's not done me before. After I'm naked I climb on to the bed and lie flat on my stomach. She goes to a tape player and puts on a tape; then she goes to the phone and flicks a switch so that the phone will not ring during the session. Very considerate of her.

The music is New Age, which I hate ordinarily but which I now find tolerably relaxing. She stands next to me, surveying me critically, as if planning some kind of strategy. She says:

"Oil or lotion?"

"Oil."

She gets some oil and pours a little on my back. She starts working it into my back and shoulders. I initially had my hands folded under my chin, but she gently undoes them and makes me place them flat against my sides. I forgot; it does work better that way.

This girl is good. Her massage is both invigorating and soothing. For the first ten minutes or so she says little while she kneads my shoulders, back, and arms. Then she notices the ring on my finger.

"You're married." It's a relatively bland comment; I don't get the impression that she wants to pry.

"Yes."

"A long time?"

"Yes."

Something about my tone makes her look sharply at me while she works. Her bush is now right in front of my nose. It has a nice fragrance. Very considerate indeed; better than the other one.

By the time she has begun working on my buttocks, she ventures to speak again.

"I get a fair number of married men. You know, sometimes it's easier to let go with a stranger than with someone you know."

I don't exactly know what she means by "let go"; I actually think she's referring merely to talking things out. I ruminate about whether I should say anything. Finally I do:

"I'm in a strange position."

She has the good sense not to reply: "I'll say you are." She says nothing.

"I love my wife," I go on. "I do. Really. But things have gone from bad to worse lately. She doesn't seem to want me to be affectionate any more. It's like she doesn't want me even to touch her. She glares at me. I think I'm even getting a little afraid of her."

She's massaging my thighs now. Her fingers feel incredibly good.

"Maybe it's time you walked away," she says, in a rather off-handed and preoccupied way.

"It's not so easy as that."

"No. I guess it never is."

I turn my head so that I don't have to look at her; can't see her very well anyway, since she's now working on my calves. "I hurt someone very dear to me to get her. I think that was a mistake. A big mistake." Suddenly I'm all choked up. I can't say any more.

Diane does nothing but massage each toe individually.

I wonder whether I should just stop this, get up, and leave. She can have the money. I don't know if I want to go through the rest of it. Suddenly it seems so crass and vulgar. So desperate.

She senses this somehow and returns to massaging my neck and shoulders. Her hands feel so good—it's like a cool drink being offered to a man dying of thirst in the desert. I close my eyes, even though I would ordinarily be drinking in her face, her breasts, her bottom, her bush. I shut my eyes tight; there are tears there.

She whispers gently in my ear: "Do you want to roll over?"

I resist for a moment, then go ahead and do so.

My eyes are still closed, but I can feel her pouring warm oil on my chest and kneading it. She even massages my neck and my cheeks, which seem very tight. They loosen a little after her ministrations. I open my eyes and find myself looking straight up at her breasts from below as they loom over me; they seem huge, so huge that I can scarcely see her face above them.

Now she's grazing her fingernails over my chest, stomach, thighs. I've only been about half-hard, but this treatment suddenly makes me engorged. My cock is actually quivering.

But when she puts her hand on it, I grasp her wrist spasmodically and cry: "No!"

I feel like a fool. I look at her, both ashamed and scared.

She is merely looking down at me with a kind of mingled pity and sympathy. She must really be very nice, but she has a boyfriend; she told me so.

"Shall I stop?" she says.

Again a sensation of unreality comes over me. Here I am, lying down naked, with a beautiful woman standing over me, her hand fixed to my cock because I've grabbed her wrist and won't let go.

Finally I say: "Yes . . . I mean, no. No. Don't stop. Go on."

She looks at me keenly to make sure I've made up my mind. She actually pats my cheek with her other hand and says: "Okay, babe. You just relax."

I let go of her wrist. She pours a little warm oil right on my cock. The sensation is electrifying. Then she begins working the shaft up and down, first with one hand, then with both. I try to relax, but I feel very tense. The pumping at my groin seems totally unrelated to my body. I develop a horrible fear that I may not be able to make it. I have visions of walking out of the place, hanging my head down in humiliation. A failure.

But she's good. She's very good. She slows the pace a little, and that does relax me a bit so that I can give all my attention to the task at hand. I keep my eyes closed. After a while it seems as if my entire being is enclosed in that cock; that I'm nothing but one big cock.

One of her hands reaches down and begins gently squeezing my balls, then rubbing the soft area right under them. God! how on earth does she know that that's my fatal spot? I've told Cassandra about that a dozen times, but she always forgets. Not that I've had to worry about it lately with her.

The double friction—on my cock and under my scrotum—does the trick. I can literally feel the juices flowing in me. I try to hold back; it's best to hold back as long as possible, then to let go suddenly.

That does it. Spurts of liquid squirt out of me, going directly up into the air before falling on her still-pumping hand and on my belly. I cry out, clutching the side of the bed with my hands. I've opened my eyes, and I see her smiling benevolently, but with a kind of triumph in her eyes. She continues to pump me, more and more gently, squeezing all the juice out of me.

"Oh, God, that was so good. . . ." I can't say more.

She just smiles at me, finally letting my cock fall back on my groin. She gestures for me to remain there while she retreats to the kitchen and gets some paper towels. She cleans me up.

I feel boneless. I don't think I could move if my life depended on it. She's gotten a little wet cloth and is toweling me off. The cool moisture feels wonderful.

Then she does something strange. Saying, "That was wonderful, sweetie," she reaches down and kisses me right on the lips.

They don't do that usually. That's not part of the routine. I don't know if she's just feeling sorry for me or is actually attracted to me. I suspect the former.

I just stare up at her. My face must be expressing a kind of dazed, confused gratitude.

I can't even remember the last time Cassandra kissed me on the lips.

I feel very strange. Very strange. There's a big lump in my throat. Suddenly, with a strangled cry, I throw my arms around her waist and bury my face in her bush. This is clearly not part of the rules—you're never supposed to touch these women—but she doesn't seem to mind, or at least is making no signs of protest. Probably more pity.

I'm sobbing like a little boy. My tears are mingling with her hair. I'm holding on tight, as if to a life-preserver. I wonder if I'm hurting her.

I do this for a long time.

It doesn't even register to me that here is a woman, whom I've known for less than an hour, standing naked in front of me. I cease to remember or care who she is: she's not Diane, the erotic masseuse; she's just a woman. All I need right now is a woman; not a woman to fuck, not even one to jerk me off, but a woman who will just hold me—or will allow me to hold her—while I cry my eyes out. It doesn't seem ridiculous that my face is in her bush; if she'd been clothed and sitting down, my head would be in the same place.

Finally I'm out of tears. My throat feels as if sandpaper has been dragged over it, on the inside. She hasn't moved, but I can't look at her. I close my eyes.

She moves away for a moment, then comes back. She has another paper towel, and is wiping my face. All this time she has not said a word. Finally, putting her arm behind my shoulders, she says, "Get up, now," and pulls me up.

As I'm sitting there on the bed, my feet hanging over the edge, I suddenly feel the absurdity of the situation. My nakedness embarrasses me, and my face feels hot. I almost leap from the bed and clumsily get my briefs on. I put my other clothes on as fast as I can, not bothering with the tie, which I'm sure I can't manage right now. Meanwhile she has gone to get a robe.

She comes back with a cheerful smile—exactly the same one I saw when I first met her—and says brightly, "Well, David, I hope you come back sometime. Just give me a call, won't you?"

I can scarcely bear to look at her. I walk out of the place with my head down. I don't think I'll be back.

27.

Cassandra Phillips
March 22, 1996, 9:06 p.m.

I'm already mad. If David weren't such a homebody I wouldn't have to trudge all the way out here for this. God, I think I'm going to fall into the East River at any moment. I was probably about twelve before I even knew there was such a street as York Avenue in Manhattan. Sounds like someplace in Brooklyn.

I ring the doorbell. I'm buzzed in. I head right to the elevator—one of those creaky old things where you have to wait for an inner door to yawn sleepily open before you pull the handle of the outer door and walk in. I press the button for the fifth floor. Nothing happens. I punch the "Close Door" button over and over. Nothing happens. The button seems like an ugly and useless ornament. I fume, wondering if I have the patience or energy to take the stairs. I don't, but just as I decide to fuck this shit and walk out of here, the elevator shakes with a kind of nervous spasm and starts going up.

Paul greets me with a chirrupy "Hi, baby doll!" but with an expression suggesting I must be some sort of dope for taking so long getting up to his place. He doesn't want to know what I'd like to do to his face right now.

I say nothing, but push him into his little hole in the wall. He's a little shocked, but is still smiling as if he finds my behavior quaintly feisty. I'm seething now.

I dump my coat—it's still damn chilly outside—on the sofa and begin almost tearing my clothes off. Without even looking at him I snarl, "Just get your stuff on, pal."

I'm already down to my bra and panties, but he's just standing there. I notice this just as I've bent down to remove my thigh-highs.

I straighten up slowly and give him an icy look. "Get moving, you little shit! What's the delay?"

He cocks his head at me and looks at me with this sweet, angelic expression. Ooh, what I'd like to do to that face! Then he pipes up: "Aren't you forgetting something, sweetheart?"

I look at him blankly. Then I say "Oh, shit!" and rummage for my purse, which has already become buried under my clothes. I unearth it, fish through it a little frantically—God knows why my hands are shaking—and find the envelope. I throw it at him.

He catches it deftly enough. He doesn't look in it; he doesn't need to. He knows I wouldn't try to shaft him.

After shoving the thing in a drawer, he undresses quick as lightning. Then he gets his other stuff on—which amounts only to a metal chain around his waist and a tight leather collar for his neck. Meanwhile I've gone to a cupboard, gotten my stuff—I keep it here, of course, on the dim chance that David might stumble upon it if it were at home—and put it on. Long leather boots that come halfway up my thighs; a leather garter belt from which a variety of chains and handcuffs dangle; a corset that pushes my breasts up; and, of course, the whip.

That whip is designed to inflict the maximum amount of pain with the minimum of telltale physical marks. God knows David doesn't see me naked much anymore, but no use taking chances.

I stand before Paul. I'm almost as tall as he is. I look him right in the eyes. I nod my head. He falls to his knees, head down, arms behind him. I go around and put a pair of handcuffs on his wrists.

I go back in front of him, looking down at the top of his head. He's going just a little bald. He wasn't when I started this.

I stand with my legs spread. I feel my mouth twisting into a snarl. I say: "Eat my pussy, you shit."

He inches forward on his knees and begins to do as I say. He starts slow; he knows his stuff. He gets me wet very fast. Just as he seems to be getting into it, I give him his first taste of the whip.

I don't hit him hard, but this first one always catches him by surprise. Or is it just an act?—he really is very good. On impact he arches his back and expels a rough breath that's almost a groan; the rush of air tickles my bush.

I shout, "Don't stop, you cunt-licker!" He immediately glues his tongue back to my crotch.

As I apply the lash a few more times, I can actually feel his grunts in my vagina. His face is covered with my wetness. I look down and see that his cock is already so hard it's quivering.

I push him away with a knee applied to his chest. He falls clumsily backward and sprawls on his back on the low bed that's virtually the only furniture in the tiny place. His cock is almost perpendicular to him.

I lunge at him, fixing my mouth on his member. I suck hard, taking it in as deep as I can without choking. I've gotten pretty good at this myself. I reach my hand up toward his mouth and make him take the whip between his teeth. I draw his cock out of my mouth so that my lips are encircling only the tip. Looking right at him, I slowly close my teeth around it.

His face registers increasing waves of pain, as he bites down hard on the whip. Fuck him!—I can never tell whether he's pretending or not. He's too damn good.

I suddenly leap up and roll him over on his stomach. I unlock the handcuffs and hurl them aside. I start whipping him hard— back, shoulders, thighs, even his cock, which is hanging stiff as a board between his legs like some useless, atrophied extra limb.

I stop, a little out of breath, and tell him to turn over. I take two pairs of handcuffs and lock his hands to opposite sides of the headboard. I attach a chain from my garter belt to the hook on his collar. Then I impale myself on his cock.

I thrust myself down hard on him; there's pain for a bit, but I gnash my teeth and take it. I ride him hard and fast, tugging at the chain so that his head bobs up and down. He does a good choking imitation. I can hear my butt slap against his thighs. He's groaning rhythmically to my thrusts, but he's too skilled to deliver the goods just yet.

I leap up from him abruptly, deftly releasing the chain from my garter belt. It lands heavily on his stomach. There he is, lying there with his arms spread wide like some obscene Christ, his cock— slimed with my juices—wobbling like a drunken blind man, his mouth agape, his tongue quivering.

All of a sudden I feel as if I'm going to throw up, but I take some deep breaths and settle down.

I unlock the handcuffs. He rubs his wrists a little, not looking at me. I almost throw the whip into his hands, get on my hands and knees on the bed, and wait for him.

Very slowly he unzips the corset and, when it falls on the bed, pushes it away. He unzips my boots and wriggles them off. I have nothing but the garter belt on, the chains hanging down impotently, but it's not going to protect me much.

Oh, this bastard is too good. He does nothing for a while. I'm facing a blank wall. I want desperately to turn my head and look at him to see what he's doing, but that's against the rules.

Then, just as I've relaxed a bit, the first lash comes. It's not hard, but a jolt of pain seems to go through my whole body. I groan harshly, scratching my throat. I wait for more.

Now he doesn't waste time. He whips me hard and fast over my whole body. After a while I feel a burning sensation all over, and can't tell when the lashes are striking me and when they're not. I feel dazed, confused, but also weirdly comforted and at peace. The pain doesn't allow me to think of anything else.

Suddenly he thrusts his cock into my pussy from behind. The lashes are still coming, although a little less frequently, and he doesn't have quite as much room to maneuver while pumping me. He's grunting as much as I am. But he's waiting for a signal from me.

I let him pound me for minutes; then, while barely able to catch my breath, I shout: "Now!"

He pulls out of me, throws the whip aside, pries open the cheeks of my ass and thrusts his cock deep into my rectum. No lubrication, of course; his cock is already wet enough, and anyway lubrication is for wimps. I feel a shooting pain proceed from my ass to my brain, where it explodes. He pulls almost all the way out, then violently in again; more waves of pain, and a burning sensation that's worse than the whip.

This is what I paid for, and this is what I want.

He's not able to last very long. In what seems like under a minute he comes violently, spurting his seed into my ass. He cries out gruffly, and I involuntarily echo him. He stays in me for a while, but it seems as if my hole is pinching him, so he pulls out and flops exhaustedly on the bed next to me.

I'm still on my hands and knees. I'm shaking and quivering like someone who's stuck his finger in a light socket. I seem weirdly fixed in this position, my elbows locked painfully; it's like I've forgotten how to send messages from my brain to my limbs. I turn my head and look down at him. Sweat is glistening on his face and chest, and he's peering up at me with a mixture of worry and a kind of expectation. He opens his mouth but says nothing.

Finally I let my whole body relax and flop on my back. I'm breathing heavily, and at each breath a little moisture trickles out of my backside. It feels very cold, wet, and slimy. My gorge is rising again.

As I turn to look at him he says in a soft, hesitant, and almost childlike voice, "Are you okay, babe?"

For some reason I don't recognize him. I don't even know where I am. I somehow expect to see David's face, but who is this thin, dark-haired, sunken-cheeked gargoyle next to me? What the fuck am I doing here?

All of a sudden I feel old—hideously old. I leap up frantically from the bed, stumble against the wall, and retreat to a corner of the room. I curl myself into a ball and press myself to the wall, almost as if I'm trying to burrow through to the other side.

I start to sob and cry. The sobs come out weirdly—harsh and gruff, like a man's.

I haven't cried like this in two decades.

Paul comes over to me and places a hand gently on my back. He knows better than to stroke me—that'll just cause my whipped back to burn some more. He croons: "What's the matter, babe?"

I want to tell him to shut the fuck up, but I can't even speak. I just shake my head wildly and continue to cry. It's like I don't want to stop; I could do this for the rest of my life.

Finally my tears run out. I'm still curled up like a ball. I wish Paul wouldn't touch me, but he still has his hand pasted to my back. I get up, facing the wall; I don't want to look at him. I push him gently away so that I can get to the couch and put my clothes on.

He's standing there uncertainly, like some shy man not sure whether he has the gumption to kiss the girl at the end of the first date. He has the sense to leave me alone, saying nothing while I finish dressing. He hangs his head a little, as if he's the one who's been humiliated.

I harshly wipe my face with some Kleenex; they tear apart uselessly in my hands, and I fling them aside. I snap my purse closed and start heading for the door.

"Wait . . . Cassandra," he whines. "Are you . . . is everything all right?"

"Yeah, everything's just fine," I say. How can I possibly explain to him what a fuck-up I've made of my life? Maybe he knows anyway.

"You gonna come back? Shall I see you again?"

He really does sound like a guy after the first date.

I turn to look at him wearily, my hand on the doorknob. "Yeah, maybe. I guess so."

Where else have I got to go?

28.

David Phillips
June 6, 1996, 8:39 p.m.

I reach down into my pants pocket and give a reassuring pat to the surprisingly heavy object there. I don't know why I should feel nervous, but I'm trembling a little. Everything is going to work out tonight; nothing will—or can—go wrong. I feel rather quaint: hero comes to rescue damsel in distress. But it's no joke: Lauren's in a mess and I have to get her out. And I will.

I casually say goodbye to Cassandra, telling her I'm going for another walk. Just like last time, and unlike the several times before, she doesn't seem to care much. Probably she doesn't give a damn about me any more.

This time I'll probably take the subway. Don't even know why I walked the time before. Jud is exactly the asshole I remembered from college—didn't even want to see me until I implied it might be worth his while.

Well, let's get this show on the road.

Justin Federlein
June 6, 1996, 8:42 p.m.

The taxi is careering up Lexington Avenue as if possessed.

That hiss over the phone is still ricocheting through my skull: *"Quick! He's heading east on 68th Street! Probably the subway! Get there, and don't blow it this time!"*

How the hell am I supposed to catch him on the subway? He only has to walk three long blocks, and this cab has to go about three miles. But the driver seems about as frantic as I am—probably thinks it's a game of some kind.

I leap out of the car before it comes to a full stop, throwing twenty bucks at the guy—about three times the amount of the fare. Can't even stop to look at his reaction. I hurl myself down the steps of the subway entrance. I have to assume David is heading south. Where else could he possibly go?

This goddamn weight in my pocket is making me walk like a cripple. I almost get stuck in the turnstile because of it. I don't see the guy anywhere— Oh, Jesus! Just as I step out on to the platform I see him at the other end. Thank God he's looking in the other direction. I turn around myself so that he can only see my backside; and just as I do so I'm overwhelmed by the subway train roaring through the station, lights flashing and horn blaring.

Sounds like an ambulance. Or a police car.

I get in the car behind the one he's in. I can see him through the windows. He has that stiff, robotic posture I saw three days ago, but there's a kind of grim, determined smirk on his face. What the hell is he doing? And where's he going?

At the Grand Central stop he gets out. I follow him. He is momentarily confused at the size and complexity of the labyrinthine station—can't find the line he's looking for amid all the stairs leading down and the signs pointing in every direction of the compass. As he looks around in my direction I hide behind a pillar. I peek out just in time to see him heading for the Times Square shuttle.

Christ, he would pick that train! It's only two cars, and conceal-ment is going to be hard. There aren't very many people waiting—it'll be minutes before the train will come—and I have to hang back so he doesn't see me. Other people jostle me and glare at me, thinking me some useless and stupid obstruction. There's one guy in a three-piece suit whose face I want to blow off. I tighten my hand around the thing in my pocket.

Finally the train comes and I get into the car he didn't go in. Only one stop: Times Square.

Can he possibly be going back to that dump in the porno district he went to before? Why the hell would he be doing that? And how am I supposed to—do the job—there? Jesus, what a mess!

Fuck you, Cassandra. Fuck you.

Cassandra Phillips
June 6, 1996, 8:49 p.m.

"Is this Cassandra Phillips?"

"Yes. Who is this?"

"Um . . . um, it's Lauren Oxley. Do you remember me?"

I can't believe my ears. I must be dreaming. Oh, you bitch, I certainly remember you.

For a moment I'm stunned at her sheer gall. Where the fuck does she get off calling me up like this? What do you want to do, girl—gloat? Gloat over how many times you've laid my husband in the past few days or weeks or months? Years, for all I fucking know.

My silence allows her to keep on yapping. "I just wanted to thank you . . . to thank both you and David."

"You want to . . ." I can't even go on.

"Oh, David didn't want me to call you. In fact, he made me promise I wouldn't." I bet he did, you cunt. "But I just had to. He probably hasn't told you anything about what's been going on, has he?"

I'm still so choked with rage that I can't utter.

"Well," she goes on in a breathless rush, "you see I got into a real jam and he's been helping me. He says it will be over tonight. I don't really know what he's going to do, but I know he'll do it. That's the way he is. He's such a sweetheart."

The room is starting to spin.

"You're so lucky to be married to him, Cassandra. He's really devoted to you. He told me so. He should have told you about this business, but he was afraid you wouldn't understand. But really, he's just trying to help a friend. He's like that."

She stops. I feel sick to my stomach. I can't speak.

She's a little confused at my silence. "Cassandra, are you there?"

I still don't answer for a moment, but finally I manage to croak: "Yes. I'm here."

"Will you just tell David how grateful I am to him? You'll tell him that, won't you?"

"Yes. I'll tell him that." It's a whisper.

"Well . . . then, goodbye."

I hang up.

Oh God. Oh God.

I know Lauren Oxley. She's too naive and innocent to make up something like this. She's telling the truth. I hear it in her voice.

I pick up the phone again and frantically dial a number. Even before the second ring I know it's useless.

Justin doesn't even have an answering machine—too poor or too cheap. Not that that would have done much good now.

God, what have I done? What have I done?

I feel tears welling up in my eyes. Oh, Jesus, what's the use of that? But then, what's the use of anything now?

I have some crazy desire to run all around the city to look for David. I almost start for the door before I stop in my tracks. Don't be a fool. It's pointless.

My only hope is that Justin will be too clumsy or stupid or scared to do what I've told him to do.

David Phillips
June 6, 1996, 8:52 p.m.

Well, I'm going to be a little early.

I don't suppose Jud will mind. He doesn't seem to spend much time outside that little room. I pat my pocket one more time for reassurance. It's there.

The Times Square station is huge—bigger, I think, than Grand Central. But I know where I'm going this time. All the turnstiles are jammed with people either entering or leaving, and you have force yourself out before someone can force their way in. This city is not for the faint of heart.

The bright lights of the street stun me momentarily. I'm also just a little confused, for I have come out at an entrance I don't immediately recognize. But I orient myself quickly, heading for the north side of 42nd Street near Eighth Avenue.

The door is ajar as before, and little Tony—probably Jud's catamite—is on his stool as before. He nods to me as if he's the one who's expecting me instead of Jud; but as I reach for the doorknob of Jud's office he suddenly grabs my wrist:

"Knock, why don't you?"

I can't believe what I'm hearing. So even two-bit porn producers are deserving of courtesy now? Sure, why not? I knock.

"Yeah?" I hear from inside.

"David Phillips."

"Yeah, okay."

I open the door. As before, he's sitting behind his little desk. No other furniture in the room except some file cabinets behind him. What a life he must lead.

He continues—or pretends to continue—working on some paperwork in front of him. The dutiful businessman, putting in long hours to feed wife and baby. How touching.

Finally he looks up at me. "You got what you said you'd bring?"

"Oh, yeah," I say, wondering what sort of smirk is on my face. "I got it."

"Let's see it."

"Not so fast, Wynn. Show me your stuff first."

He looks at me as if I've committed some sort of faux pas, then shrugs. Reaching behind him while not turning his eyes from me, he pulls open a drawer of a file cabinet and pulls out a folder. He places it on the desk, not far from his fingers.

"Let me see it," I say.

"You come here and look at it."

I expel a breath heavily in irritation and approach the desk. I open the folder. It contains many negatives along with three or four 8 × 10 prints. One glance tells me all I need to know. Or almost all.

"This is all of them?"

"Yeah, that's all." He looks weary and disgusted.

"You better not be shitting me, Wynn. You'll be worth shit if you are."

"Keep your pants on, Phillips. You give me what I want and I'll leave your precious Lauren alone."

He pauses, expecting me to do or say something. Then he loses patience:

"So give it to me, asshole! Stop wasting my time."

Without a word I take the thing out of my pocket.

I throw the fat envelope derisively on the desk. It hasn't been sealed, so some of the bills fall halfway out of it. For a moment Wynn is stunned at the sight. He picks up the envelope gingerly, as if it's made of crystal.

"Don't bother to count it," I say. "It's what we agreed."

He flips through the bills, then places them carefully back in the envelope. He slides the folder toward me.

"I didn't think you'd do it, Phillips," Wynn says. "I didn't think you could get the money so fast. And I didn't think you'd really go so far to help your little friend. I hope she's suitably grateful."

I'm so tired all of a sudden that I don't even want to say anything to him. I just want to get out and go—

Justin Federlein
June 6, 1996, 8:56 p.m.

Jesus, he's going back to the place he was at before! What the fuck am I to do? That little dark boy is sitting up there on his stool. Oh, God—someone please tell me what to do!

No. I'm not going to blow it this time. I can't face Cassandra's wrath again. I gotta do it now! I gotta do it!

David Phillips
June 6, 1996, 8:57 p.m.

The door bursts open.

A crazy man, hair streaming behind him and sweat drenching him, is standing there, huffing as if he's just run a hundred-yard dash. There's a gun in his hand.

"What the fuck?" Wynn says, more outraged than frightened. "Who the fuck are you?"

The guy doesn't respond. He's just looking back and forth between Wynn and me. The hand with the gun is shaking—almost quivering.

Oh, Jesus God. Justin Federlein? Can that be him? God, he looks awful. What the bloody hell is he doing here?

"Justin, is that you? What is this—?"

Justin shouts back: "Shut up, David Phillips. This is the end for you!" The words ring through the room; but, loud as they are, they come out with a weird kind of hesitancy, as if he's saying things he's expected to say.

Wynn turns to me: "Who the hell is this guy, Phillips? What's he doing here?"

Without tearing my eyes from Justin or the gun I say: "I don't know, man. I don't know."

"You'll know in a minute!" Justin screams.

The gun is aimed right at my stomach. I'm frozen, stunned by what's happened. This seems like some dream-fantasy of a drug-crazed horror writer. Justin's finger is on the trigger, but he can't seem to pull it.

"Jesus fuck!" Wynn cries, pulling open a drawer. "I've never seen such stupid shit!"

He scrabbles around in the drawer for something. He pulls out a Saturday night special. He aims it at Justin.

Justin's eyes grow huge, but he's still looking at me. Then he wheels and fires the gun at Wynn. A bullet drills into Wynn's forehead and blows the back of his head off.

Wynn's gun, still clutched in his hand, goes off spasmodically an instant later. But the bullet flies over Justin's head and embeds itself in the wall.

Justin turns to look at me. There seem to be tears in his eyes. His hand goes slack, and the gun falls to the ground. Its impact on the floor is very loud.

Justin turns to the wall and begins to cry.

Justin Federlein
June 6, 1996, 9:01 p.m.

Oh God, what have I done? I've killed a man. I've killed a man I don't even know. There's so much red spattered on that wall.

David Phillips comes up to me. He kicks my gun away. He puts his arm on my shoulder.

"Justin, what got into you? What are you doing here?"

I'm crying so hard that I can't even speak. "I . . . you . . ." I can't tell him about Cassandra's plan. "You were . . . you were fooling around with Lauren, weren't you?" It comes out like a whiny plea.

He seems startled for a moment; then he says: "No, Justin. I wasn't. What made you think that?"

I'm totally confused. He doesn't sound as if he's lying. But I still can't tell him. "I just thought so. . . . But you weren't?"

"No, I wasn't. I wasn't."

I want to claw my way through the wall. Maybe I should just grab that gun and blow my own head off with it.

David shakes me a little. "Justin, we gotta get out of here. Now. God knows who heard those shots." I don't hear any sirens, though.

I nod to him. I turn like a zombie to the door of the room. David is behind me, having grabbed a folder and a fat envelope from the desk.

I open the door. The little boy on the stool isn't there—he ran off after I waved the gun at him. I can't see anyone at the foot of the stairs.

Out on the street there's just the usual crowd. It's as if nothing had happened. Maybe nothing has. Maybe this has been just a dream. Maybe I'm a dream.

David is hailing a taxi. It slows down in front of us. He pulls open the door and almost shoves me in. "Justin, just go home and forget about it. Don't say anything to anyone. Okay?"

I stumble into the taxi like an automaton. When I don't reply to him he says again, sharply: "Okay?"

I look up at him. "Okay." Who am I going to tell anyway?

He closes the door of the cab. It roars off.

In the rearview mirror I see him hail another one for himself.

I'm not even aware of telling the driver where to go. I just lean back in the cab and close my eyes. Wake me up when it's over.

Or maybe I shouldn't wake up. Being in this dream is so much better.

29.

David Phillips
June 8, 1996, 5:27 p.m.

"It's over, Lauren. It's all over."

She looks at me as if she wants to believe me but can't quite manage it. She sounded the same when I phoned her two nights ago. But what can I possibly tell her?

That twerp Justin isn't going to say a word—he's scared out of his skin. I wish I knew what had gotten into him. Imagine stalking and trying to kill me just because he thought I was having an affair with Lauren! I know he doted on Cassandra in college, and probably still does; but isn't this carrying the knight-in-shining-armor bit a little too far? How did he even know I was seeing Lauren, anyway? The little snoop. Well, he'll not utter a peep now.

Strange that there hasn't been anything in the papers about Wynn's death. I guess a murder in New York has to be particularly heinous for it to be reported. Or maybe the newspapers care as little as the police do when lowlife gets offed. Just as well.

Lauren looks at me as if she wants me to say more—but what does she want? "You don't have to worry about Wynn any more," I say as reassuringly as I can. "He's out of the picture."

"But can't you tell me what happened? Was it as simple as that?"

"Sure it was. I just gave him the money and he gave me the negatives and some prints. I burned them immediately." I add hastily: "Without looking."

She turns away. I'm not going to question her about that. It was so long ago, and she was so young. God only knows, though, what was going through her mind when she did it.

Over her shoulder she says: "Do you want some coffee?"

"Sure."

I sit down on the couch, fidgeting a little as if I'm on a first date. There's no reason why I should feel uncomfortable in her presence, but I do. Maybe it has something to do with the way Cassandra has been behaving lately—really lovey-dovey. Can't imagine what's got into her.

I watch Lauren as she pours water into the coffee maker. Her hands are still so sleek and thin—almost fragile, like china. She's already changed from her formal work clothes and is dressed comfortably in jeans and a halter top. She looks good. Better than good.

She hands me the coffee and sits down next to me. I give her what feels like a crooked little smile, and she smiles back warmly. We've known each other such a long time; maybe that's why I always feel young with her. I think of all the things we've been through from the eighth grade onward. . . . Suddenly I get choked up; I look away from her and take a big gulp of coffee.

Maybe she's thinking the same thing. She's just sitting there, sipping coffee, nestling just a little against my shoulder. I don't want to move; I don't want her to move. I'm very comfortable.

But then she does get up, a little abruptly. Looking down at me, she says: "Would you like to listen to some music?"

I shrug. "Sure. Whatever you want."

Her stereo—with the smallest speakers I've ever seen—is in her tiny bedroom, so she goes there. I hear her putting on an LP—she doesn't have a CD player. The music starts.

This can't be by accident. And it isn't: she comes back into the room with a big smile—a little naughty at the corners—on her face.

She's put on "Summer Breeze."

It's the most natural thing in the world for me to take her in my arms and just rock her there on the couch. Her arms slip around my neck, her head rests on my shoulder. We don't do anything but hold each other until the song is over.

She sighs heavily after it's finished. I find there are tears in my eyes. She looks up at me; there are tears in her eyes too.

"Oh, David . . ." she starts.

"No. Don't say anything."

To bring the point home, I place my lips on hers. I don't kiss her hard, but we remain like this for a long time. Our faces are wet.

I pull her halter off. She has no bra underneath. She's scrabbling at my clothes, trying to take my shirt and trousers off at the same time. I push her away a little, stand up, and finish the job myself. She whisks her jeans off in an instant.

There's nothing to do but go to the bed.

* * * * * * *

Afterward, I lie back in exhaustion. She's resting her head on my chest; each breath tickles my chest hairs. Her hand is gently playing with my genitals; she wants more, and I'll give it to her.

But I have to do some thinking first. There's no use kicking myself for the mistakes I've made over the past fifteen years. That's all over. But there's always time to start again.

Cassandra will be the problem, though. I can't divorce her: she's been too shrewd to let any of her money fall under my control, and I don't imagine there's much employment value in a mediocre writer who's never held a job. So it'll have to be on the sly. I think Lauren can deal with that; what choice does she have? I want her, and she wants me. She'll understand. And especially now that Cassandra seems to have become so meek and affectionate, deception will be easy.

I have a good feeling about this. Things will be all right.

Not just all right. Great. Things will be great.

30.

Cassandra Phillips
June 9, 1996, 9:18 p.m.

I wish David would speak to me.

He's said almost nothing since he came home three nights ago. Not that that's much different from before—we haven't talked much, or done much, for years. He can't possibly know what happened—what almost happened. Justin called me and said he simply couldn't find David—spent the night wandering around the city, both by subway and on foot, until he finally just went home. I told him that was okay, that the plan was off.

He's sitting on the couch, reading. How do I approach him? It's like I'm afraid of him now. But I really didn't do anything to him ... I didn't. Nothing happened. How can you be afraid of your own husband?

I know I've wronged him. For years and years I've not treated him well. But that doesn't mean things can't be different now. People can change; couples can start over. We have money, a nice place, a lot of time on our hands. We're luckier than most people. Why doesn't David realize that?

I have to try to be different. I *will* be. I'll change.

I sit down next to him. He looks at me briefly, with a kind of crooked smile. The same sort of shy smile he used to give me way back in college, when I first knew him. It wrings my heart just to see that smile.

I put my arms around his neck. He dutifully puts the book down. I nestle my head on his chest, and feel his arms go around me. He's not holding me very tight, but at least he's holding me.

"David, you're such a sweet man," I say. "You mean so much to me." I look up at him. I'm sure my face has this pleading look that it hasn't had for a long time. Maybe never.

He strokes my head as if I were his daughter and says, "You mean a lot to me too." I try to read his expression, but it's just kind of blandly benign. I can't tell if there is any feeling behind his words.

I don't care. At least we're touching. This is a start. I can't expect things to change overnight.

I'll make sure things are better from now on. I'll get him things that he wants. I'll try to do whatever he wants me to do. We'll take vacations wherever he wants to go. If he wants to write all day, I'll let him do that.

I reach my hand slowly down to his crotch. I try to unzip his fly, but he grabs my wrist—not hard, but firm.

"Oh, sweetheart, not just now, okay? Maybe later."

I'm disappointed, of course, but it's all right. I can wait. We'll do whatever he wants.

He lets go of my wrist, and I put my arm around him again. I keep resting my head on his chest. I wish I could take his shirt off and rub my face against his hair, but maybe he wouldn't like that. Maybe later.

I have a good feeling about this. I'll do my best to make everything work. Things will be all right from now on.

Not just all right. Great. Things will be great.